The
Canal Boat
Café
Christmas

Cressy was born in South-East London surrounded by books and with a cat named after Lawrence of Arabia. She studied English at the University of East Anglia and now lives in Norwich with her husband David. When she isn't writing, Cressy spends her spare time reading, returning to London or exploring the beautiful Norfolk coastline.

If you'd like to find out more about Cressy, visit her on Twitter and on Facebook. She'd love to hear from you!

 /CressidaMcLaughlinAuthor
 @CressMcLaughlin

Also by Cressida McLaughlin

Primrose Terrace series

Wellies & Westies
Sunshine & Spaniels
Raincoats & Retrievers
Tinsel & Terriers

A Christmas Tail – The Complete Primrose Terrace Story

The Once in a Blue Moon Guesthouse series

Open For Business
Fully Booked
Do Not Disturb
Wish You Were Here

The Canal Boat Café series

All Aboard
Casting Off
Cabin Fever
Land Ahoy!

The House of Birds and Butterflies series

The Dawn Chorus
The Lovebirds
Twilight Song
Birds of a Feather

The Cornish Cream Tea series

The Cornish Cream Tea Bus

Don't Go Baking My Heart
The Éclair Affair
Scones Away
The Icing on the Cake

The Cornish Cream Tea Summer

All You Knead is Love
Beauty and the Yeast
My Tart Will Go On
Muffin Compares to You

Cressida
McLaughlin

The Canal Boat Café Christmas

HarperCollins*Publishers*

HarperCollins*Publishers* Ltd
The News Building
1 London Bridge Street
London SE1 9GF

www.harpercollins.co.uk

This paperback original 2020
2

First published in Great Britain as two e-serial books in 2017 by HarperCollins*Publishers*

Copyright © Cressida McLaughlin 2017

Cressida McLaughlin asserts the moral right to
be identified as the author of this work

A catalogue record for this book
is available from the British Library

ISBN 978-0-00-844431-0

Set in Birka by Palimpsest Book Production Ltd, Falkirk, Stirlingshire

Printed and bound in Great Britain by CPI Group (UK) Ltd, Croydon CR0 4YY

To anyone who believes in the magic of Christmas

Part One

Port Out

Summer Freeman placed an electric, flickering tea light in the pumpkin nearest the bow doors, and stood back to examine her handiwork. The café looked both celebratory and spooky which, she supposed, was the effect she was going for. The six tables inside *Madeleine*, her canal boat café, were adorned with black and orange streamers and the glint of metallic, pumpkin and skull-shaped confetti. The chair-backs were cloaked in white sheets, tied with glossy orange ribbons so it didn't look like they were simply in the process of redecorating, and Halloween bunting – bats and cartoon ghosts and skeletons – hung in swathes along the length of the café. It certainly gave it a different feel to her usual, summery, bunting, but it still looked smart.

As she turned towards the blackboard behind the counter, Summer thought about the couple who had decided on a Halloween-themed engagement party. Was it just that the timing was right, and they were piggy-backing on the existing Hallmark occasion, or did they have a shared interest in all things supernatural? Emma and Josh had seemed down-to-earth when she'd met them a few weeks ago to plan their event; both in their mid-twenties, Emma with auburn waves and a face as open as any she'd seen, and Josh, slightly more reserved but with a light in his blue eyes that conveyed easily to Summer how much he loved his fiancée. Josh had grown up in Market Harborough, the Grand Union Canal on his door-step, and when a friend had told them about the canal boat café, and that it now ran private parties as well as serving daily bacon sandwiches and brownies, they'd known it was the perfect way to celebrate their engagement.

Summer hadn't questioned their theme, why would she? But as she took in the transformation her café had undergone, she wondered again if it was something she would consider: celebrating the start of a new life together, while simultane-ously looking the afterlife in the face. She shook her head and smiled; she needed to stop being so serious. Halloween had a distinctly American feel about it these days – it was fun and frivolous rather than macabre.

She remembered her dad refusing to answer the door to trick-or-treaters when she was small, despite her mum's entreaties, and the idea that she and her brother Ben might dress up as a witch and a skeleton to knock on doors them-selves was nothing short of scandalous. But now it was embraced, it demanded as much decoration as Christmas, and the streets were filled with laughter as children tried to out-sweet each other.

The previous evening's pumpkin carving hadn't exactly been downbeat. Summer had corralled her best friend Harriet, fellow liveaboards Valerie and Norman, and of course Mason, into helping her.

She ran her fingers over Mason's pumpkin. He was her boyfriend of just over a year, and owned *The Sandpiper*, the beautiful narrowboat moored next to her. A nature photographer and journalist, he spent many cold, damp days crouching in bushes or hides, his lens trained on some rare visiting bird, hoping to capture their moment of take-off, or the vividness of their plumage as the sun emerged from behind clouds. Every time Summer thought about Mason, a flame of happiness lit up inside her, and even now, tracing her finger round the rather lopsided shape of the carved wolf's face, she couldn't help but grin.

None of their designs came close to Norman's. In his seventies, he spent the time when he wasn't fishing from the deck of his boat *Celeste* whittling, producing beautiful, intricate wooden carvings. When Summer had first arrived in the sleepy fenland village of Willowbeck he had left some anonymously on the deck of her boat, but now his secret was out, and Summer sold the models, of frogs and birds and suns and otters, in her café. His pumpkin, a take on the traditional grinning face, was terrifying.

The door of the café clicked open and Latte, her Bichon Frise, who had been dozing unperturbed on the floor close to the counter while Summer worked around her, jumped up and raced to greet the familiar visitor. Summer tried not to copy her dog.

'Hello, I – wow.' Mason stood inside the doorway and ran his hand absent-mindedly through his dark, unruly curls as he stared around the café. 'This looks . . .' His words trailed away and he gave Summer a bemused smile.

'Spooky?' she asked.

Mason nodded, crouched to ruffle Latte's springy fur and then wrapped his arms around Summer, resting his chin on the top of her head. Summer hugged him back, breathing in his familiar, citrus scent and luxuriating in the feel of his strong body against hers. She would never get tired of this, would never fail to get a thrill from being so close to him. That conviction was growing more with every day that they were together, and had recently planted a seed of an idea in her thoughts.

'You've done a fantastic job,' he said, his words vibrating through her.

'I'm not sure about Norman's pumpkin. I'm worried it's too scary for an engagement party.'

'That face was in my dreams last night,' Mason said, pulling back from her and running his thumb softly over her cheek.

'You were tossing and turning a bit,' Summer said. 'Remind me not to make you watch the new horror film that's appeared on Netflix. Have you seen the trailer?'

'Nope.' He smiled down at her, his brown eyes with their usual intensity, his expression one of pure contentment. He looked the same way she felt. 'Is there anything I can help you with? It seems I've turned up too late.'

'Perfect timing, then.' She folded her arms in mock disapproval.

'I've been trying to finish my article,' Mason said. 'It's due in tomorrow and it's been so difficult to write. I don't know why. But now I'm done, and I've decided it's actually brilliant. I'll give it a final read through and then send it to my editor.'

'At least you're being humble about it.'

'As always,' he replied solemnly, then grabbed her hand. 'So if you're done here, and the guests aren't arriving for a couple of hours, does that mean we can spend some time together?'

'Possibly,' she said. 'What did you have in mind?'

'I thought we could take Latte and Archie to the big field, let them get as damp and muddy as they want, and then when they're exhausted I can seduce you with one of my trademark hot chocolates.'

Summer pursed her lips. 'I'm not sure I've got time to be seduced. Harry's arriving at six to put the finishing touches in place.'

'So let's take the dogs for their walk, and I can do the seduction bit when you come back tonight.' He pressed his face into her neck, kissing her softly, his hair tickling her skin.

'OK,' she murmured, closing her eyes. 'Sounds like a plan. But only if you stop kissing me now, otherwise tonight's going to seem like a very long way off.'

Mason gave her a rueful smile and planted a kiss on the tip of her nose. 'The things we do for those dogs, eh?'

Summer stared down at Latte, who was looking up at them, her big, doggy eyes pooling with innocence. 'If only they appreciated it more.'

Willowbeck, the small, riverside village on the Great River Ouse, looked pretty even with the apt autumn mist that had descended throughout the day. Now it hung lightly over everything, hitting Summer with a much-needed burst of cool moisture as she stepped outside. *Madeleine* had originally been called *The Canal Boat Café*, but she had renamed it last year in memory of her mum, who had died suddenly, and left her the boat and business in the hopes that she would take over from her. It hadn't been an easy decision, but Summer knew now that it had been the right one.

Hers was one of four boats permanently moored up in Willowbeck. Her café was adorned in red and blue; the cakes and coffee cups, the gingham trim, had all been painted by her own fair hand, along with its new name, when she'd taken it to the boatbuilders the previous year. Next to her was *Cosmic*, owned by Valerie Brogan, who had been her mum's best friend. *Cosmic* was an incense-filled, spiritual haven, from which Valerie did fortune-telling, psychic readings and all manner of other things that Summer tried not to delve too deeply into, watched over by her silver tabbies Mike and Harvey. On Summer's other side was Mason's boat *The Sandpiper*, an almost regal boat in red, gold and black, that was as smart inside as it was out. Norman's boat was the last of the four. Painted traditionally in red and green, it was called *Celeste*.

As Mason went to retrieve his Border terrier, Archie, from *The Sandpiper*, Summer sat on one of the picnic benches at the edge of the towpath, realizing too late that the film of condensation would make her jeans damp. But she was about to tromp through the fields with the dogs, so she didn't mind too much. She would get changed before the party guests started to arrive. The picnic benches belonged to the Black Swan, the pub that overlooked the river, its gentle grass slope running down to the towpath. In summer the benches were usually packed, but on a misty late October afternoon, any punters would be inside, Jenny and Dennis, the couple who owned and ran it, giving everyone a cheerful welcome.

The stillness of the afternoon was shattered by the loud crack of a door banging open, and a familiar shout of 'Archie, no!' Summer held firmly onto Latte's lead as her young dog bounded towards the commotion. Archie, his fur recently trimmed, raced forward leadless, and greeted first Latte and then her with the enthusiasm of someone who'd been held captive for weeks. Mason followed, the lead dangling from his hand, his handsome face crumpled in confusion as if this hadn't happened hundreds of times before. While firmly in control of every other aspect of his life, Mason had never been able to assert himself as Archie's master, and the love-able, mischievous dog was always getting the better of him. Summer found this chink in Mason's character wholeheartedly endearing.

'Archie, come here,' Mason said, a hint of exasperation in his voice.

Archie continued to snuffle at Latte and Summer, his tail wagging, and ignored him.

Mason crept up behind his dog and, dropping to his knees, clipped the lead onto Archie's collar in one fell swoop. He grinned triumphantly at Summer, and Archie turned and gave his master a big, slobbering lick up the side of his face.

'Archie, for God's sake!'

'True love.' Summer stood and held out her hand. Mason took it and hauled himself up, and the four of them set off down the towpath, the dogs racing ahead, searching for new scents to sniff, Summer blissfully content with Mason at her side.

As Emma and Josh appeared, wide-eyed, at the entrance to the café, closely followed by their guests, the familiar surge of adrenaline kicked in. Summer turned to Harry, who gave her a nod of encouragement. Her friend's long, sleek hair was tied up in an elaborate plait, a smile flickering on her lips. It would be so easy for the two of them to be giddy, almost schoolgirlish – they were hosting parties on board a narrowboat, and what could be more fun than that – but they knew they had to start out friendly but professional, then adapt to whatever mood the occasion took on.

Emma and Josh, it seemed, were up for fun. As Harry handed a glass of champagne to each of the guests, and turned the lights down low to maximize the effect of the glowing pumpkins, the chatter and laughter filled the café and echoed outside, the sound spilling onto the bow deck. Summer gave everyone enough time to greet each other, and then cleared her throat.

'Welcome aboard *Madeleine*, our canal boat café, for a celebration of all things Halloween – oh, and Emma and Josh's engagement!'

After the whoops and cheers had died down, there was a round of introductions. Summer and Harry met Beth, the maid of honour, and Luke, Josh's best man, along with their other, closest friends. There were twelve guests altogether, six men and six women. Emma had told Summer, during that first meeting, that her mum wasn't keen on boats, so they were organizing a separate, larger party for the family at a later date.

She noticed that two of the men, Mark and Stuart, looked slightly awkward, folding their arms and hunching their shoulders, as if the space was too small for them. Not everyone was used to being on a narrowboat, but she knew that once they'd spent some time on it, and the champagne had worked its magic, they'd begin to relax.

'We're going to be travelling for about thirty minutes,' she continued, 'and while it's obviously dark, there are some riverside villages that are creative with their lights and look beautiful even at nighttime. I'd ask that you don't go on the deck while we're travelling, though of course once we've stopped you're more than welcome to, and please shout if there's a problem or you want to ask anything. I'll be at the helm of the boat, but Harry will be on hand the whole time. Now sit back, relax, and enjoy the ride.'

Summer waited for the smattering of applause, and then made her way across the kitchen that serviced both the café and herself, through her snug living quarters, and to the stern deck of the boat. She started the engine, its thrum low and reassuring. The chill was equal to the time of year, and she zipped her fur-collared coat up to her neck. Latte sat at her feet, loyal despite the less than cosy conditions, and Summer couldn't help thinking of later, when she would be curled up with Mason in *The Sandpiper*'s luxurious interior, a hot chocolate and his presence warming her cold limbs. If there was a better reward for an evening of work, she couldn't think of one.

The stop that she was taking them to wasn't even a village, but an area where an old river warden's hut stood, deserted since the job became defunct, and the last warden hung up his hat for the final time. When Summer had first passed by, it had been covered in ivy, the tendrils bursting through cracks in the window and roof, grass and wildflowers growing up through the floor. But inexplicably, several months ago, someone had taken it upon themselves to clear it out, to paint the hut turquoise with a magenta roof, and wrap it in multicoloured, solar fairy lights. She had asked the people who cruised regularly up and down the waterways, but hadn't been able to find out who was behind the makeover. Summer found the spot enchanting, beautiful whether in daylight or darkness, and so it was where she cruised to whenever she had a private party, a talking point for her guests.

It had taken her a while to get used to night cruising, but she didn't want to limit this new branch of her business by only being able to take the boat out during the day or on summer evenings. With Mason's help she had become a pro, and now had only the slightest frisson of nerves every time she set off on one of her after-dark adventures.

The journey was straightforward; Summer had got so used to travelling this stretch of the river, she knew that — even if she didn't have her boat's lights or the towpath lamps to guide her – she would know every curve, every turn of the tiller. The moment when it twisted right, the bank of ash trees on the left making way for a view over open fields, now just a different shade of black; the place where a weeping willow hung low over the water, giving each boat a leafy hug as it passed. She regularly checked in with Harry on the walkie-talkies they had purchased in a fit of over-excitement, but which had proved useful when Summer was steering and Harry was in sole charge of hosting.

'All OK?' she asked now. 'We're only a couple of minutes away.'

'Full of good cheer,' Harry confirmed, in her calm voice. 'I'll start plating the canapés.'

'Fab. See you back there.'

Soon, the river warden's hut came into view, its multicoloured lights glowing softly, standing out against the dense, countryside darkness. Summer slowed her speed and cruised gently up to the side of the towpath, stepping expertly off the boat with the rope and securing *Madeleine* at one end, and then the other. Once the boat was firmly moored, a couple of the women came out onto the bow deck and admired the decorated hut.

'It's beautiful, isn't it?' Summer said.

'It's amazing,' laughed Beth. 'Why is it like that?'

'I haven't been able to find out.' Summer shook her head. 'The waterways are more close-knit than you'd think, considering the stretches of open river, and yet nobody seems to have any idea who's given the hut a makeover – it used to be derelict.'

'Maybe everyone involved is sworn to secrecy?' said Aliana, her eyes widening at the possibility.

'Could be. There's an old-fashioned air of mystery about this lifestyle, this area. Lots of traditions, lots of strange stories.'

'It must get hard in the winter though,' Beth said, shivering in her cream parka.

'Oh, it does.' Summer felt a twist of nerves. Tomorrow was the first of November, the winter was on its way, and she had only one year's experience behind her. There were challenges to being a liveaboard all year round, and she wondered what this Christmas would bring, especially with the idea that had been steadily growing, gaining shape and substance in her thoughts. 'Shall we go in?' she asked. 'It's food time!'

The café's interior was welcoming, the orange glow from the pumpkins and their electric tea lights adding to the effect, and the mood was jubilant. Summer joined Harry in the kitchen and they took out trays of nibbles, refilled everyone's drinks and made them feel pampered.

As well as the champagne, there were cocktails and mocktails made with blood orange juice, and a range of canapés – fingers of pâté on ciabatta, discs of courgette and pea bruschetta, smoked salmon and horseradish blinis and tempura prawns with sweet-chilli dipping sauce. They had stopped short of producing full-on Halloween-themed food, such as lychees as eyeballs or biscuits shaped like fingers, Summer reminding Harry that, while it was All Saints' Eve, it was also an engagement party for adults rather than children.

While the guests laughed and ate and drank, Summer and Harry stood side by side behind the counter.

'What are Greg and Tommy up to tonight?' Summer asked.

Harry wrinkled her pretty nose. 'Greg's taking Tommy trick-or-treating. Reluctantly, I might add. We don't have a lot of close neighbours.'

Summer's best friend, along with her husband Greg and eleven-year-old son Tommy, lived in an idyllic country cottage with roses around the door. It was stuck out on the edge of a Cambridgeshire village, and Summer could imagine Greg stalking along the country roads with a torch, his shoulders bunched up against the cold while Tommy, ever enthusiastic, took his pumpkin bucket to the front doors of houses that sometimes had a half-mile stretch of nothing in between them.

'What's he dressed up as?'

'A Stormtrooper,' Harry admitted, and they both laughed. 'What's Mason doing tonight? I hope he's not going trick-or-treating with Archie.'

'Do you think he'd risk that? If ever a scenario spelt disaster, it would be that one. No, he's tinkering with his latest magazine article.'

'Is that still going well?'

'It is! Sometimes he feels the pressure of having something new to write about, but he always manages it, and it's always interesting – even for someone who's not as much of a nature buff as he is.' Mason had recently won a contract with an eastern region nature magazine to write a regular article, complete with his own photographs, about the seasonal high-lights and unusual sightings in the area. It gave him focus, as well as a new challenge, and Summer was sure it would lead on to other things. She wasn't the only one who had made leaps and bounds career-wise, and she wondered if it was partly due to them both feeling happy and secure.

As Josh, stooping slightly beneath the narrowboat's low ceiling, tapped a spoon on the side of his glass and, staring adoringly at Emma, proceeded to tell the group of close friends how much he loved her and how excited he was to be marrying her, Summer knew she was grinning idiotically. The young couple seemed wonderfully happy, and it was clear they had so much to look forward to. Summer's applause was more profuse than most when Josh raised his glass for a toast, and when she returned from the kitchen carrying more bottles of fizz, icy-cold from the fridge, Harry gave her a curious look.

Everyone was fully in the party spirit by the time Summer manoeuvred the boat slowly round and began the return journey. The canapés were finished, more champagne was drunk and *Madeleine* seemed to vibrate with laughter. Even Mark and Stuart had relaxed, listening intently while Aliana told everyone about the last time she had been on a boat, a ferry over to France, and her younger brother had spent the whole time with his head in a bucket, his face greener than the pea bruschetta.

As the clock struck ten, the guests thanked Summer and Harry, Emma enveloping Summer in a sweet-smelling hug, and stepped from the deck onto the towpath in turn. Several taxis were waiting in Willowbeck's small car park, engines running, exhausts puffing out into the cold night sky in much the same way as Summer's breath. She stood on the deck and watched them all go, giving Josh a final wave as he climbed into the back of the taxi.

After the short flurry of activity, the riverside village was suddenly still. The butcher's, newsagent's and gift shop that faced the river were all quiet, and only the Black Swan was aglow with life, its large windows golden and inviting. Summer's mind was firmly fixed on finding Mason, getting the hot chocolate he had promised her, and sinking into his arms. But Harry wasn't ready to let her go.

'What's going on?' she asked, as they gave the café a final check, ensuring everything was tidy, the appliances switched off. The pumpkins would remain until tomorrow but, even though electric tea lights were safer than real flames, she removed them all and switched them off, with the exception of Mason's wolf. She tucked his pumpkin under her arm as she let Latte, who had spent the evening sitting at her feet as she steered the boat, or snoozing on her sofa, and then Harry onto the deck. She didn't sleep on *Madeleine* very often these days, *The Sandpiper* being much more comfortable and having the significant added bonus of Mason on it, but occasionally he had to take his boat away for work, and so her cosy living quarters weren't entirely abandoned.

'What do you mean?' Summer asked, focusing on locking the door, securing her boat for the night.

She heard Harry sigh behind her, and turned to meet a look that was entirely penetrating, even under the soft glow of the towpath lamps.

'Don't play the innocent with me, Summer Freeman. What was all the smiling, the nervous energy about tonight? Your bounce has gone up several levels, and when Josh was talking about marrying Emma . . .' Her words faded away, and she gasped into the darkness. 'Has Mason proposed? Oh my God!' She glanced at *The Sandpiper* as they stepped onto the towpath, and took Summer by the shoulders. 'Why didn't you tell me? How could you keep this from me?' The words were a loud, squeaky whisper, and Latte, sensing the excitement, let out a loud yip.

Summer realized, then, that she wouldn't be able to keep her idea to herself; she was too transparent, and her best friend knew her too well. Besides, in only a few minutes Harry and Latte combined would have woken the whole of Cambridgeshire's wild dog population with their high-pitched squeaking. She knew she could trust her.

'No,' she said, 'Mason hasn't proposed, but . . .' she paused, took a deep breath. 'I'm going to.'

Chapter
2

'You're what? Oh, Summer, when? How?' Harry clapped her hands together, and Latte upped her barking. Suddenly the dark towpath was charged with excitement, and the last thing Summer wanted was for Mason to overhear the commotion, come outside and rumble them. *Madeleine* was all locked up now, and she didn't want to have to go through the process all over again, so she pointed towards the pub.

'I've got half an hour before I have to leave,' Harry said. 'I want to know everything!'

'You have to promise not to tell anyone else.'

'Of course, of course.' Summer could see her friend's eagerness, recognized in her jitteriness the way she had been feeling for the last few weeks, as the thought had taken hold.

She held the pub door open and Latte skittered inside, followed by Harry. It was warm to the point of gentle furnace, and Summer knew she would have to work hard to stay awake after the cold of the river.

'Summer, Harry,' Dennis called, raising a hand in greeting. Dennis, in his early fifties and with a mild, approachable manner, owned and ran the pub with his wife Jenny. Summer had known them both for years, ever since her mother had bought the boat and moored it in Willowbeck, and their friendship had grown over the last year – though it hadn't been without its complications. 'How are you? How did it go tonight?'

'It was very successful, thanks. The spirit of celebration wasn't dampened by all the gurning pumpkins.'

'Like that one, you mean?' Dennis said, pointing, reminding Summer that she had Mason's wolf tucked under her arm.

'This is the least scary, believe me.'

'What can I get you both?'

'Two mulled wines,' Harry said. 'One alcoholic, one non. I'm driving back shortly, to see if Tommy's overdosed on Haribo.'

'Coming up.'

They took their drinks to a table by the window, and Latte settled at their feet as Summer pressed her cold hands against her burning cheeks.

'It's warm in here,' she said.

'Never mind the temperature,' Harry said. 'When did you decide you were going to propose? How are you going to do it? I need to know.'

Harry's eyes were dancing, and Summer was reassured that her best friend was clearly enthusiastic about the idea, and wasn't going to try and persuade her against it.

'It's been the last few weeks,' she said, cradling her mug of hot, spiced wine. 'Mason and I are happy. More than happy – this last year has been the best of my life. Perhaps all the complications at the beginning meant we used up our quota of difficulties, but whatever the cause, whether it's fate or destiny or simply that we just fit together, I can't imagine

18

not being with him. I don't want to. I love him, and I want to make it permanent – officially permanent.'

'This is the *best* thing,' Harry said. 'I'm so excited for you. What are you going to do? How will you pop the question? Will you get him an engagement ring?'

'I'm not sure if he'd appreciate me buying him a ring that he'd feel obliged to wear. He's not really the jewellery type.'

'But you can get lovely rings for men, something special but not sparkly. If you're doing the proposing, you need to get him a ring.'

Summer wrinkled her nose. Would Mason like a ring?

Unperturbed, Harry continued. 'Will you go down on one knee?'

'Maybe,' Summer said. 'I hadn't got much further than making the decision, and wanting to do it at Christmas. It's our second one together, and I want to make it extra special.'

'It'll be perfect. Anything I can do to help – distract Mason, string lights along Willowbeck's bridge – I'll be there. We should brainstorm!'

'We should,' Summer said, drumming her fingers on the table. She wondered, now she had revealed her plans to Harry, if she should also tell her about the one thing that was holding her back, dampening her enthusiasm ever so slightly. But she didn't need to wonder, because Harry had already picked up on her hesitation.

'So what's worrying you? You don't actually think he'll say no, do you? Summer,' she pressed her palms flat on the table, 'anyone can see he loves you. People passing on the towpath who have never met you would realize that much. And you've said how happy you are with him. What else is there?'

Summer sipped her drink so she could get her thoughts in order before she replied. 'Will he want to get married again, after what happened with Lisa? Maybe he's content to be with me, but won't want to go through all that again.'

Sadness darkened Harry's eyes. 'What happened to Lisa was tragic, but it had nothing to do with their married status. She wouldn't have been saved if they'd only been partners, boyfriend and girlfriend. It's usually divorce that makes people reluctant to go through it again, or Hugh Grant in *Four Weddings and Funeral* – having all that bad luck with his friend's weddings.'

Harry's words made perfect sense, and she wasn't finished.

'He was reluctant to get involved again, to open himself up to love, but he cared about you enough to risk his heart. That was the hard part for him, and it's proof that he wants to be with you, that what you're doing, planning, is wonderful and exciting, and is the right call. You love him, you want to be with him for the rest of your life, and I'm sure he feels the same. Do you ever talk about Lisa?'

'Sometimes,' Summer said. 'He's become better at talking about her, about their life together, before she died. He's started to accept the happy memories without being clouded by the terrible ones. But I've never spoken to him about re-marrying. We talk about the future – what we'll do when we're in our sixties, whether our bones will creak as much as the tiller on *Celeste* when we're cruising, or if we'll still be able to work the locks without help. But it's always flippant.'

Harry was nodding, her expression patient and under-standing. Summer wondered why she hadn't talked to her before now, why she had been reluctant to tell her about her plans, and the worries that came with them.

'So maybe,' Harry said, 'you need to have a chat with him, a more serious one. Try and gauge his thoughts before you pop the question – if you're concerned, which I don't think you need to be.'

'I'm not sure I could get away with it. How do you do that subtly when your whole mind is focused on not giving away the secret? It's like trying to avoid a bunker on a golf course, and all you're thinking about is avoiding the bunker. Inevitably you end up in the sand.'

'There'll be a conversation, one day, when you realize you can change direction slightly, slip it in.'

'You sound very confident about that, Mrs Poole.'

'I have faith in you, because you're brilliant and determined; when you want something you go for it.'

'I think you've confused me with someone else,' Summer said, laughing. 'Think how long I dillydallied over taking over Mum's café, how long it took me to realize my feelings for a certain, curly-haired nature photographer.'

'OK, but when you decided you wanted the café, you made a huge success of it – you've just hosted a cruising engagement Halloween party for God's sake, who else can say they've done that? And with Mason, it was complicated. For both of you. You got there in the end, and you've not had a moment of doubt since. Go for it, Summer. You'll soon have a wedding to plan on top of everything else.'

Summer's shoulders relaxed, the tension ebbing out of her. 'You're the brilliant one, Harry. What would I do without you?'

'I don't know, but you're temporarily going to find out, because I have to get back to my boys and see what chaos they've caused. Normal time in the café tomorrow?'

'Come in after lunch,' Summer said. 'The morning rush isn't quite as rushy now it's getting colder, so I'll be fine on my own.'

'You've worked late too,' Harry said, standing and shrugging on her coat.

'Yes, but it's my business. Besides, it's not like I have the same commute as you. Take the morning off.'

'Thank you.' They hugged, Harry's squeeze a little tighter than usual. 'And don't worry. Mason loves you, he wants to be with you, and you need to focus all your energy on planning the perfect proposal rather than fretting about his past. But if you want reassurance, try to subtly sound him out first. I don't think you need to, but it's an option. Now, go and find him.'

Summer assured her friend she was going to do just that, and after they said goodbye and Harry hurried to her car, Summer strolled with Latte down the path that cut through the grass in front of the Black Swan, back to the towpath. She thought of everything her friend had said, that Mason's commitment to her was enough, that he was unlikely to be against marrying her because his first marriage had ended so tragically. Could she be sure that was the truth, or if not, could she talk seriously to him about it without him getting suspicious? She was going to have to come down on one side or the other soon, or she would derail her own proposal plans before she'd even got out of the starting blocks.

She opened the door of *The Sandpiper* and was met with a familiar scene. Beyond the galley kitchen, with its black, marble-effect worktops and curved wooden cupboards, the open-plan living area held two figures. One, Archie, lay stretched out along a sofa, and the other had his back to her, leaning forward and peering at the screen of a large desktop computer, set up on a tiny desk squashed into the far end of the space. She had fleeting thoughts about creeping up on him, making him jump, but Latte had already bounded forward, greeting her doggy companion first, and then looking for Mason's affection. He turned at the sound, reached a hand down towards Latte but looked straight at Summer, his face breaking out into one of the smiles that made her heart beat faster.

'How did it go?' He abandoned his computer and wrapped his arms around her.

She accepted the embrace willingly, smiling into his soft jumper, the firmness of his chest beneath. 'It was great,' she said, 'better than I could have hoped.'

'And no weirdness, with the celebratory terror crossover?'

'None,' Summer laughed. 'And I bought you a present.' She nodded towards the kitchen counter where she had put Mason's wolf pumpkin, still flickering with electric light.

'To remind me of my crap handiwork? Couldn't you have brought Norman's instead?'

'I'm not having that monstrosity in a place of rest and relaxation. How's the article?'

'OK. I've been working on the photos to accompany it. Here – come and have a look. It's for the run-up to Christmas, and everyone thinks that robins are cute on their Christmas cards, but not many people know a lot about them. I didn't even need the zoom for these – that's how tame it was.'

Summer followed him to the computer and he pulled her onto his lap, then scrolled through the photographs. They were spectacular, as his photos so often were, the feather detail, the beadiness of the bird's eye, captured in perfect clarity. She felt a swell of love for him, for the way he got excited about the everyday wildlife surrounding them, his tenderness towards each creature, whether rare or mundane. She kissed the top of his head, inhaled the lemon scent of his shampoo, turned her attention away from proposals and her niggling worries, and gave it all to Mason and the festive robin redbreast on his computer.

The following morning, as they lay under the duvet in Mason's cabin, she wondered if they'd reached the point where he could read her mind.

'What do you want to do this Christmas?' he asked. 'It's now officially November, so it's not that far away.' It was after midnight, all the souls of the dead would have hopefully been appeased, so it was time to start thinking about the next celebration.

I'm planning to propose to you, she thought; *so stop trying to catch me out*. 'Oh God, you're worse than the supermarkets. It's still two months away, one-sixth of a year. As much as Sainsbury's would have you believe, we don't need to start our Christmas shopping now. The John Lewis advert hasn't even aired yet, and you legitimately don't need to worry about anything Christmas-related until that point.'

'All right,' he chuckled, stroking her hair. 'Have I hit a sore spot? Do you want to leave everything until Christmas Eve this time? I remember you were uber-organized last year.'

'That's because it was my first Christmas as a liveaboard, and I was paranoid that the river would freeze over and we'd be completely stuck, so I wanted to be prepared.'

'Even though your car was sitting in the car park, waiting to transport you to the nearest shopping centre if you so desired?'

'Hey,' she slapped him lightly on the chest, and he feigned hurt. 'I was nervous. I hadn't done it before, and with Dad and Ben coming for dinner on the boat . . . Everything needed to go right.'

'And it did,' he said softly. 'So maybe it's fine to leave things a little later this time round.'

'You were the one who brought it up, said we needed to decide!'

'I didn't,' he protested, laughing. 'I just asked what you wanted to do. We don't need to firm up the plan for ages, we can stay here, in bed, while it gets colder and grimmer outside the window, safe in our snug little cocoon . . .' He rolled over, kissing her collarbone.

'We will need to eat at some point,' she murmured, 'and I have to open the café.'

'Right now?'

'Not quite yet, but I'll need to get started on . . .' All her arguments drifted away at his touch, as they so often did. 'Bacon sandwiches,' she blustered, as his kisses went lower.

'Do you know what?' He looked up, his eyes bright with amusement. 'That's the most romantic thing you've ever said to me.' And he returned to the important business of kissing her.

Valerie Brogan intercepted Summer as she was rushing to open up the café, her watch displaying 8.05. Valerie's long red hair was flowing out behind her, her dress a shimmering green, and her approach brought with it the usual cloud of sandalwood incense, despite the icy air.

'Summer,' Valerie said. 'Happy All Saints' Day. I trust you're well?'

'Very well thanks, Valerie,' Summer replied, fumbling with her keys in her haste to open up the café. She had several regulars now: Toby, who detoured along the towpath for an Americano and bacon sandwich on his way to his bus stop; Charlotte and Sammy, who had a permanent mooring further down the river, but often passed through Willowbeck and always bought a generous portion of homemade brownies; and Mrs Ramsey, who brought her Cairn terrier Destiny for a walk every morning without fail, and would be even more in need of her usual cappuccino now the weather was turning colder.

Summer pushed open the door and raced inside, Valerie following, wafting incense, as she turned on the coffee machine.

'Are you OK, Summer dear? You seem somewhat in a flap.'

'I'm running a bit late this morning, that's all.' Summer pushed a strand of frizzy, strawberry blonde hair behind her ear. She'd had to leave it to dry naturally after the world's quickest shower, and it was making the most of its freedom, being unruly and unhelpful. She dug in the pocket of her jeans and was disproportionately overjoyed to find a hair-band nestling at the bottom. She scooped her hair up into a ponytail, checked the coffee machine was making all the right noises, and opened the hatch onto the towpath, letting in a rush of welcome cold air. How had she let herself get so flustered already?

'Did your Halloween party go well last night? With that young couple?'

'Yes thanks,' Summer said, rushing into the kitchen to take yesterday's remaining brownies out of the fridge, and the lavender and honey, fruit and cheese scones out of the purple storage tins she kept them in. She would have time to make more this morning, after the early rush which, she had to accept, would be only those few regulars and a couple of other passers-by. She had been worked off her feet throughout the summer, Harry had been a permanent help and, on several occasions, they'd even called on Mason to clear the outside tables she used in warmer weather. Now, she'd be lucky if, at any time during the day, she'd have visitors at all six of the tables inside the café.

Once the counter looked inviting with sweet and savoury offerings, the coffee machine was heating up, and bacon was sizzling on the hob, Summer swiftly removed all last night's pumpkins from the tables and put them in her small living space. The bunting was still up, but Summer decided she liked it, and having ghosts and bats hanging from her ceiling a few days into November wouldn't offend anyone, surely? In a couple of weeks, she realized with excitement, she could make and put up Christmas bunting.

'Valerie, I'm so sorry. Can I get you a drink? Any breakfast? I've just put the bacon on.'

'Thank you, my dear, a latte wouldn't go amiss. Where is the little puffball, by the way?'

'Mason's looking after her. He's going to take her and Archie for a long walk this morning, seeing as we ran out of time before work.'

'Ah. So lovely of him. He's a keeper, that man of yours.'

Yes, Summer thought. *That's what I've been thinking.* 'He's not too bad,' she said, smiling.

She started to make the hot drinks, and felt a surge of relief when there was a familiar rat-tat-tat at the hatch, and she turned to find Toby standing there, his usual grin on his face, a smart navy overcoat covering his business suit. She hadn't missed him.

'Toby! How are you? Any trick-or-treaters last night?'

He gave her a pleasantly exasperated look. 'My wife took it upon herself to organize a Halloween party. Twelve over-excited seven-year-olds that we had to chaperone around the neighbourhood. I know fancy-dress outfits have improved a lot recently, but they were mini nightmares. I felt quite sorry for the people we passed on the street.'

Summer laughed, starting to make his Americano automatically. 'Didn't frighten any old ladies, did you?'

'Ah, no. We have a strict rule to only visit the houses that have a pumpkin in the window, inviting the madness upon themselves. Billy and Ella now have enough chocolate to last until the festive influx, though they'll plague Sal and me to let them eat it all in one go. I can see you got in the spirit, too.' He pointed at the bunting.

'We had an event last night,' Summer said, unable to keep the pride out of her voice. 'Halloween engagement party, of all things! It went well.'

'So there are more strings to your bow than making the best bacon sandwiches in Cambridgeshire?'

'Speaking of which.' She held up a finger and raced into the kitchen where her bacon, on a low heat, was sizzling and crisping up nicely round the edges. She sliced a flour-dusted bap in half and, knowing Toby was a brown-sauce fan, squeezed it liberally on the buttered bap, and then added rashers of bacon. She wrapped it in a couple of paper napkins and put it in a paper bag, expertly twisting the corners. She handed it to him, along with his Americano, with a flourish.

'Thank you,' he said, handing over the right amount of money. 'You seem particularly sprightly this morning.'

'Aren't I always?' Summer asked. And then, leaning forwards and tapping the side of her nose, said, 'Plans are afoot.'

Toby gave her a curious smile, and then a single nod, as if he was a fellow MI5 agent and they were in the midst of a covert operation. 'Say no more.'

He thanked her again, and continued on his way.

'What plans are those?' Valerie asked.

'Oh, it's nothing.' Summer chewed her lip, debating whether or not to tell her. She loved Valerie – she had been the right mix of forthright, stubborn and supportive when Summer had been fighting an internal battle over whether to return to Willowbeck and take over her mum's café – and the two were much closer since the events of the previous summer. But she hadn't planned on telling anyone, and not only had she taken Harry into her confidence, given a ridiculous, pointless hint to one of her regulars, she now had Valerie asking questions. Why had she done that? How was she going to organize a romantic, unique proposal for Mason when she couldn't even keep the fact that she was doing it a secret?

It was nerves, she decided. The lingering fear that he might say no, that what had happened to Lisa was still haunting him, too big an event in his past for him to fully move on with her. Of course he loved her, Summer didn't doubt that for a second, but was this a step too far for him, too soon?

'It's something big,' Valerie said, nodding decisively when Summer put their drinks on the table and sat down. 'You've got grand ideas, Summer Freeman, that much is clear. Now, are you going to spill the beans?'

Summer stirred the froth on her cappuccino. 'I don't think I can yet,' she said quietly. 'If that's OK? I mean, when I'm ready . . .'

Valerie patted her arm, her kind face breaking out into a reassuring smile. 'Of course, Summer my dear. You tell all when it's the right time, just know that I'm here for you, and I'll always help if, and when, you need me.'

'Thanks, Valerie, you're amazing.'

'And so are you, remember that. Whatever may have happened in the past, all anyone can do is look to the future.'

Summer smiled weakly, wondering not for the first time if Valerie somehow knew more than she should. She tried not to ask too many questions about her beliefs. She wasn't sure what she'd discover, and Valerie's insistence that her mum's spirit was still around, that she could pass messages on from beyond the grave, had never sat comfortably with Summer. But sometimes, the older woman would say something that would send a chill running down her spine.

As she heard dogs barking further down the towpath, and Mason's exasperated voice trying to call Archie to him, she realized that Harry's suggestion was seeming more and more sensible. She needed to sound Mason out before she took the plunge. If he wasn't ready to get married again, then she would rather not ask him. Better that they stay together, in an untroubled relationship, than she risk ruining it by asking him for the one thing that he wouldn't be able to give her.

Chapter 3

'We should go out on Friday,' Summer said to Mason when she'd closed up for the evening, and had returned to *The Sandpiper* to find him in the midst of making a prawn stir-fry. The smells of Chinese spice filled the boat, making Summer's mouth water.

Mason turned away from the hob, his eyes crinkling at the edges as he looked at her. He was wearing scruffy jeans and a thin black cotton jumper that clung to his torso, his feet bare.

'What?' she smiled, stepping forwards and placing her cold hands against his warm cheeks. 'Why are you looking at me like that?'

'You look beautiful,' he said, the words indistinct as he tried to speak through the press of her hands.

'Why, because my hair's a frizzy mess and my nose is running from the cold?'

'Is it? I hadn't noticed. You look . . . glowing.'

'I'm not pregnant,' she rushed. 'Did you think—'

'No no,' Mason replied, his words equally hurried. 'No, I

wasn't suggesting . . .' He ran his hand through his hair, sending it into disarray. 'I just meant you look particularly happy, your eyes are shining and . . . I shouldn't have said anything. I'm floundering here – rescue me?'

'Maybe you've used up all your eloquence on your article.' She wrapped her hands around his waist, and he kissed her forehead, turned so he could stir the vegetables. 'I look happy because I am happy,' she added. 'And I think we should go somewhere on Friday. Just us.'

'A restaurant, or a nightclub?' He said the last word hesitantly, as if it was the last place on earth he wanted to go, but wouldn't rule it out if she did.

'No, I don't mean on Friday night. Harry's got the café covered, it's my day off, and I thought we could find some-where along the river, take Archie and Latte' – both dogs pricked their ears up at their names – 'and go for a mammoth walk, a nice lunch somewhere. The summer was so busy, and we've not done something like that for ages. You thought I wanted to go *clubbing*?'

'There's a first time for everything.'

'I don't even know where we'd go! It's been such a long time since I had a night out like that. So what do you think? You're not due at a reserve on Friday, are you?'

'Nope, I'm all yours. And I'd love to.'

'Great,' Summer said, her stomach flipping. She could do this. She could be subtle, bring the conversation round to the future and what he thought of the holy institution of marriage. She wrinkled her nose. As long as she didn't put it like that. 'Can I help with dinner?'

'You can pour out two glasses of wine, and then make yourself comfortable.'

'That sounds like the best job.'

'I saved it especially for you.'

As they ate Mason's delicious prawn stir-fry – a recipe she'd taught him and which he'd now taken on as his own – she thought back to his earlier comment. Had he really thought she was pregnant? She tried to recall his expression at that exact moment, whether he would have seen that as good news or bad. Maybe that could help with her dilemma, because surely if he was happy at the thought she might be having their baby, then a marriage proposal couldn't fail to be positive. She knew she was over-analysing everything, but she'd got herself stuck in that rut now. Friday would help. After then, she'd know for certain if she could give Operation Proposal the green light.

Friday greeted them with sunshine and an extra burst of crispness that stung Summer's skin as she stepped outside. They would need lots of layers, on the boat and on their walk. Mason, used to rising early to find wildlife and get stunning dawn photos, chugged *The Sandpiper* out of Willowbeck while the rest of the village was still asleep. This was one of Summer's favourite things, cruising up the waterways when there was nobody else about, and the prow cut through a glass-like river, its wake rippling out on either side. She stayed on the stern deck with Mason, sipping hot, milky coffee, the dogs alternately sitting with them, or racing inside to cause their own particular brand of havoc.

'So, where are we going?' Summer asked. Once Mason had agreed to their day out, she had let him decide where to go as his knowledge of the area was so much more extensive than hers.

'Haddenham Country Park,' he said. 'It's got some wonderful trails through the woods and across the parkland.

It's dog friendly, and the tracks are well maintained so it shouldn't be too muddy, even now. The house is privately owned, but there's a great pub on the estate, where I thought we could go for lunch.'

'I knew I could leave it to you.'

They fell into an easy silence, absorbing the quiet of the morning, greeting the helmsmen and -women they passed. They reached the river warden's hut, its solar lights muted but the colourful paintwork making it stand cheerfully out from the autumnal landscape beyond. Once they'd cruised past it, Summer was into less familiar waters. She had been further afield on several occasions, but not that often, and not recently. The river was constantly changing, the view from the boat never boring as they passed through wooded areas, open fields, small villages similar to Willowbeck. The colours were the ambers, browns and golds of autumn, instead of the lush green of spring and summer, but it was still beautiful, and very peaceful.

Two years ago, Summer Freeman had wanted to stay as far away as possible from Willowbeck and the river, and hadn't pictured herself ever going back to the place her mum had died, but now she couldn't imagine a different way of life. She felt Mason's hand on her shoulder, and put her own on top of it, feeling a small hole in the finger of his glove. She'd have to add new gloves to the list of all the other things that came with surviving winter on board a canal boat. It was an idyllic existence in lots of respects, but it wasn't always straightforward.

'Here we are,' Mason said, as they cruised round a wide bend in the river and open parkland and a few visitor mooring spots appeared on their right-hand side. The parkland sloped gently upwards, and on the top of the hill was a copse of evergreen trees. Summer wondered if the private house was nestled amongst them. She could see several dog walkers, their bright coats standing out against the grass, and Archie barked loudly at her feet. Mason steered *The Sandpiper* towards one of the moorings, and when he was close Summer jumped onto the towpath and secured the central rope, before going to the stern end, then the bow, tying the knots tightly. Mason clipped Archie and Latte's leads on with surprising ease, and they set off.

The park was beautiful, with large open spaces, trails leading to hidden areas, woods and rose gardens and a walk where, in early spring, Summer knew the rhododendrons would burst out in a riot of colour. They picked a wide, wooded trail, letting Archie and Latte off their leads, strolling gently behind them while blackbirds and robins trilled from the trees, the smell of rain and vegetation all around them. The November sun broke through in thin, dappling rays.

'We don't do this enough,' Mason said.

Summer nodded her agreement. 'The café's so busy in the summer, and now, with the events beginning to take off, at least the winter won't be too empty. More consistency would be good, and I'm proud of how it's going, but we don't get much time to do things like this.'

'We'll have to make the most of your days off. But at least we can spend every evening together, you're virtually living on *The Sandpiper* now, and I – no, Archie! Don't do that.' The Border terrier was pulling vigorously at a long trail of ivy that was wrapped around a large oak tree, as if it was the tail of a vicious monster. Mason rushed towards him, crouching and coaxing his dog away from his helpless victim, and then rewarding him with a treat as he turned his nose away and began trotting amiably alongside Latte.

'That dog's going to be the death of me,' he said, slipping his hand into Summer's. 'Why is he so antagonistic?'

'Because he's a cheeky Border terrier, and you're a pushover.'

'A pushover?'

'With him, I mean. I think you must have let him get away with too much as a puppy, so now your relationship is ingrained. He misbehaves, you can't bring yourself to give him anything other than a gentle reprimand, and it starts all over again. You're never going to be able to control him properly. But he's not *that* badly behaved, and watching you struggle with him is adorable.'

Mason didn't respond immediately, and Summer glanced at his profile, his firm jawline, dark brows and unblinking eyes staring straight ahead. 'So what you're saying,' he replied eventually, 'is that you think I'm an adorable pushover? That's not going on the CV any time soon.'

Summer laughed, and nudged his shoulder affectionately. 'I'd choose you. And why would that credential make you any less desirable in the eyes of wildlife professionals?'

'"Pushover" might even endear me to them, come to think of it. At least when it comes to my employment rights.'

'I didn't mean you were a total pushover, just with Archie.'

'And you,' Mason said. 'I'd never say no to you.'

Really? Because if you knew what I was planning . . . Summer thought.

'Wow, that's good to know,' she said instead. 'So . . . what if I asked you, for our next day out, to take me to Paris?'

'It would take some organizing, but I could do that – as long as you didn't want to go next week. It's much prettier in the spring.'

'You could?' Summer was teasing, speaking in hypotheticals, but the idea of Mason taking her to Paris filled her with excitement. 'Great, OK! And what if I told you that I'd like to convert *The Sandpiper* into a party boat that I could use for my events, while we slept in my compact and bijou cabin on *Madeleine*. You know how popular it would be, the interior of *The Sandpiper* is stunning.'

She bit her lip, holding in her laughter as Mason wrestled with the outlandish request. He loved his boat, and had put months and months of effort into designing it, working alongside the boatbuilders to turn it into the ultimate, luxury narrowboat. And she loved it too. It was both serene and welcoming, a sleek but cosy hug of a living space that she looked forward to going home to every evening.

Mason sighed, his thumb rubbing her hand nervously. 'Well,' he said. 'I mean, we could, maybe . . .'

'Oh God, I'm joking, I'm joking! I'd never ask you to do that, or want you to. *The Sandpiper* is perfect; I wouldn't change a single thing. I'd convert *Madeleine* fully into a café if I was going to do anything, not the other way around.' But she felt a flush of warmth that he was genuinely trying to come up with a way to avoid saying no to her. She flung her arms around him. 'You're the best. And not a pushover, see?'

He narrowed his eyes, and she wondered if he was trying to work out what had got into her, whether it was more than just the freedom of spending a whole day together. Or maybe she was just projecting, sure that the secret she was keeping was as clear on her face as if she'd written it on her skin. Could he know? He had said, the other evening, how glowing she looked. She needed to lose her nervous energy, and the best way of doing that, she decided suddenly, was to run across the glorious open parkland, the dogs at their heels.

'Are you up for expending some energy?' she asked.

'Sure,' Mason said, as laid-back as ever. She couldn't remember ever having seen him run, except for that one time . . . the time she didn't want to think about, because it still gave her nightmares occasionally; the smoke, the threatening crackle, the horrendous wait to hear his voice, to know he was safe. And if it still did that to her, then it must be a hundred times worse for him. She shook the thought away. Mason wasn't a runner. He kept himself trim with hours of walking, crouching, tromping for miles across rough terrain to find a perfect spot or elusive bird of prey. Now, though, she was going to force him to run. It might make his suspicions grow, but at this moment she didn't care. She wanted lungfuls of the crisp, November air, and she was taking him with her.

'Come on then.' She grabbed his hand. 'Let's go!'

They ran along the wide path, the trees either side, twigs cracking and breaking beneath their feet. Latte and Archie were whipped into a frenzy at the unexpected game, and yelped and raced alongside them, their tails wagging frenetically.

'Summer,' Mason said, his voice breathless with laughing and running, 'why are we . . .'

'Because it's fun!' she called back, slowing when Latte, her legs too short, started to lag behind. 'Because I need to!'

'We could buy you some trainers if you want?' he panted.

She shook her head and swerved left, through the trees and out onto the open parkland, the river below them to their left, the gold and red of *The Sandpiper* glinting in the distance. The grass was spongy beneath their feet, sprinkled with an overnight littering of orange and brown leaves, though their sparseness showed that they were picked up regularly, the park well maintained.

Archie bounded towards a cluster of crows pecking in the grass, scaring them off, and Latte, not wanting to feel left out, also went on the attack. She pounced on a large oak leaf, and as she got it in her mouth it whipped away from her, dancing in the breeze. She chased it, barking furiously.

Summer slowed her pace, laughter bubbling up as she felt a pang of tenderness for her ridiculous dog, and her attempt to impress Archie. She wished she could make her understand that it was OK now, that Mason and Archie weren't going anywhere. She waited until Latte had let the leaf go and then crouched in the grass, pulling her dog's warm, wriggling body against her, despite the mud on her paws.

Mason stopped and bent double, his hands on his knees, his dark curls dangling towards the ground. 'That,' he said, pulling himself slowly upright, 'was unexpected.' His cheeks were tinged with pink, obscuring his light dusting of freckles, and his chest was rising and falling rapidly. 'I am so unfit.'

'What a load of rubbish,' Summer said, trying to bring her own breathing back to normal. 'You walk for hours.'

'I'm not run-fit though, clearly. Maybe trainers aren't a bad idea. We could do that couch to five K thing they keep going on about.'

Summer had never considered taking up running, and it hadn't been part of the plan to encourage Mason to, but if it was something else they could do together, then she wasn't going to say no. She could certainly do with improving her fitness. 'How about as a New Year's resolution?'

'I'd forgotten it'll soon be time for all that, but I'm game if you are.' Mason reached for her hand and Summer took it, releasing Latte to her leaf-chasing. 'There's something I want to show you.'

'Sure,' Summer said, frowning slightly. 'Lead the way.'

He took her across the grass and through another copse of trees, the leaves above them amber and gold, the sun reaching through the canopy much more easily, giving everything a glowing, dreamlike quality.

'This,' he said, 'is one of the park's hidden treasures.'

She could hear the excitement in his voice, the breathlessness that, this time, was nothing to do with a lack of fitness. They emerged onto a twisting path, flanked on either side by flower beds that would be bursting with the intricate leaves and heady scents of herbs in the spring, and then Mason stopped.

Summer stared for a moment before the gasp came, because it took a few seconds for her brain to process what her eyes were seeing.

They were standing on the edge of a large lake, its wide, calm expanse stretching away from them. It was surrounded by trees, some evergreen, some the burnished colours of autumn and others the bold, vibrant red of a post box. It was as if they had stepped through a door into New England, not a country park in Cambridgeshire. The water was slate, glassy, the smattering of clouds reflected in it as perfectly as if it were a second sky, the mirrored trees lining the edge. Beneath the clouded glass were fish. There were koi carp as orange as autumn leaves, some milky yellow with dark spots, other, smaller fish a fleeting flash of black or silver, almost invisible in the depths. They circled and turned, then flicked their tails and shot a few feet forwards, before doubling back on themselves.

'Wow.' She didn't know what else to say. It was like a fantasy world tucked into the impressive, but mostly traditional, parkland. The whole thing was mesmerizing.

'It's special, isn't it?' Mason said. He sounded awestruck, despite having seen the sight before. 'I knew you'd love it.'

'Why is it so hidden?'

She felt his shoulders shrug next to her. 'It's not. On maps of the parkland it's there – Haddenham's lake – I just don't think they do a good job of advertising how spectacular it is, especially at this time of year.'

'What are the red trees?'

'They're a mixture of Japanese and red maples, and red oak trees. Whoever crafted this lake, or designed the foliage around it – and it must have started centuries ago because some of the trees are so mature – knew what they were doing. You get heron, kingfishers in the more secluded areas of shoreline where the boughs overhang, because there are rich pickings.' He indicated the fish, then cleared his throat. 'I discovered this place when I first moved to Willowbeck, and I used to come here a lot. It's a good place to be quiet. The trees look like they're on fire, don't they?'

His voice had become strained, his hand in hers much more rigid, and she knew what he had been thinking about, as he stood or crouched or sat at the side of this lake, looking out over a view that was more like a Photoshopped desktop screensaver than reality.

'You thought about Lisa?' she asked softly.

'It was years after she died,' he said. 'You know I only arrived in Willowbeck a few months before you came back, but by then I'd started to accept what had happened. Not get over it, exactly, but work out how to live with it. I started to remember my life with Lisa, before. This place became like a magnet, it seemed to accept me and my thoughts, as if its beauty and serenity somehow absorbed the pain, and I could focus on the positives.' He turned fully towards her, taking both her hands in his. 'I'm sorry I haven't told you about it until now. At the beginning I didn't want to share it, it was somewhere I could be with my thoughts of Lisa, but then after we got together, I wondered if you'd understand, if you'd worry I wasn't wholly committed to you once you knew I spent time here.'

'I would never think that,' she said. 'I know how important Lisa was – and always will be – to you. I'd never ask you to give up your memories, or hide them away from me.'

His smile was soft, his eyes shining. 'I know you wouldn't. But now, I feel it's the right time. I want to share everything with you, Summer. I wanted to share this, I didn't want to hold onto it by myself any more.'

Summer tried to swallow, the lump of emotion thick in her throat. She felt sad and elated and guilty all at once. The thought of Mason coming here alone, forcing himself to confront his loss, made her want to reach back through time and comfort him, and yet she knew what he was giving her today was more important than any object, than any token of his affection. This was precious; he was giving himself wholly up to her, banishing any secrets they might have still had between them.

It wasn't a torrid or harmful secret, it was simply the way he'd dealt with his grief, but it meant he was letting her in. She felt guilty that she had orchestrated this day partly so she could bring the subject round to Lisa, to find out if he was ready to move forward. And here he was, without any prompting, doing exactly that. She should have trusted him, believed in his love for her, and believed in herself, too.

'It's the most beautiful thing,' she said, knowing she sounded choked up, no longer looking at the lake.

He glanced at his feet, then back up at her. 'Summer, I—'

There was a loud, strangled yelp, and they both turned

towards the sound. Archie was in the water, his front paws scrabbling desperately at the bank, his fur wet and spiky.

'Shit.' Mason let go of her hands and crouched at the river's edge, taking hold of his dog under the front legs and hauling him out of the water. Archie thanked him by shaking himself thoroughly, spraying Mason and Summer in the process. 'Archie!'

'Where's Latte?' Summer's voice was high with panic, but her white cloud of a dog came bounding through the foliage and stopped at their feet, eyeing the bedraggled Border terrier warily. 'Oh, thank God. He must have jumped in further round and then swam to us when he realized the bank was too steep to climb out by himself. I hope he hasn't eaten any fish.'

Mason shook his head. 'Not a chance. A fish with bones in would be too much like hard work. He'd be hand-fed prime cuts of pork while he lounged on a cushion if he had his way. He may have chased a few fish, but it's all bluster.' He sighed, looked up at her and grinned. 'I think it's time for the pub, don't you?'

Chapter 4

The sunshine had been deceptively warm, and with all their exercise Summer felt quite toasty, so she wasn't prepared for the wall of heat that hit her when they walked inside the Duck and Duckling pub. The dogs raced ahead and settled themselves on the rug in front of the crackling fire. Mason went to the bar, while Summer found a corner table close to where the dogs were stretched out, but far enough away that they wouldn't melt. Even after all this time, she wasn't sure how Mason felt about large, open fires, but she certainly wasn't as happy near them as she once had been – the wood burner on her boat was as much as she could deal with.

'Is this OK?' she asked when Mason returned with two glasses of red wine and some menus.

He glanced behind him, then turned to her and smiled. 'It's fine, honestly. I promise I'll tell you if I ever feel uncomfortable.'

'You will?'

'Scout's honour.'

They turned their attention to the menu, and the wealth of winter warmer dishes it offered: sausage and mash, chicken casserole, hearty fish and chips, beef stew served in a giant Yorkshire pudding. Summer's stomach rumbled as she read, and it took her a long time to narrow down her options, eventually deciding on the chicken casserole and dumplings.

As Mason returned to the bar to order, a spatter of mud up the back of his jeans, Summer sipped her wine and wondered why she had been so worried. Asking someone to marry you was a huge thing, a show of eternal commitment not to be taken lightly – however much some people did these days. Summer wanted to spend the rest of her life with this man and she was sure, now, that he felt the same way about her.

She watched Archie and Latte lying next to each other on the rug, their bodies close, Archie's fur drying after his dip in the lake, and realized she was happier than she'd ever been. Their future looked bright, full of possibility and hope, and she felt suddenly impatient, wanting – now she was sure – to pop the question immediately. But Christmas would no doubt come hurtling towards them, and she needed to be careful what she wished for.

As she and Mason chatted over lunch, trying to scoop bits of food off each other's plates without covering the table in gravy, Summer's mind turned to her proposal. How was she going to do it? She had already decided on the day – Christmas Eve – but beyond that, she was at a loss. It had to be intimate, but also unique. She'd thought about decking out the café somehow, taking him on a personal tour up the river, and popping the question somewhere along the waterways that was beautiful or stand-out. She would have to do some research. Or she could hang a large banner from

Willowbeck's brick bridge, saying: *Mason Causey, will you marry me?* While that might lack a certain grandness, she loved its simplicity, and with her background as a sign writer she would be able to make the banner striking – better, at least, than a protest banner on a motorway bridge.

'Hello, is anyone home?' Mason tapped her temple, and Summer realized she was holding her fork aloft, chicken gravy dripping over the table as she imagined Mason saying yes and sweeping her into his arms, after putting on the ring. That was another thing. She needed to find him a ring. He didn't wear much jewellery, he didn't still wear his wedding ring, though Summer thought he must have it somewhere on board *The Sandpiper*. Was it too macabre to look for it, so she could get the right size without asking him?

'Earth to Summer,' Mason tried again, and Summer shovelled the forkful of food into her mouth and wiped the table with her napkin.

'Sorry, sorry. Miles away.'

'Fresh air and exercise, followed by food and wine – it's a lethal combination. The beauty of arriving by boat is that we can have a nap before we head back to Willowbeck, if you want?'

'That's tempting,' Summer said, 'but we'll never want to go home if we're curled up in your cabin. It'll be too hard to go outside in the cold to steer home. Or we'll sleep for too long and end up cruising back at night.'

'I wasn't being that serious,' Mason said. 'But I have loved today, and you're right that we need to spend more time together away from Willowbeck, broaden our horizons. Besides, I think I have a trip to Paris to plan.'

'Oh yes, you do!'

'Right then.' Mason nodded decisively and finished his wine. 'I'll just settle up.'

46

'I'll gather up the dogs, which might take a while.'

'Give me a couple of minutes, between us we might be able to coax them away from the fire.'

Fifteen minutes later they were back on board *The Sandpiper*, and Mason was expertly turning the narrowboat round so that it pointed in the direction of Willowbeck and home.

Saturday at the café was busier than it had been for a while; it was lunchtime before Summer had a chance to stop and think, wipe down the tables and check the stock levels of her macarons, brownies and pastries. She would spend late afternoon baking, and start to draw up a menu of Christmas specials. She had two festive parties booked in for early December, something she was very proud of. Not many people thought of the river as an ideal spot for a pre-Christmas knees-up; they thought that narrowboats would be damp, draughty and uncomfortable. She hoped that, over time, she would prove more and more people wrong.

Her mobile rang as she was stacking the dishwasher and, glancing at the screen, she grinned.

'Hello?'

'Ahh, Summer,' said a familiar voice with a hint of a Welsh accent. 'How are you?'

'I'm good thanks, Claire, how about you? How are Jas, Ryder and the others?'

Claire was bold, positive and larger than life, the first person Summer had met when she left Willowbeck, not long after moving aboard *The Canal Boat Café*, unsure of what she wanted and with no real plans about where she was going. Claire had taken her under her wing, and Summer had spent a couple of months travelling the waterways with her band of roving traders, opening her café alongside Claire's music boat, an antiques barge, sandwich boat and several other floating businesses. They had formed a firm friendship, and Claire and the others had visited to trade in Willowbeck on several occasions. It had been a few months since they had seen each other, but they stayed in touch via phone and online. Claire had started posting the most wonderful Instagram photos and Summer wanted to know all her tricks.

'We're all grand, thanks. Moseying along as ever, trying out new places, new people. And look, we've had this idea and we want you to be a part of it.'

'Ooh, what is it?' Summer leaned against the counter, keeping an eye on the hatch and the doorway for any new customers.

'A Christmas fair! A barnstorming, beautiful, boatiful Christmas fair. Will you join us? Cinnamon-spiced lattes and chunks of Christmas cake would certainly help to fuel the punters.'

Summer thought of the music festival they had hosted the previous summer. The buzz and busyness, the fun they'd had working long days serving customers, getting together to swap stories and listen to the bands in the evenings. It was relentless, breathless, and one of the best things Summer had ever done.

'It sounds amazing!' she said. 'I'd love to. Where are you thinking? Are you coming back to Willowbeck? I know it's small, but if we advertised well enough – remember how popular the music festival was.' If they were here, then she could organize her proposal at the same time, perhaps finding inspiration from the other traders.

'Yeah,' Claire said, dragging the word out, 'that's the thing. Willowbeck *is* beautiful, and it's perfect in the summer, it's got the whole picturesque, pretty English countryside vibe going on, but it's not right for Christmas. We're going to London.'

Summer blinked, wondering if she'd heard right. 'London?'

'Little Venice. Have you been? It's a stunner. A haven of water and boats and magic in the middle of the city. But it's London, and it's touristy, so even on a cold, dark day, our boats will be busy. We can adorn them with Christmas lights, make them shine.'

'London?' Summer repeated, unable to take it in. She had visited the area with her mum, years ago, and remembered its fairytale quality, how it was unlike any other part of the capital. But taking the café there seemed like madness. 'Can we even get our boats to London?'

'Of course, Summer! The canal network is pretty well established, and I've been down to London a lot – I've got friends there, and they've secured us visitor moorings for seven days, which is no mean feat I can assure you.'

'When?' Summer's voice was faint. Was she really prepared to take *Madeleine* to London, for Christmas, at such short notice? What about Harry, Mason – what would Willowbeck do without its café? How would Toby cope without his bacon sandwich in the mornings?

'We've got the slot three weeks before Christmas, and even that was touch and go. But it'll take us a couple of weeks to get there. All the way along the Grand Union canal, it's a wonderful journey and it'll open your eyes, I promise you.'

'So five weeks altogether?' Summer asked, thinking it through. They would be home just before Christmas Day. No time to organize a proposal in Willowbeck, and she would have to cancel her festive parties, which wouldn't be ideal when she was just getting that side of the business off the ground. But it was a great opportunity to be part of the hubbub and festive fun of London's canal community in the run-up to Christmas. She remembered her mum telling her that it had been visiting Little Venice that had made her want a boat in the first place, that in the middle of the traffic fumes, noise and endless busyness, was this mirage of tranquillity. If Summer didn't take the chance to be part of it, with friends who knew what they were doing, she would regret it.

'Five weeks, Summer,' Claire pushed, sensing her uncertainty. 'Five short weeks. And think how much fun it will be, being part of the band again. Remember the good times when we were travelling together. You must miss it just that teensy weensy little bit.'

She felt a pang. She did miss it. But she knew she would miss something else more if she went. 'What about Mason?'

'Bring him with you!' Claire said. 'He'd be welcome, absolutely, and you'll need help in the café, it's going to get busy.'

Summer grinned. Claire and Mason had known each other years ago, before either of them knew Summer, but their friendship had ended when Mason walked out of a relationship with Claire's friend, Tania. Claire had thought Mason was a love rat, and hadn't been too pleased when, once she and Summer had got to know each other, Mason had turned up on Summer's boat, and she had seen how much Summer cared about him.

Mason had finally given up his secrets and told Summer that his marriage had ended in tragedy, that when he'd met Tania he'd been grieving for his wife Lisa, and hadn't been ready for a new relationship. He knew that he'd messed things up, that Tania had been collateral damage in his grief, and had regretted it ever since. Summer had encouraged Mason to tell Claire the truth, and since then her boyfriend and her roving trader pal had got on well.

Summer didn't know if Claire was still in touch with Tania after all this time, but she knew that, now he was beginning to move on, Mason was keen to face up to his past and apologize to Tania for the way he'd treated her. Summer would do anything to make Mason happy, but the thought of him seeing Tania again unsettled her. From what Claire had told her at the time, it was clear that Tania's feelings for Mason had been more than just fleeting.

'I'll have to check what his plans are,' Summer said. 'He might have time scheduled on the reserve.' But already she knew she wanted him to come, to share this adventure with her.

'Have a think about it,' Claire said. 'Give me a call in a couple of days with your answer.'

Summer was pretty sure what her answer would be, but she had to get all her ducks in a row before she could say yes.

'Five weeks away from Willowbeck, just before Christmas. *This* Christmas?' Mason asked, his brows lowering, his expression suddenly stormy.

'It's not going to be next Christmas,' Summer said, trying to keep the levity in her voice. 'You think Claire would plan that far in advance?'

Mason rubbed his cheek. He was sitting at his desk, his chair swivelled to face her. He had his dark-rimmed glasses on, the sleeves of his grey jumper rolled up, a hole in the toe of his sock. He looked gorgeously dishevelled, but now he also looked disgruntled.

'I know it's a bit of a bombshell,' Summer said. 'Short

notice, a long way, a hectic week sandwiched between lots of travel. But it's exciting too, isn't it? Little Venice at Christmas – it could be the title of a film. It sounds romantic, and I don't want to go without you.'

Mason rested his elbows on his knees and looked at the floor. 'It's so soon, and – my articles, I need to submit them up until the twentieth of December. The reserves have got a lot of migrating birds at the moment, there are some other things . . .' He drifted away, clearly mulling it over. 'I can't drop everything at a moment's notice!'

'You don't have to decide now,' Summer rushed, surprised by the sharpness of his tone. 'Claire wants me to call her back in the next couple of days, so we can sleep on it.' She stepped forward, sinking onto the sofa next to his chair, putting her bare foot over his, covering the hole in his sock. 'When I first met Claire and the others, it was a difficult time. I was trying to decide what I wanted to do, if it was too hard being back in Mum's café, whether I could cope with all the shit that was happening with Jenny. Claire was a good friend to me, didn't put up with any nonsense, and wouldn't let me dwell on things. I enjoyed seeing that different side of living on the river. I know you were a rover for a long time before you came to Willowbeck, and I know that you're settled now, that this is our home, but this doesn't have to change that. It's only five weeks, Mason. An adventure.'

He fixed her with the dark, intense look that still captivated her. 'I know all that,' he said softly.

'And even though we didn't know each other very well when I left, I spent so much time wishing you were there to share it with me, to go on those weird storytelling evenings, to explore the different villages. And now we have that chance.'

He took her hand. His fingers were warm, and he threaded them through hers absentmindedly.

'And,' she said, swallowing, 'you showed me Haddenham's lake yesterday, told me how it had helped you, reminded you of the good times you'd had with Lisa. In some ways, those months I had with Claire helped me sort out my feelings, too; what had happened with my mum, how I felt about Willowbeck, how I felt about you. It was a defining time, and it would be wonderful to recapture that, but this time with you at my side.' She hoped he could see that she wasn't trying to emotionally blackmail him, she just wanted to be as honest with him as he'd been with her.

'Let me think about it. There are a couple of things I have to sort out.' He looked away, frowning at something over her shoulder. 'I'll check with the reserve, and my editor. I can't promise, but if it's possible then I'll come with you.'

'OK,' she said quietly. She could see from his hunched shoulders, the uncharacteristic edge to his voice, that he wasn't convinced, and she wondered whether it was just that it was unexpected, or if there was something more significant that was bothering him, making him reluctant to go. She tried hard not to think what that could be.

Monday morning was cold and grey, a fine mist of drizzle casting Willowbeck in a melancholy pall that meant hardly anyone ventured onto the towpath, though Summer and Harry did a good trade in hot drinks to passing helmsmen and -women. They spent most of the morning baking; Harry worked on a gooey salted caramel cake that would make even the coldest punters feel cheered, and Summer conjured up cinnamon and almond flavour macarons. She had never attempted macarons before she'd taken over *The Canal Boat*

Café, but they were now one of her favourite things to make, eat and sell. They were dainty portions of loveliness, the flavour possibilities endless, and were good as treats or gifts. Mason was her chief flavour-taster, a job she knew he relished.

The slow custom also gave Summer the chance to talk over her latest concerns with Harry.

'So let me get this straight,' Harry said, her lips twitching, 'you're now entirely confident that Mason wants to spend the rest of his life with you and will accept your marriage proposal, but you're worried that he doesn't want to come to London with you on Claire's mega Little Venice river trip?'

'Yup,' Summer said, recalling Mason's frown. It wasn't that he didn't ever frown, but that his frowns were mostly in puzzlement rather than genuine unhappiness, and the darkness of his expression when she'd told him, along with the sharpness of his voice, wasn't sitting right with her.

'And you think it's more than the initial surprise of having it sprung on him?'

'It could be,' Summer said. 'I was wondering if there might still be some tension between him and Claire, though whenever she's visited Willowbeck, and since he told her about Lisa, they've seemed fine together, so I don't think it can be that. But what else is there?'

'You've just got yourself in a spin about the proposal, and it's seeping into everything else like spilt red wine. It's a fantastic opportunity,' Harry added, ruefully.

'I'd love you to come, if you could get away. But with the boys . . .'

'It's not practical, I know. Greg's got work tidying up people's gardens before the frosts start to hit, and of course there's school for Tommy. I can't leave them to fend for themselves for five whole weeks, the horror doesn't even bear contemplating. You'll have to send me endless photos, and Skype me every night.'

'And I'll still pay you,' Summer said. 'It's an unusual situation, the business owner denying her employee hours because she can't get to her place of work any more.'

'You don't have to do that,' Harry said.

'Yes I do, and I will. Anyway, you can still do some baking for me. I won't get much of a chance to cook while we're travelling, so you could make sure there's enough stock for when we're back in Willowbeck.'

'And what about when you're in London? Do you want me to do some batch baking over the next couple of weeks so you have cakes stored in the freezer for while you're there?'

'That,' Summer said, 'would be perfect.'

Harry laughed and tried her cake batter, closing her eyes in ecstasy so that Summer was tempted to do the same.

'Oh God, that's good.' Summer dipped a fresh teaspoon in for a second taste. 'Why are you laughing?'

'I just wish you could be as forthright about the rest of your life as you are about your café,' Harry said. 'You have a great business head on your shoulders, making this café the glorious hideaway that it is, planning those private parties which are really beginning to take off—'

'Don't you mean cruise off?' Summer asked. 'Anyway, I'll have to cancel a couple of those now, which isn't good for business. I'm going to offer them freebies in the New Year to make up for it.'

'It's one time, extenuating circumstances. They'll understand – especially when you tell them how you're making it up to them. You're so in control with *Madeleine* now, isn't it time you did the same with Mason? The guy is head over heels for you. If he seemed reluctant about travelling to Little Venice then it's understandable – it would be an upheaval at any time, but it's the run-up to Christmas, and everyone gets an extra, irrational layer of panic at this time of year. He's probably wondering when he's going to pick up your Christmas present.'

'We'll be in London,' Summer reminded her. 'He'll have much more choice than either a pound of bacon from the butcher's or a furry doorstop from Carole's gift shop.'

'Fair point,' Harry said. 'But it's irrational panic, remember? When will I get a chance to cook the pigs in blankets, do I need to get a different type of chair in because of Auntie Ethel's hip, will the Christmas tree from the garden centre be too big for the living room, or the Homebase one be too scruffy? Even if you don't have an Auntie Ethel, or in your case a living room, these fears go through everyone's mind.'

'You, Harriet, are a wise woman. Mason's probably just worried about keeping on top of his articles. It'll be a busy few weeks.'

'You've settled into life here, so five weeks out sounds like a long time. But personally, I think it'll be good for you both. Settled is lovely, but so is a change of scenery. Go, explore the world with your gorgeous man, Summer.'

'That's what I'm trying to do! I need to give him a bit more time, that's all. I'm sure you're right.'

'And think of all the wonderful inspiration you'll find in London for your proposal. Are you going to delay it until you get back, or do it while you're down there?'

'I was thinking about New Year's Eve, which in some ways is even more special than Christmas. We can ring in the New Year with fireworks, champagne and – hopefully – an "I will".'

She looked up from her macaron mix to find Harry grinning like the Cheshire Cat. 'It sounds perfect.'

'I hope so.' Summer could picture it: the glitter of fireworks shattering the darkness, reflecting on the river, Mason's arms around her after he'd uttered those life-changing words. It would be the icing on the top of the Christmas cake, only a few days later. But first they had another challenge to navigate, a Christmas fair in Little Venice with the roving traders, and the excitement and trepidation of four weeks cruising along Britain's waterways. The thought sent a thrill of excitement through her, memories of torch-lit nights in the woods, homemade wine and busy, bustling days, new villages to cruise through, different faces at the door of her café.

She wanted to do it so much, to spend time with her friends and show Mason a little bit of what she'd experienced. She just hoped that – on this occasion as well – Mason would say yes.

Chapter 5

When Summer locked up the café at the end of Monday, the sun was already beginning to set behind the trees, leaving a cold chill that reached easily through her layers. She stepped outside in her thickest coat, boots pulled up over her jeans and, shooting a quick glance in the direction of the empty mooring where *The Sandpiper* usually was, began walking down the towpath in the opposite direction. Latte was bouncy and interested in everything after an afternoon of snoozing on Summer's sofa.

Mason was spending the day on one of the local reserves, and had called her earlier to say he would be back late, that one of the rangers was doing a study on the local bat population, and had asked if Mason would like to look at the data with him. Summer had heard the thrill in his voice at the opportunity to investigate the habits of the nocturnal mammal, and had said she would keep her fingers crossed that they found something interesting. At the back of her thoughts was the niggle that he needed more time to think about Little Venice, that she was right about his uncertainty being down to more than the short notice.

She stepped under the brick bridge that marked the edge of Willowbeck, and into the riverside wilderness. The towpath was still well-kept here, lights along it beginning to spark on now that dusk was falling, but the further she walked, the more the countryside encroached. On the opposite side, the river was lined with mature trees, the occasional bench nestling in the undergrowth, and to Summer's immediate left, after she'd passed the copse of trees that edged the Black Swan's land, were open fields. Tall hedges, their leafless branches twisted and gnarled, acted as a border between the fields and the towpath.

Latte snuffled close to the hedge, an unlikely tracker dog, and Summer let her go as far as she wanted. It was unusual for her pampered pooch to be quite so enthusiastic about something that didn't involve a soft cushion, and she thought their trip to Haddenham Country Park might have woken up something inside her little dog too.

When they returned to Willowbeck, the mooring next to *Madeleine* was still empty, and instead of returning home, Summer turned towards the Black Swan. The pub wasn't heaving, but it was gratifyingly busy, the atmosphere humming, enveloping her with warmth. Summer found Jenny behind the bar, her dark hair pulled up into a messy pony-tail, serving a customer with practised efficiency.

Summer's history with Jenny was complicated. They had been at loggerheads when Summer first returned to Willowbeck. Jenny was angry for an entirely justifiable reason, but she had directed it at the wrong person, and Summer had spent a long time wondering if it was worth staying in the riverside village. But since the events of last year, they had been able to put the past behind them, and Summer knew she wasn't the only one who felt the burden lifted from her shoulders. She waited until the older woman turned in her direction, and returned her smile.

'Summer, how are you? How's that boat of yours? We've got mulled wine if you need warming up.' Despite living on the river's edge for years, Jenny had never quite got over her conviction that narrowboats were eternally damp, cold places. Summer had even given her a tour of Mason's boat, which was more luxurious than most of the houses she'd been in, but Jenny still wasn't convinced.

'A glass of red wine please,' Summer said. '*Madeleine*'s good, heating's working fine. We'll have to do the usual round of checks before the winter sets in, but she had a thorough going-over when I repainted her last year, so she's in great condition.'

'*Madeleine*,' Jenny repeated, shaking her head. 'It's so strange to think of your boat as *Madeleine*, and you referring to it as "she". I sometimes wonder if she's been reincarnated into the boat. You know . . . your mum.'

As she spoke, her words became less certain, and Summer bit her lip to try to stop herself from laughing. Not that long ago, she wouldn't have found this flight of fantasy remotely funny, and definitely not coming from Jenny.

Jenny's face creased into a frown. 'Ignore me, Summer, I don't know where that came from.'

'You've been spending too much time with Valerie,' Summer said. 'But in some ways you're right. She was my mum's boat, her café, and I'm keeping her memory alive every day that I open it and serve my customers – some of them were her customers, too. It made sense to rename the boat after her, so there's lots of my mum in there. Maybe not her spirit, but . . .'

'Indeed,' Jenny said, suddenly businesslike. 'Any food this evening? Mason out on one of his jaunts?'

'Yes and yes. I'll browse the menu and order in a minute. Things OK with you?' she asked, wanting to dissolve the awkwardness that had appeared between them.

'Oh sure, fine. Great, mostly,' Jenny said. 'Gearing up for our Christmas menu, and Dennis is thinking of getting some reindeer and penguins for the lawn.'

Summer's eyes widened.

'You know, models that light up, all very cheerful. He's found some tasteful ones – his words – and seems rather overexcited at the prospect. He said we don't have to worry about offending the neighbours, but I've realized we do. There's you and Mason, Norman and Valerie. I'm not sure how Norman would feel about pulsing purple penguins outside his boat.'

'I'm sure Norman will love them,' Summer said. 'Even if he's not prepared to admit it.'

'I might do a bit of door-knocking anyway, as a courtesy.'

'Well, you have my full approval. I love anything Christmassy.' Summer paid for her wine and selected a booth, Latte happy to curl up at her feet after their long walk.

Summer ordered a cheeseburger and chips and, though she had told herself she would wait until Mason had made up his mind, nevertheless she found herself looking at tourist websites for Little Venice. The photos were small on her iPhone screen, but immediately she could see that it was as charming as she remembered. She read about the variety of boats and riverside attractions; there was a permanently moored canal boat café already, and Summer felt a twist of nerves that she wouldn't be welcome. But then, she reasoned, there were so many other cafés, restaurants and food stalls

– it was London after all – they couldn't begrudge her being there for seven days.

She read on, laughing at the discovery that there was a puppet theatre on a boat. The whole area seemed alive with creativity and interest. In some of the photos, it looked as calm and tranquil as Willowbeck, but she knew that would be far from the truth. Little Venice was at the point where the Grand Union Canal met Regent's Canal; it was a walk away from Regent's Park and London Zoo. It would be a whirlwind of different sights, sounds and smells; the still water and lone, echoing footsteps of her fenland village replaced by constant chatter, the comings and goings of a busy waterway in the heart of the capital.

A young barman Summer knew as Ed brought her food to the table. She thanked him, and ate the chips with her fingers while she scrolled. She *had* to go to Little Venice. She would regret it if she missed the opportunity. Of course, there was nothing to stop her and Mason going on their own, but Claire knew people, Claire was a roving trader with experience and unwavering confidence, and people who could sort out visitor moorings three weeks before Christmas. And Summer wanted to be amongst her old friends, to be swept up in their adventure.

As she finished her burger, her phone rang.

'Hello?'

'Summer,' Claire said, her voice jubilant. 'How are you? What's the answer?'

How she would love to say yes. 'The answer is hopefully. Mason's got a couple of things to confirm with work before he knows if he can have time away, but I should be able to call you tomorrow.'

'And if Mason can't get away?'

'Then I'll make a decision, and I'll let you know one way or the other.' Summer hoped she wouldn't be faced with that dilemma.

'We'd all love to have you,' Claire said, 'you know that, right? Mason too, of course, but if he can't make it then it's not the end of the world.'

Summer swallowed. 'I'm sure he'll be able to come. Who'd want to miss this?'

'Exactly,' Claire said. 'You work your magic on him, Sum. He'll make the right call.'

They said goodbye and Summer swilled her wine in her glass. Of course she could go away without Mason. There was nothing wrong with being apart, but five weeks seemed like a long time, especially before Christmas, and especially when she was gearing up to propose to him. Claire was used to being independent, so wouldn't fully understand Summer's reluctance to make the trip without him.

She browsed the dessert menu idly, wondering if she had room for apple pie and custard, and looked up as Jenny slid into the seat opposite, putting two full glasses of wine on the table.

'Hi.'

Jenny pushed a glass towards her. 'On the house.'

'Thank you. What for?'

'A apology, for being so insensitive.'

'There's no need. What you said made a weird kind of sense. Except I see the café as mine now, which I hope doesn't seem insensitive either.'

'Not at all. You've done so much with it, Summer. You've given it a new lease of life, and – while I'm not the right person to be saying this – your mum would be so proud.'

Summer smiled. 'I know,' she said quietly. 'And I don't mind you saying it.'

The silence between them seemed thick with unspoken words, and Summer had the urge to fill it.

'How will you and Dennis spend Christmas?'

'We'll be here,' Jenny said. 'Open on Christmas Eve, and we're trying to decide whether to open for a select few on Christmas Day too. It's usually just the two of us, and it's not that we don't want to spend time together – things are much better between us than they were – but it seems a shame not to open our doors when we've got the space, the catering facilities. What did Norman do last year, do you know?'

Summer folded her arms, thinking. 'I don't. I invited him to the café. Mason and I had my dad and brother for the day, Valerie came for the meal and I wanted Norman to come too, but he said he was fine – you know what he's like. But if the pub was open, maybe he'd be more willing. I'm sure he thought my invite was out of pity. Which it wasn't, of course, but he's a proud man, underneath all that gruffness.'

'So you think it's a good idea?'

Summer never thought she'd see the day when Jenny would be asking her advice about something. It showed how much had changed since she'd returned to Willowbeck on that cold, February morning. 'I do if there are a few more people you can invite besides Norman.'

'Will you and Mason be here?'

'Yes,' Summer said. 'I think we're going to have a quiet one, just the two of us.'

If they were getting back to Willowbeck close to Christmas Day, she might not have a chance to arrange for her dad and Ben to visit, but if her brother was staying with her dad in

Cambridge she could see them between Christmas and New Year.

'We might even come to the pub, too. That would be really useful, if—' she stopped, not wanting to mention Little Venice until it was confirmed. She wasn't about to blackmail Mason by making it a certainty in other people's eyes.

'If what?'

'If things work out how I want them to,' she said, feeling her cheeks redden.

Jenny peered at her closely. 'Things?' she asked, with a gentle smile. She was inviting Summer in, coaxing the words out of her. And Summer was tempted, because in her mum's absence it would be nice to have the perspective of an older woman. She was close to Valerie, but somehow Jenny was more objective. She hadn't been her mum's best friend – far from it – and maybe her cool detachment was exactly what Summer needed.

'I have this plan, that . . . I mean, it's changed a bit now and there's this other potential thing that's come up, so . . .'

Jenny rested her chin on her hand, a puzzled smile on her face. 'Sounds great.'

Summer laughed self-consciously. 'You promise you won't tell anyone? Not even Dennis?'

Jenny hesitated, and Summer realized her mistake. The last thing they needed was any more secrets between them. 'It's nothing terrible, or huge – not for you or Dennis I mean – but it is – it could be – for Mason and me. The thing is . . .' She chewed her lip. 'How did Dennis propose to you? Or did you propose to him?'

Jenny's expression morphed from confusion to delight, and she glanced around self-consciously, as if her smile alone was giving the game away. 'Has he proposed?' she whispered, leaning across the table.

Summer shook her head. 'I'm going to. At Christmas – New Year now, probably. We might be going away for a couple of weeks first, but I want to know how to do it. Is it best if I go all out, guns blazing, or should I do something small and intimate? Ordinarily, I would say small, but he loved his surprise birthday party last year, so I don't know if should make a bigger splash and involve everyone. That's obviously a more risky option, especially if he turns me down, but I have to get it right.'

'Firstly,' Jenny said, 'that's wonderful news. Secondly, he won't turn you down, and thirdly, of course it will be right, because you'll be asking him to marry you. That's all that matters.'

'I want it to be special.'

'Summer, you could wait until you'd both fallen off your boat trying to make a difficult turn in the river, and were standing waist-deep in green slime, and he'd think it was special.'

'What if I'd dropped the ring onto the riverbed?'

'Don't run with my hypotheticals. He loves you, Summer.'

'I know, but I want to go the extra mile. I was thinking a banner, hanging from the bridge here – if I have a chance to design it – plus fireworks, champagne.'

'See? You've got it completely sorted. A little bit of your individual style, a lot of sparkle, and the main thing – looking into his eyes, asking him to be with you for the rest of your lives.' Jenny's voice wavered at the end, and without warning she reached over and put her hand on top of Summer's. 'Your mum's not the only one who would be proud of you, you know. Dennis and I, we feel like we're family. I know Valerie feels the same. This community is a lot more closely knit than it ever was before.' She swallowed, took a large gulp of wine. 'Now, is there anything I can help you with, towards New Year's Eve? And I know you said not to mention it to Dennis, but I promise you he won't spill the beans.'

'I know he won't,' Summer said. 'Of course, talk to him. I'm concerned that the more people that know, the more precarious it is, but you and Dennis – no problem. And once I've firmed my ideas up I'd love some help.'

Jenny patted her hand and got up, the movement disturbing Latte who stood suddenly and blinked, as if trying to remember where she was, and then pawed at Summer's shins.

'Oh, and Jenny,' Summer said, as the older women turned towards the bar, 'I see you as family too.'

When she stepped outside, the cold closed in around her, the soft glow from the towpath lights impeded by a mist that reminded Summer of Halloween. But nothing could hide the fact that *The Sandpiper* was back in its rightful place, nestled in between the café and Norman's boat *Celeste*. She hurried down the path, Latte pulling on her lead, and Summer laughed at the fact they had both been hooked by their respective men; Latte was as smitten with Archie as she was with Mason.

'Hello?' She knocked on the door, pushing it open when she heard his voice.

'Hey.' He was still shrugging off the navy wool coat that would have been too smart for him, except within days of buying it Archie had chewed a hole in the pocket. His cheeks were pink with cold, and he came towards her while his arms were still tied up in his sleeves. He flapped to try and get them over his hands. 'I missed you,' he said, their faces close, his arms behind him as if he was handcuffed.

She laughed, kissed his icy-cold lips. 'Here, let me. You've just got back?'

He turned around and she pulled on his sleeves, tugging his hands free. 'Yup. It was interesting, but freezing. Deepest Cambridgeshire in the dark, in November. I didn't go fully prepared.'

'It was spontaneous,' Summer said. 'Are you glad you stayed, though?'

'The data they're gathering is groundbreaking. It's fascinating, and Shaun, who's running the project, says I can cover it exclusively for the magazine. I'll work closely with him – there'll be rules about what can be revealed when – but it could be a whole series of articles, a real scoop. Or as much as these things can be called scoops, anyway.' He gave her a one-shouldered shrug, but she could sense his excitement.

'In the nature world, it'll be a *huge* scoop! I'm so happy for you! And worth losing a couple of fingers for, then – did you even wear gloves on the journey back?'

'I did, but they're a little on the airy side.' He pulled one out of his pocket, and Summer saw that the hole in the finger she'd noticed the other day had grown considerably.

'Have you eaten?' She pressed her hands over his, her fingers steepled.

He shook his head. 'You?'

'I had burger and chips at the pub, and a catch-up with Jenny.'

'How is she?'

'She's good. Dennis is going to cover the lawn in sparkly Christmas animals.'

'Oh God, seriously?'

'It'll look wonderful.'

'It'll look tacky.'

'Don't be a Grinch. There are going to be penguins. Penguins in Willowbeck, just imagine! They'll give the crested grebes a run for their money.'

'You are ridiculous, Summer, you know that?' He was grinning.

'Go and have a hot shower, and I'll cook you something.'

'You will?'

'A pasta dish, with extra cheese. Now go, get warm. How will you be able to type groundbreaking articles if your fingers have fallen off?'

He did as he was told, and Summer set to work, conjuring up a simple but delicious meal that, despite her huge dinner earlier, gave her pangs of food envy.

When Mason emerged wearing jeans and a grey jumper, his curls dampened into shiny ringlets, she handed him the bowl, and he held it close to his face and inhaled. 'Bacon?'

'And tomatoes, broccoli and condensed mushroom soup. If this doesn't warm you up then you're beyond hope.'

'You didn't have to do this,' he said, tucking in hungrily.

'I wanted to.' She left him to it, finishing the washing-up while he ate. He made short work of it, and then, as Summer went to take his empty bowl to the kitchen, Mason took hold of her wrist.

'Come and sit down a moment.'

'I'll just wash this—'

'I'll do that. I wanted to say sorry, for how I reacted yesterday. It was so out of the blue, this plan of Claire's, and I'd got set in my head how the run-up to Christmas would be. I was being selfish.'

'I did spring it on you,' Summer said. 'It's understandable that you wouldn't be sure about it.'

'I've had a chance to think, to talk to my editor about everything I need to submit by the twentieth of December. So . . .' He drew the word out.

'So?' Summer's heart thumped in her chest. Little Venice, at Christmas, with Mason. That was what she wanted.

'When do we leave?'

She waited a beat, waited while his face broke into one of his killer smiles, and then a flicker of confusion lowered his brows. 'Summer?'

'You're coming?'

'Yes, I'm coming. If you'll still have me? You seem unsure.'

'No. No no no. Not unsure, but – I thought you wouldn't. I thought work would stop you, or . . . you're coming?'

'Yes, Summer,' Mason laughed. 'Though God knows what I've let myself in for. I've seen what you and Claire can be like when you get your heads together.'

'So join in with us, embrace the madness! Oh, Mason, this is going to be amazing! Have you seen what Little Venice looks like? Imagine if it snowed.'

'Summer,' Mason said, 'it is not going to snow in London at Christmas. The winters have been steadily warming up for the last—'

'Sshhh.' She put her finger over his lips. 'Don't spoil my fantasies with your nature buff knowledge. Just think of twinkling lights, roast chestnuts, carol singers serenading us from the little blue bridge.' She couldn't help it; she was elated. It was as if he had said yes to everything all at once. 'We can make gingerbread lattes and mince pies, and wear Santa hats while we work . . .'

'Fantastic,' Mason said dryly. 'Santa hats have been missing from my life since I don't know when.'

She flung her arms around him. 'Thank you, Mason. For coming with me.'

'As if I could leave you for five whole weeks,' he said into her ear. 'You beat this lady hands down.' He tapped the arm of the sofa, and Summer blinked, taking a moment to realize what he meant.

'Oh, *The Sandpiper*.'

'I assume we can't take both, I'm sure the moorings in Little Venice are limited, not to mention pricey. We'll go on *Madeleine*, leave this girl to have a cosy Christmas in once we return.' She thought she could detect a hint of sadness in his voice, which would be entirely understandable. She loved the minimalist luxury of *The Sandpiper* too, but the thought of the four of them, all living in *Madeleine*'s smaller quarters, snug in her tiny cabin, Mason helping her in the café, exploring the sights of London together, was thrilling. A proper adventure, with the person – and pets – that mattered most.

'She'll be fine,' Summer said. 'We can get Valerie, Dennis and Jenny to keep an eye on her, and make sure the heating's on when we get back.'

'I know,' Mason said lightly.

'I'm going to call Claire, give her the good news.'

He nodded, taking his empty plate to the kitchen. As she brought up Claire's number, Mason glanced at her, and Summer smiled. Her sense of relief was huge, almost eclipsing the excitement. She'd got her Christmas wish, now she just needed to keep that momentum going through to New Year's Eve.

'Claire, it's Summer. Guess what?'

Chapter 6

The first thing Summer heard was the music, and it took her back to a time when she had felt very differently. Today everything was grey outside, but inside Summer was anything but, her life falling into place in a way she hadn't imagined. Whereas that spring, when she'd first returned to Willowbeck and then made her escape up the river, the sun had shone while she struggled. Now, the soothing tones of London Grammar drifted towards her from upriver, and Summer knew that Claire and the others were on their way.

The café had been surprisingly busy for a bleak November morning, but it was a Saturday, and she wondered if people were being galvanized into activity, knowing they should be starting Christmas shopping with just over a month to go. She served a couple who were walking a pair of poodles along the towpath, and who had taken up her special offer of a gingerbread latte and a chocolate twist, the perfect snack to eat while walking. Summer knew this, because she'd done it a bit too often since perfecting the recipe a couple of weeks ago.

Her Christmas specials were all in place. She and Harry had worked in the quiet periods, browsing recipe books and online sites, injecting their own personalities into the recipes. As well as the chocolate twists, Harry had come up with a mince pie lattice, which was delicious and indulgent and sprinkled with icing sugar. Summer had developed some new macaron flavours – Christmas pudding, brandy butter and rich chocolate log. They'd created a cranberry jam to go in the bacon sandwiches, and Summer had even ordered some turkey from the butcher's, to add an extra festive element. When they were on route, she'd defer to Ralph who owned *The Sandwich Shack*, though she was sure he wouldn't mind her selling her bacon and turkey special.

All that, along with her cinnamon and gingerbread lattes, a special chai tea, and a creamy hot chocolate with a dash of almond syrup, meant that Summer was fully in the festive spirit. Harry had been making batches of their new recipes for her to store in the freezer and take down to London, and the two of them had spent the previous day decorating the café, to bring *Madeleine* up to their Christmassy standards.

Gone were the bats and ghosts hanging from the ceiling, which admittedly Summer had kept up for a bit too long, and now the bunting was made of pennants in silky green and red, interspersed with glittering gold and silver. She had a mini Christmas tree on the counter, its coloured lights fading in and out, and with a wooden star on the top that Norman had carved especially for her. It was five-pointed, hollow at the bottom so she could pop it on the top branch of the tree, and was of the same, beautiful quality as the rest of his whittling work. She could have painted it gold, but she loved the pale wood, the way the lights reflected off the matt surface. A sprig of mistletoe hung in front of the counter, ready to catch out unsuspecting customers.

When they had arranged the date to set off for London, Summer had suggested that she and Mason could meet Claire and the others further west, where the River Nene met the Grand Union Canal, but Claire had said she'd come to them, that she knew the area like the back of her hand. Mason protested at first – he had been a rover for several years before finally settling in Willowbeck, and was confident navigating England's waterways and locks – but Claire had insisted. They would do the journey together, united as one raggle-taggle band of traders, stopping to sell their wares along the way.

Summer's stomach was knotted with excitement and, as the café was momentarily empty, she rushed onto the bow deck, waiting until *Water Music* appeared under the bridge, then *Doug's Antiques Barge* and *The Sandwich Shack*. Others followed, and then Ryder, in his beautiful navy and silver narrowboat, *The Wanderer's Rest*, brought up the rear. Slowly, they manoeuvred into the visitor moorings on the opposite side of the river, Claire giving Summer a cheery wave once she'd secured her boat to the towpath.

'Summer,' she called. 'We made it! How are you?'

Summer waved back. 'Good! Come across.' She indicated the bridge, and Claire disappeared inside, her music volume lowered but not turned off. It had moved on to Crowded House now, reminding Summer that *Water Music* played anything and everything, her soundtrack able to drag long-forgotten memories and nostalgia out of anyone in its vicinity on a regular basis.

She waited for Claire on the towpath, and let herself be scooped into a bear hug. Claire's dark hair was longer than the last time she'd seen it, but other than that she was unchanged, her eyes alive with mischief, her snug-looking jumper in a bold, pumpkin shade.

'Willowbeck's looking grand,' she said, 'despite the miserable weather. One of the prettiest places we've visited, though you wait until you see Little Venice. You won't want to come back.'

'Not sure about that,' Summer said, laughing. She thought of Valerie and Norman, Jenny and Dennis. Even Adam in the butcher's and the river warden's derelict but decorated hut would be hard to leave for good. There was too much here, even with the promise of excitement and bright lights ahead of them. 'But I'm fully prepared for a Christmas adventure.'

'I'll ask you again in a few weeks,' Claire said. 'See if you've changed your mind. Everyone's here.' She pointed, and Ryder and Jas waved from the deck of *The Wanderer's Rest*, where they were drinking tea out of tin mugs. Jas's Irish wolfhound, Chester, had accompanied Jas to Ryder's boat and was sitting next to him, docile as ever, while Latte bounded excitedly at her feet. Summer wondered if she remembered the larger dog, or it was just someone new to be interested in.

'How are you and Ryder?' Summer asked.

Like Ryder himself, Summer had never been able to pin down the nature of her friend's relationship with the wild man of the group. With his blond hair and effortless charisma, not to mention the kind of ambiguity surrounding everything he did – his business dealings, his boat, his stories – that made him a classic bad boy, Ryder flirted mercilessly, and never apologized for anything. He'd been interested in Summer when she'd temporarily joined their group, and Summer, while never being worried, had found his attention

75

claustrophobic. But once she'd made it clear nothing was going to happen between them, Ryder had backed off, and become entertaining instead; his sporadic, seemingly opportunistic trading – buying and selling whatever he could get his hands on, often to order, always with an air of shadiness – raising a laugh or an eyebrow.

Currently, his bow deck was adorned with about seven, three-foot-high fake Christmas trees that she was sure he was planning on flogging. She could see the fibre-optic stars on top, translucent without electricity to light them.

'Same as ever,' Claire said, refusing to give anything away. Summer was sure that Ryder was interested in Claire in a way that surpassed mere flirting.

'Fantastic,' Summer said dryly.

Her friend rolled her eyes. 'Give us a chance to turn the engines off before you go fishing for gossip. We thought we'd stop here for a couple of hours, then set off around lunchtime, so we can get a good chunk of travelling in before dark. OK for you?'

'Sure, we're ready to go.'

'And where is the lovely Mason?'

'Ah,' Summer said, wondering how long she could stall.

Claire narrowed her eyes. 'Ah?'

'Mason's sort of disappeared. He left me a message saying he had to do something crucial, and he's taken my car – though I'm surprised he got it to start. He's not answering his phone, but that's probably because he's driving back. If we're not going for a couple of hours, then it's fine.'

'Does he do this often, this disappearing act?' Claire smiled, but it was a tight smile that Summer wasn't used to. She knew Claire was thinking of a couple of years ago, and wanted to remind her that Mason wasn't the only one who had left Willowbeck under an emotional black cloud. And before that, with Tania, had been entirely different.

'Of course not. He's just gone to pick something up for the journey. Is anything wrong?'

Claire didn't reply for a moment, and then she sighed. 'No,' she said. 'Not at all. I just need to make sure that we stick to our travelling schedule if we're going to make the most of our moorings in Little Venice. To say it's a popular spot is an understatement.'

'I get that,' Summer said. 'And Mason's looking forward to it as much as I am.'

'But he took a bit of convincing, didn't he?' She said it gently, but Summer squirmed.

Claire was a great friend, but she always spoke her mind, however uncomfortable it made things. Summer didn't want to be reminded that Mason hadn't originally been thrilled by the idea, even though his change of heart had been swift.

'It was the short notice,' she said, defending him. 'I sprung it on him and he had to sort out a few things with work. Who wouldn't be flustered, especially so close to Christmas? I'm asking him to uproot his whole life, leave his lovely boat behind, for over a month.'

'God, Summer, I know all that. I'm sorry – I wasn't thinking. I spend my life roving, I'm firmly in that mindset and sometimes I find it hard to believe other liveaboards don't feel the same. And this opportunity, Sum, it's so good. Little Venice, just before Christmas. It's the kind of thing that doesn't come around very often.'

'I know – and we're coming! We're both excited, even if Mason has, as usual, left it to the last minute to get organized.' She smiled, hoping to dispel the tension that had worked its way between them.

To her relief, Claire laughed. 'Good old Mason. Café still the same? How are your events going?'

'They're great,' Summer said. 'Come and see the wooden decorations Norman's made for my tree.'

'Ooooh, is he still doing that?' Claire's voice warmed instantly at the mention of Summer's elderly neighbour.

'I've convinced him to make some that I can sell for him in Little Venice. I'm sure they'll be popular.'

'Too right.' Claire followed Summer inside *Madeleine*, and Summer was thankful that normality seemed to have been restored.

Summer's rusty old Polo screeched into Willowbeck's car park forty-five minutes before they were due to leave, and Summer rushed out to meet Mason.

'Where have you been?' she asked, almost before he'd climbed out of the driver's seat. It came out harsher than she'd intended, Claire's comments putting her on edge.

Mason grinned, his hands going up in submission. 'It took longer than I thought, I'm sorry.' He kissed her, and Summer's irritation disintegrated.

'What did?' she asked softly.

'This!' He opened the boot triumphantly, and Summer took in the words and photo on the box that filled the cramped space: *Jumbo Christmas lights. Five settings. Superior LED bulbs.* 'For *Madeleine*. To turn her into a Christmas cruiser.'

Summer stared, first at the lights, then at Mason. 'You don't think they're tacky?'

'We've got four weeks of travelling ahead, and I thought we could be a leading light – as it were – of Christmas spirit on the waterways. Besides, we'll need to stand out once we reach London. Are they here?'

Summer swallowed, touched by Mason's thoughtfulness. 'Claire was wondering where you were.'

'Now we can tell her. I may not have been part of the welcoming party, but I come bearing sparkly lights. She can't be annoyed about that.'

'You're right,' Summer said. 'She can't. Let's go and give *Madeleine* her Christmas costume. Thank you for getting them, she's going to look wonderful.'

'The belle of the ball,' Mason agreed.

Claire came out of Valerie's boat *Cosmic* while Mason was on *Madeleine*'s roof, securing the fairy lights to each corner.

'So, the wanderer returns.' Her smile was wide.

'Claire.' Mason climbed down and jumped onto the towpath, wiping his hands down his jeans. 'Good to see you.' They embraced, and Summer watched from inside the café. Did Claire still have reservations about Mason that Summer didn't know about – was that why she had brought up his initial reluctance to come with them? Or was she reading too much into it, still worried that there was something more behind his uncharacteristic annoyance when she had first mentioned the trip?

Feeling unsettled, Summer left them to chat, taking a fresh batch of scones out of the oven, Latte hovering at her feet as if warm, cheesy dough was her favourite treat.

When it was time to set off, Ryder tooted his horn.

Summer gave Valerie a hug on the towpath, the older woman squeezing her tightly as they said goodbye.

'Be careful, Summer,' she said. 'And believe in the ones you love.'

'What does that mean?' Summer asked, laughing nervously.

'Just have a wonderful time.'

'See you for Christmas,' Summer said. 'And keep Norman company.'

'I'm going to teach him how to read tea leaves,' Valerie said, and Summer was left with that disturbing but hilarious image as she made her way to the stern deck of *Madeleine*, untying the ropes as she went.

'All set?' Mason asked, giving a quick, wistful glance at his beloved boat.

'All set,' Summer agreed, patting the side of *The Sandpiper* before jumping up beside him. 'Let's get this show on the road.'

Mason started the engine, the low thrum obscured as Led Zeppelin blared out from *Water Music*'s speakers, and Summer and Mason followed Claire, Ryder and the band of roving traders out of Willowbeck. Peering ahead, as *Madeleine* followed in the wakes of the other narrowboats, Summer noticed that Claire had a small banner hanging from the back door of her boat, visible when she changed position at the helm. It said *Bruisin' for a cruisin'*.

The weather was grey but still, the sun and wind both muted, the water flat, the going easy but cold. They made good progress, and slowed as they reached a small marina in a place called King's Corner, just after a particularly tight lock. The marina was decorated beautifully, with blue, twinkling Christmas lights and a Christmas tree alongside the towpath covered in silver baubles and fake snow.

'So this is our stop-over for the night?' Mason asked. 'I'm not sure I've ever stayed here before.'

'And I definitely haven't.' The festive sight made Summer feel giddy with excitement for their trip, glad that they were on their way, and that the moment of frostiness between her and Claire hadn't lasted. She kissed Mason, distracting him from turning the boat into the mooring.

He tried to see past her and huffed. 'Summer, do you want a hole in the side of *Madeleine*?'

'Sorry,' she said, stepping back, trying to hide her smile.

She waited until they were in place, and hopped onto the towpath to tie the ropes. 'See,' she said, once she was back on board and Mason was feeding Archie and Latte in the kitchen. 'No damage done.'

'Only because of my astute navigational skills in the face of women throwing themselves at me.' Mason flashed her a grin.

Summer shook her head, trying not to laugh, and then flung her arms around him, the scratchy wool of his coat – which he hadn't yet taken off – tickling her cheek. 'Let's go and see what the plan for tonight is.'

The plan turned out to be a slightly scruffy pub a hundred yards along the towpath, where they ordered fish and chips with a tangy, homemade tartar sauce and got reacquainted with each other. Mason had met everyone when they'd put on a music festival the previous year, and Claire's band of roving traders had visited Willowbeck a couple of times since then, but he didn't know them as well as Summer did. Ralph still had his sandwich shack, and delighted in telling them all about his Christmas offerings. They included bacon and Christmas pudding, and roast beef and brandy butter. Mason made a guttural moan when he said he was trying out turkey, cranberry jelly and a custard relish.

'I'm calling it turkey trifle,' Ralph said, grinning. 'I might even add a bit of nutmeg stuffing.'

'Was that a moan of pain, or longing?' Summer asked Mason.

'Don't you think it sounds delicious?'

'Custard, Mason. With turkey.'

'I can't see custard ever being a bad thing.' He shrugged.

'And I thought I knew you.' Summer placed a hand against her chest dramatically, and Ralph laughed.

'Seems like I've got a fan,' he said. 'And don't worry Summer, there's plain old turkey and cranberry, or beef and horseradish. I never forget about the people with unadventurous taste buds.'

The group slipped into a familiar, easy chat. They caught up on the last few months' gossip, the goings-on at Willowbeck, the different places Claire and the others had ventured to, the quirkiness of life as a roving trader. There was a woman who had spent two hours on *Water Music* in stifling heat, searching every shelf for Boyzone LPs and CDs, even though Claire had directed her to the right section to begin with. Doug told Summer and Mason about a couple who had bought a miniature portrait to his antique barge for valuation, and he had told them he didn't have enough money to take it off their hands because he was sure it was an original John Smart, and they could pay off half their mortgage if they took it to an auction house.

Summer was in the process of telling everyone about the Halloween-slash-engagement party when Ryder leaned languidly across the table, his blond hair flopping in front of his eyes, and spoke in a voice that was loud enough to bring all other conversation to a halt.

'So Mason,' he said, 'I noticed you've been writing these pieces, about the nature reserves around here. How's that going?'

Mason seemed as taken aback by the question as Summer was, but then she glanced at Claire and thought that maybe her friend had been prepping Ryder, perhaps suggesting he needed to make an effort to seem interested in other people.

'It's a great job,' Mason said, 'having a regular column. I can build up a picture of the reserve slowly, look at the changes throughout the year, the seasonal highlights, and I don't have to cram everything into a couple of thousand words. I've had good feedback from readers so far.'

'Getting a fanbase already?' Ryder leaned back, giving Summer a quick, smug glance.

'It's three letters,' Mason laughed, 'from bird watchers. They're interested in the area, so—'

'Not those Byronic curls? Sure one of your twitchers isn't really a groupie in the making, masquerading as a sixty-year-old man?'

Mason frowned. 'Pretty sure. It's not really the specialism for attracting adoring fans.'

'You never know. Best stay on your toes.' Ryder tapped his nose, and then turned to Doug, who was looking equally bemused by the younger man's warning.

'What was that about?' Mason asked out of the side of his mouth.

'It was Ryder being Ryder,' Summer said.

'He's not happy unless he's stirring the pot,' Jas added.

In his mid-twenties, with a neat black beard and thick hair that was often hidden under a baseball cap, Jas wrote a blog about living on the waterways, which had grown slowly before taking off, appealing to a younger audience than the subject matter suggested, gaining followers into the hundreds of thousands. Summer remembered his kindness, his quiet, unassuming nature, his online appeal more about the warmth of his posts – and his Irish wolfhound, Chester, who featured heavily – than anything flashy or show-off. He left all that to Ryder.

'But,' Jas continued, 'you shouldn't underestimate the power of your words, and the number of people who are passionate about the same things as you, even if it doesn't seem, at first, like the kind of thing that would reach a wide audience.'

'Speaking from experience,' Mason said.

'Nobody's more surprised about how my blog's grown than I am. Have you ever thought of doing one? It would sit well alongside your magazine work. They'd feed off each other.'

'I hadn't. If there was any interest, it would be a small, select few.' Mason looked to Summer, who squeezed his leg under the table.

'You're being too modest,' she said. 'Jas is right, he knows what he's talking about. You just need to be able to commit, to have the time to do it regularly.'

Jas was nodding. 'Absolutely. Build up your followers, make sure that it's consistent, manage their expectations. Talk to them. And,' he said, his dark eyes alive with amusement, 'a good photo of you with those Byronic locks wouldn't hurt either.'

Mason ran a hand self-consciously through the hair in question. 'I don't know.'

'Let's get together at some point – it's not like we'll be short of time – and I can show you around my blog, give you a feel for what it would be like. Then any decision you make will be informed.'

Mason chewed his lip, and Summer could almost see the battling factions in his head: the opportunity to reach out to more people, to spread his love of nature, against his love of being in it, of not being stuck behind a computer screen – except when he was sorting through his photos or writing about what he'd seen. She knew that spending hours replying to comments, endless tweeting, would have him running for the hills.

'Have a think,' she said. 'You don't need to decide now.'

'No. Thanks, Jas, it's a kind offer.'

'Sure,' he said amiably, 'any time. I'm not going anywhere.'

Later, curled up in *Madeleine*'s snug cabin, blanketed in quietness, Summer let the familiar and unfamiliar settle around her. She could hear the occasional snuffles and knocks from Archie and Latte next door, as they both tried to monopolize the sofa to sleep on. A nighttime cruiser sometimes drifted past, causing the rhythmic swaying of the boat, hollow clunks as *Madeleine* knocked gently against the side of the towpath. There was a tawny owl in a tree not far away, its hoot soothing and reassuring.

She had enjoyed their first day cruising, had slipped back into it so easily, the relaxed evening in the pub, the banter and the teasing, Ryder getting under everyone's skin. She hoped that Mason hadn't been too put out by it, that he was enjoying it as much as she was. Because already, Summer knew that it had been the right decision. She had missed Claire and Jas, Ralph and Doug – even Ryder – more than she'd realized, and the thought of spending five weeks with them, of being in the centre of London in the run-up to Christmas, filled her with happiness. And this time, she thought, as she snuggled closer to Mason, his hair tickling her face even while he slept, it was even better, because she was with the man that she loved.

Chapter 7

The following day they cruised out of King's Corner after an early breakfast, and Summer held her head high, breathing in the cold, fresh air as she followed behind *Doug's Antique Barge*, waving at helmsmen and -women and people on the towpath. Even though it was daylight, the lights on her boat sparkled, and Claire interspersed her usual soundtrack with Christmas carols, keeping the volume low in deference to the unknown territory and wildlife. Once they were moored up in Little Venice – and in their other stops along the way – Summer knew she would blast the songs out, the perfect advertisement for the boat that sold CDs and LPs, and sold them well despite the digital age.

Now they were heading south-west, soon to join the Grand Union Canal and meander their way along it towards London. The views were new and fresh, the villages different, all with their own, unique character. The terrain changed too, becoming hillier, the stretches of fields replaced by sloping banks, the canal sitting in valleys, evergreen or skeleton forests sometimes hugging close to the water's edge, obscuring the land beyond.

Over the next few days, Summer did more than her lion's share at the helm, enjoying the fresh air, the sights and sounds. Mason often joined her, and they took it in turns to make hot drinks, keeping the cold at bay.

As the journey to London would take most of the two weeks, they had only fleeting opportunities to open their businesses: a couple of hours in the morning before they left a mooring, an afternoon when they arrived at their next destination. Whenever they did, Summer and Mason worked as a team in the café, Mason proving excellent at chatting to the punters, coaxing strollers on the towpath over to the hatch for a coffee and a pastry. He'd helped out during the summer when she was rushed off her feet, but had focused on clearing tables, loading and unloading the dishwasher, leaving the serving and interaction to her and Harry. Now, though, he was getting stuck in.

'That's an Egyptian goose,' he said, leaning out of the hatch and pointing to a pale brown and grey goose with darkish red-brown patches around its eyes and on its tail feathers. A couple nearby, who were taking photos and holding out stale bread, looked up. 'They're not native,' Mason continued, 'they escaped into the wild after being brought to this country as an ornamental bird.'

'Really?' The man, in his late forties, Summer guessed, straightened. 'I've not seen one before. Unusual markings.'

'You only get them in this region,' Mason added. 'I've always thought that they're particularly beautiful. And not as aggressive as the Canada geese.'

'Oh, those blighters!' The woman spoke now. 'I've given up getting my bread out when they're around, they're like attack dogs.'

'They're becoming a bit of a nuisance in some places,' Mason agreed. 'Not their fault really, but they're not the most tactful of beggars.'

The man laughed, approached the hatch and carried on the conversation while ordering two gingerbread lattes and a bag of six mince pies. Summer watched from the table she was pretending to clear, feeling a flush of pride.

'Who knew the *Springwatch* sales technique would prove so successful?' she asked, once the customers had gone away happy.

Mason smiled at her. 'I love Egyptian geese.'

'So you weren't even trying to reel them in?'

He shook his head. 'I wasn't, but I might do now. Though I expect it only works when you're not trying too hard. I'm not a natural salesman.'

'You could have fooled me! But you don't have to be very often,' Summer said. 'The boat usually entices people in; the idea that they can have a cream tea on a narrowboat is tempting enough. Maybe there is something to this leaning out of the hatch business though.' She pondered, looking at him, and ran her fingers through his unruly curls. 'Maybe Ryder's right about the hair. It is very good hair, and attached to such a lovely face, too.'

Mason rolled his eyes. 'Ryder's a wide boy. I don't believe anything that comes out of his mouth.'

'You used to be a rover too,' she said quietly, knowing this was uncertain ground, that he'd made the move after Lisa had died, and might not want to talk about it.

'I did. I was younger, and in a bad place when I became a liveaboard. I might not have done everything the right way, but I wasn't manipulative, and nowhere near as sure of myself as Ryder is, even if I tried to pretend I was. Confidence radiates off him like the sun, and it's unnerving.'

'I wish I'd known you then,' Summer admitted. 'I know that you were struggling, that it wasn't easy at the beginning, but I'm intrigued about your wild side.'

Mason leaned against the coffee machine, and briefly closed his eyes. 'I was never wild, Summer. I was grieving, blundering through this new lifestyle with blinkers on, barely able to see past my own nose. If we'd met each other then, I don't know if we'd be together now.'

Summer nodded, her eyes directed to the floor. 'Tania?' she asked softly.

Claire's friend, the woman Mason had been with all those years ago, who he'd left without a proper explanation – not just in the emotional sense, but in the physical too, taking himself and his boat away from Tania without looking back. It was why Claire hadn't had much to say in Mason's favour when Summer first met her, and he'd turned up on her boat one evening when they were moored up in a market town called Foxburn. Claire hadn't been happy that Summer knew Mason, already feeling protective of her despite their fledgling friendship. But once Mason had explained what had happened – that he should never have got together with Tania, that he had been too damaged by his grief, nowhere near healing – Claire had forgiven him, embraced him with open arms.

'Tania,' Mason repeated, the word coming out as a sigh. 'It was a disaster. I treated her so badly. I'd like to think that, had I met you back then, things would have been different, because, believe me, Summer, the way I feel about you . . .' his voice hitched, and he shook his head. 'But I was barely making it through each day. I put on a front, pretended I was just a new liveaboard getting the hang of the lifestyle, and I thought being close to someone again would help to patch me up. But it was selfish, and she paid the price. So . . . I wasn't a wild, enigmatic rover like Ryder. I had a broken spirit, and no way of knowing how to fix it.'

Summer swallowed. Mason suddenly looked so forlorn. She went round to the other side of the counter and took him in her arms, kissing his forehead, trying to kiss away the memories. 'I'm sorry, I shouldn't have brought it up.'

'No, of course you should. I often wonder what it would have been like if I'd met you sooner, if you'd been on your mum's boat helping out when I'd passed by – a couple of years later, once I was slowly getting back on track.'

'See, that's when I'm talking about. Not at the very beginning, but once you'd established yourself as a wildlife photographer. You, Archie and *The Sandpiper* cruising up and down the waterways, dazzling everything in your path with your beauty—'

'I hope you're talking about my boat, there.'

'I bet you were a force to be reckoned with, Mason Causey.' She smiled, and his eyes danced back, his face transformed by a sudden grin.

'As opposed to the staid, boring old codger I am now, you mean?'

'That's not what I meant!'

'And you're highly romanticizing everything, by the way. It wasn't like that. The only reason I sold any of my photos was because of the contacts I'd had before. You're imagining this confident, dynamic guy—'

'I'm not imagining him, Mason, I'm standing in front of him.'

'Just a girl, standing in front of a boy, asking him to love her.' He raised an eyebrow, but Summer's breath stalled in her throat.

'Now who's romanticizing?' she managed. His words were too close for comfort to the proposal she'd been imagining. 'And when did you learn all the words to *Notting Hill* off by heart?'

Mason looked shifty. 'Sometimes when you're busy in the café and my article refuses to write itself, I turn to the television for company.'

'Specifically Richard Curtis films?'

'Not exclusively.'

Summer tried to slow her pulse. 'I despair—'

'Hello, are you open?'

'Yes of course.' Summer spun so quickly that she knocked into the counter, smiling widely at the family as they stepped inside. 'Please, come in. Have a seat and I'll be over to take your order in a moment.'

She watched as they took their coats off and picked up the menu, the children aged around eight and ten, wide-eyed at being on the boat, uninterested in sitting while there were so many windows to look out of.

'Can you go and check on the brownies in the oven, Hugh?'

Mason turned in the kitchen doorway. 'I think you'll find that line belongs to Julia Roberts.'

Summer shook her head and went to greet her new customers.

The Grand Union Canal was much busier than the fenland waterways, as if they had turned onto the M25 of canals. The going was much slower, the routes narrow in places, wide in others, so they often found themselves getting up a head of steam, cruising at a regular speed and then having to slow to negotiate a tight bend, while other boats tried to manoeuvre through from the opposite direction. But despite being harder work, it woke Summer's eyes up to the buzz and chatter of a busy, good-tempered waterway.

Welcomes were exchanged, there was time to talk to the other helmsmen and -women as they queued for locks or tackled bends, and everyone was cheerful despite the cold weather. Life as a liveaboard wasn't without its challenges, but it was certainly a slower, less stressful pace of life. And *Madeleine* wasn't the only festive boat. They passed narrowboats with Christmas trees on their decks, one with fake snow covering the roof (Mason wondered aloud how long that would take to clean off once Christmas was over) and many that were also adorned with lights, though Summer secretly decided none were as vibrant or sparkling as theirs.

One evening, a week into their journey, they ended up on *The Wanderer's Rest*, Ryder's narrowboat. It had a small bathroom and open-plan kitchen towards the bow end, the engine at the stern, and then the rest of the interior was like a shell, a single, open space scattered with beanbags and oversized cushions. Ryder opened up his boat for the use of others, and when there was no pub to convene in, and on the nights when the group of travellers came together rather than hunkering down in their own cabins, this was often where they came.

On this occasion, Ralph had cooked a Christmas curry, which Summer eyed suspiciously before tasting and falling instantly in love with.

'Oh God,' she said, closing her eyes as the flavours burst on her tongue, 'what's in this?'

'Best not to ask, I always think,' Claire said, her eyes glinting in the low light. There was a small log burner glowing and crackling in the corner, which Summer thought was a new addition since the last time she'd been on board. 'If you enjoy it, leave it there. Don't go digging for something you might not want to unearth.'

'Good point. As long as it doesn't have any kind of offal in it, I'll be fine.'

'Offal adds so much flavour,' Ralph cooed, and Summer's next mouthful hovered inches from her lips.

'Ignore him,' Claire said, laughing.

'It's delicious, Ralph. I'd love to have the recipe sometime.'

'The secret,' Ralph said, 'along with the turkey and the spices, is sweet potato and aubergine. Remind me and I'll bring the full recipe round in the morning.' He gave her a thumbs up, his thin, fair hair wispy around his face, and went back to stirring the large pot on Ryder's tiny stove.

'So,' Claire said, leaning back against the wall, curling her legs up beneath her, 'what's it like being back on the road again, so to speak? As good as last time?'

Summer twirled her fork in the rice. It was so different from last time. 'We've not been able to spend as much time together. And we've been travelling so much that I've barely opened the café. It's been great to come further afield though, to see the different canals – see how busy it is here. I can't imagine anyone actually gets anywhere during the summer. If it's like this now, then . . .'

'I know,' Claire laughed. 'You grow a good chunk of patience. But we all get where we're going eventually, and nobody's ever in as much of a rush as they are on land. The water slows everything down, puts us all under its spell.'

Summer nodded. It was a good way of putting it. She had fallen under Willowbeck's spell. It had been a slow burner, admittedly, but once it had her in its grip, it was never going to let go, and Summer was completely fine with that. 'It's a shame we can't go to the woods this time, and terrify each other with ghost stories.'

'The fairy glade.' Claire's voice was soft with nostalgia. 'Yeah, that was a good time. Doesn't mean we can't get our storytelling on here, though. You need space, a bit of wine – which Ralph's always got – and then create the atmosphere yourself. Fairy lights are an added bonus. Yours are spectacular, by the way. Almost like a disco barge.'

'They're very bright,' Summer agreed. 'Hopefully no chance of getting into any scrapes, because every other narrowboat can see us coming a mile off.'

'It's a good tactic, that.' Claire sipped her homemade wine. 'And Mason seems to be getting on with everyone.'

Summer followed Claire's gaze further up the space, where Mason and Jas were sitting against the wall, deep in conversation. They had a trio of dogs lazing around them in various states of consciousness: Chester, Archie and Latte who, Summer was surprised to see, was licking their empty food bowls. She could usually guarantee that it would be Archie who would get to that first, but the Border terrier was sparked out, his front paw twitching as he slept.

'He's very sociable, despite his geeky habits.' She and Claire exchanged a smile.

'I'm glad that he's found his feet with this regular column,' Claire said, 'it sounds just right for him. And I hope you told him to ignore Ryder's idiotic comments.'

'He chose to do that all by himself,' Summer said.

'That boy needs a good talking to, though it wouldn't change anything. Ryder is Ryder. He's not fond of new alpha males joining the pack, always has to exert his authority.'

'Mason's not a typical alpha male, but I can see why he feels threatened.'

'That's because you've got love goggles on. Mason's definitely a catch though, and all the more for it because he doesn't realize how hot he is. He was always like that, even back when I first knew him. Much tidier then, his hair short, because he'd only just started being a liveaboard, but still walking around deep in his own thoughts, unaware that every pair of female eyes followed him greedily. That was part of the problem, I suppose.'

Summer glanced at her friend. She seemed sad, rather than annoyed, and Summer didn't know whether to push further or let her speak. In the end, she couldn't help it. 'With Tania, you mean?'

Claire's lips pressed together. She nodded.

'He never meant for it to happen. You know that now.'

'Oh God, of course. He was in the worst possible place, dealing with something I can't ever imagine having to go through. I guess, though, that made him even more oblivious to how hard Tania had fallen for him. He thought he was trying something new, testing the waters again, seeking comfort in company, and she was falling in love with him.'

'Do you . . . have you seen her again? Does she know what happened?'

Claire glanced at her, looked away. 'Yeah, I told her. I'd not seen her for a while, but our paths crossed not that long ago, and so I repeated what Mason had told me.'

'And?' Summer swallowed. She was surprised Claire hadn't offered up the news before now, and wasn't sure what response she was hoping for, whether she wanted Tania to be thoroughly understanding, or if she'd prefer her to stay angry with Mason. She shouldn't feel threatened – there was no reason to – but she couldn't help it. Tania had loved Mason, and he had at least cared for her, however blinded by grief he was at the time.

'Tania's a very forgiving person,' Claire said, almost a whisper.

Summer's palms prickled with heat. 'That – that's great, that she understands. Mason would never intentionally hurt anyone.'

'Course not. As I said, he's a total catch. Sweet guy, hot as that log burner over there. You've fallen on your feet, Summer. And look, there's something I should have mentioned, before, about how we got our moorings in Little Venice.' She shuffled round to face her and Summer did the same, waiting to hear about some other spectacular fair that was going to be on at the same time as them, or that the static narrowboat café had found out they were coming and was refusing to let Summer trade.

'What is it?'

Pain flashed momentarily across Claire's face. 'The thing is, Sum—'

'How's it going over here?' Ryder slid to the floor, somehow managing to come between them and drape his arms around both their shoulders. 'How are you enjoying the GU, Summer?'

When she frowned, Claire interpreted. 'Grand Union. Actually, Ryder, we were in the middle of something.'

'Oh great,' he said, his blue eyes bright despite the gloom. 'I love a *something*.'

'It's not . . .' Claire sighed, giving Summer a meaningful look that said *Later*. Summer nodded.

'Oh.' Ryder did fake-petulant. 'So, ladies, if you won't spill the beans, then I'll have to. It turns out our esteemed friend Jas is, at this very moment, convincing your better half to set up his own blog, all about birdies and fish and snakes, and whatever else it is you get out here that he goes all paparazzi over.'

96

'Your ignorance is astounding, considering how long you've been on the water.' Claire shook her head, exasperated.

'There are more exciting things to focus on than the immediate surroundings.' He was airy, false, and Summer wondered if he actually had a guidebook about wildlife on the British waterways in his back pocket. The idea made her grin.

'Someone's enjoying themselves,' he said, quick as a flash. 'Imbibing your fair share of Ralph's homemade wine, Summer?'

'Nope. Just having a good time. And I think Mason writing a blog is a great idea. Some people love knowing more about the wildlife outside their window, and Jas's online following proves that narrowboats aren't unfashionable. If Jas gave him a bit of a plug, he'd be bound to get lots of followers.'

Ryder nodded. 'You play the dutiful wife well, I'll give you that.'

Summer felt her cheeks redden. 'I'm not his wife.'

Ryder narrowed his eyes. 'Oh, and is that a sore spot?'

'Sod off, Ryder.' Claire shoved his shoulder and Ryder shrugged, kissed Claire on the forehead and sloped off to annoy someone else.

'Why does he have to be so irritating?' Summer asked, noticing that Claire was gazing after him, her expression unreadable.

'Because he loves winding people up. It's his superhero power, he's scarily good at it.'

'Ugh.' Summer shook her head, trying to clear her thoughts, but Claire, eagle-eyed, had picked up on the last exchange.

'Is it a sore spot, that you're not married? You've only been together a year and a bit, Sum.'

'It's not, it's just . . .' She chewed her lip, wondering whether to let Claire in on her plans. But she'd already told Harry, and Jenny, and Jenny would have told Dennis by now, and while they were good friends, Claire was close to Ryder and everything would be ruined if he got his hands on the information. 'I love him, and I want to be with him. I don't want anything to get in the way of that.' It was a lame explanation, but she didn't know what else she could say.

'What would get in the way?' Claire asked quietly.

'I don't know.' Summer glanced at Mason. He was gesticulating wildly, explaining something to Jas that had the blogger doubled over in laughter, and a smile curved her lips automatically. 'It was so complicated at the beginning, so much delayed us admitting how we really felt – the past, misunderstandings, Ross – and then there was the fire. Even though we love each other, and we're good together, I get this irrational fear that it's more fragile than it is, that something's going to come along and change everything.' She stopped, wondering where the words had come from, realizing they'd been dragged up from deep inside her.

Claire's smile was reassuring. 'I get that fear, it's totally understandable. Worried it's too good to be true, waiting for something to go wrong. But you know Mason loves you, right? Even if something *were* to happen, something totally unexpected, you'd be strong through it. I know you would, because I know you, Sum. Everything will be fine.'

'Thank you. I don't know why I said all that. I'm excited about our future, I have so many plans, and along with that comes the fear that they'll be derailed, but there's nothing behind it. Besides,' Summer said, feeling buoyed by her friend's encouragement, 'what could possibly go wrong?'

Chapter
8

They cruised into Little Venice on the second of December, the time when, usually, Summer's excitement about impending Christmas turned into terror, and she became frantic and panicked, even though there were still over three weeks to go to get everything ready. But this year she didn't have time to worry about that, because her entire brain was taken up with falling in love with Little Venice on sight.

They'd cruised down the Grand Union Canal, through Uxbridge and Watford, to their destination. They were in the middle of London, but this was a part of the capital that was so different to the busy, crowded streets, the endless buildings, the noise and clamour.

Here, nestled amongst it all, was an oasis. The weak winter sun reflected off the water, the boats moored along both sides of the canal – sometimes two abreast – were colourful and welcoming, the skeletons of trees bowing above them. It was more bustling than Willowbeck, but no less picturesque. And it felt instantly friendly.

She turned to Mason, who was at the helm, and saw his expression mirrored hers.

'Isn't it beautiful?' she asked.

Further along the canal she could see a bridge, similar to Willowbeck's arched brick structure, but more ornate, its royal blue paintwork vibrant. She had seen this in the photos, and now it was in front of her she wanted to walk over that bridge, to gaze on the boats from above, to look down on her café and remember it in this iconic place, this kingdom amongst Britain's waterways.

'It's stunning,' Mason agreed. 'Better than I imagined.'

His curls were tucked inside a grey beanie hat, his nose red from the cold. She took his hand and he squeezed it, their gloved fingers holding on as they slowed, following the instructions Jas was shouting, his boat in front of theirs.

People on the towpath and on the street above stopped to watch their convoy arrive, this new influx of beautiful, brightly coloured boats, decked out in their Christmas finery. Some of them, children especially, waved down at them, and Summer couldn't help but wave back. Mason tooted their horn, and then Jas and Ryder joined in, and soon they were all tooting and waving, and other liveaboards emerged from the narrowboats already moored along the canal, standing on their decks as they cruised slowly past.

Their visitor moorings were along the approach to the blue bridge, and Summer knew from her research that beyond it was the permanent riverside café, stationed at the point where the water opened up, and the Great Union Canal met the Regent's Canal and the Paddington Basin. She hoped that if they stayed here, where the water was thick with narrowboats, and didn't pass the café, then she wouldn't be seen as competition – perhaps wouldn't even be noticed by the other café owner. She'd had nightmares of being drummed out of Little Venice, a Wild West scenario with narrowboats instead of horses, pushing *Madeleine*'s throttle as hard as she could, Latte and Archie barking furiously while the angry café manager hurled abuse, and possibly scones, in her direction.

Mason rubbed her shoulders, squeezing the knotted muscles. 'We made it. We've voluntarily travelled for miles and miles to participate in a week of London madness before Christmas.'

'We have! That other narrowboat café . . .' she turned to him.

'They won't even know you're here, and if they do, they'll embrace it. It's London, and we're here for one week. What could they possibly do?'

She was speechless. 'How—?'

Mason's smile was gentle. 'I did some Googling before we left. I have been excited about this too, you know, and I wanted to see what I was letting myself in for. OK, here we go.' He focused on manoeuvring *Madeleine* into her new mooring, Jas and Ryder giving slightly contradictory hand gestures from their boats. Despite that, he slid it expertly into place, and Summer surveyed their position.

It was perfect.

They were between *Water Music* – always helpful as an alarm clock if she was ever tempted to have a lie-in – and *Doug's Antiques Barge*. The towpath was a constant flow of people in black overcoats or brightly coloured jackets, trailing scarves and woolly hats, all slowing to examine the new arrivals, to read the signs and noticeboards on the sides of the trading boats.

'We're going to be rushed off our feet, aren't we?' Mason asked, his gaze following hers.

'The busiest week of our lives.'

It was half past two, and the sun was already beginning to

sink behind the buildings. The shadows were long, creeping their icy tendrils towards everything, and Summer shivered. Latte barked and, with their ropes secured, they headed inside, stamping their feet to try and get the feeling back in their toes.

Claire knocked on the door a few minutes later.

'What do you think?' she asked, throwing her arms wide.

'I think it looks amazing,' Summer said. 'And busy. Are you opening up for a couple of hours, or starting afresh tomorrow?'

'You don't need to close when the sun goes down.'

'So we're opening late?'

'Open whenever you want, for however long you want. But you can make a killing if you've got the stamina. Meet up later for drinks, yeah?'

'Sure,' Summer said, waving her goodbye. Mason switched on the coffee machine.

'Right then,' he said, wiping the blackboard clear and handing her a red chalk pen, 'let's introduce *Madeleine* to London town.'

They stayed open until six o'clock, serving and chatting to a constant stream of customers. Christmas had most definitely arrived in London, and they saw groups of friends and work colleagues, some loaded up with bright shopping bags crammed with presents, others clearly on the way to an evening out, glittery dresses under their coats, a few with reindeer headbands or Santa hats. They admired *Madeleine*'s exterior designs of cakes and coffee cups, the sparkly lights trailed around its roof, and the Christmas bunting inside. Summer laid a small selection of Norman's carvings on the counter, and they were soon snapped up. She would have to ration those throughout the week. Her supply of cakes and brownies was decimated, and she realized the stock she had set aside for the following day wasn't going to be enough.

Mason served customers at the hatch and cleared tables when there was a momentary lull, and they worked to a backdrop of Christmas carols and songs, 'Fairytale of New York', Wham and Slade, 'Silent Night' and 'God Rest Ye Merry Gentlemen' from *Water Music*, the sound quieter than usual to meet Little Venice's strict noise regulations, but still very festive. Summer put some of Harry's mince pies in the oven, and the sweet, fruity smell wafted through the café, while she adorned gingerbread lattes and hot chocolates with a dusting of chocolate or cinnamon using her new, snowflake-shaped stencil.

'This is new, isn't it?' asked a young, suited man as he approached the counter, an attractive blonde woman sliding into a chair at one of the tables.

'New to Little Venice,' Summer confirmed. 'We're only here for a week, part of a temporary Christmas market. You should check out the other boats – you can buy music, antiques, and some seriously impressive sandwiches – though not until you've had cake here.' She grinned. 'What can I get you?'

'A selection of macarons and two hot chocolates, please. Where are you off to after this?'

'Back home. We come from a village near Ely. It's similar to Little Venice in lots of ways, but nowhere near as busy.'

'You're in London, a few weeks before Christmas!' He gave her an amused smile. 'Hopefully you didn't come here for a rest?'

Summer laughed. 'No, not at all. But however much you imagine something, it never lives up to the reality, does it?'

'Very true.'

'Go and take a seat, I'll bring everything over once it's ready.'

He sat opposite the blonde woman, his hand landing on top of hers, but not before Summer had noticed the ring on her left hand, the diamond glinting like ice. She found that she was staring, only snapping out of her daydream when a burly man with a white beard, who looked like Father Christmas on dress-down day, waved a hand in front of her face.

'So sorry,' she said. 'What can I get you?'

'How many mince pies do you have left?'

Three pies remained on the plate under the glass dome. 'I've got these, and a few more out the back.'

'Can I have seven?' he asked.

She resisted the urge to check he didn't need eight, one for each of the reindeer, and rushed into the kitchen. When she returned, Mason was loading hot drinks into a cardboard cup carrier for a woman in a scarlet woollen coat and white sparkly hat who was standing at the hatch. Mason's customer seemed reluctant to leave once she'd got her order, and Summer couldn't help noticing how glossy her hair was, and her perfect eye-makeup.

'You're a new face along the towpath.' Her voice was low and silky, as if she had honed it in seductress classes.

'We only arrived this afternoon,' Mason said. 'We're here for a week.'

'Oh. Shame. I've just started thinking about Christmas presents.'

'We're really only a café,' he said, smiling patiently. 'But I could do you a selection of macarons in one of our gift boxes? We've got some festive flavours.'

'I was thinking about a present for me,' the woman said slowly. 'And I was hoping for more than a few macarons.' She looked at Mason from beneath long eyelashes. 'What are you doing this evening? I don't mind getting my gift a few weeks early.'

Mason stared at her, and Summer tried to hide her smile as she put dress-down Santa's mince pies in a bag. This was a more brazen level of flirting than Mason was used to, and it was clear he'd been oblivious to the woman's intentions until that moment. She felt the slimmest twinge of jealousy, but was more curious to see how Mason would respond.

'That's very flattering,' he said, slowly. 'But I'm busy tonight, and I hadn't planned on ending up under someone's tree in a bow. Well, not unless it's Summer's tree.' He gestured towards her, and Summer received a steely look from Mason's admirer. 'I hope you enjoy your coffee.' He gave the woman a kind smile.

She returned it with a quick, defiant one, then disappeared into the crowd, her shoulders held high.

Mason worried his hand through his hair. 'Bloody hell.'

'I'm going to have to stay on my toes, aren't I?' Summer asked, elbowing him gently in the ribs.

He looked mortified. 'Summer, I didn't encourage—'

'I'm joking.' She squeezed his hand. 'She was quite forward, wasn't she? Maybe Ryder's right, and you need to be more aware of predatory women in highly populated areas.'

Mason rolled his eyes. 'It was one woman, and I'm sure if you'd been at the hatch all afternoon you would have been hit on by at least a dozen men.'

Summer laughed, unsure what to say, and then realized dress-down Santa was still standing at the counter, grinning at them through his white beard.

'I'm so sorry,' she said again. 'Did I forget to give you your change?'

'No no,' he said amiably. 'I'm enjoying the entertainment.'

'Oh.' She felt her cheeks flush.

'We've only been here a few hours,' Mason explained. 'We're not total country bumpkins, but it's our first time with the café in London, so . . .' he shrugged.

'Oh, mark my words,' the older man said, 'women throwing themselves at you will be the least outlandish thing you have to deal with. Expect people sleeping on the deck of your boat, wild river swimmers—'

'In December?' Mason interrupted, incredulous.

He kept going. 'Singers, dancers, people using the boats as floating stages for dramatic re-enactments. You might even get an escaped animal. We're quite close to London Zoo here, and the chimpanzees are notorious.'

'OK, now I know you're having us on.' Mason folded his arms. 'I have a few contacts in that area, and a chimpanzee has never escaped from London Zoo.'

Dress-down Santa laughed, a big belly laugh that shook his beard. 'Lion tamer, are you?'

'He's a nature journalist,' Summer said proudly.

'Be prepared for a lively time, that's all I'm saying. And thanks for these, I'll be back for more tomorrow if they're up to scratch.'

'They will be,' Summer called to his retreating back, feeling a rush of affection for their new, amused customer.

'People swimming?' Mason said, turning to her. 'In the canal, in December?'

'That was the weirdest thing you took from that?'

'I'm feeling naive all of a sudden. Take me back to Willowbeck and Valerie's fortune-telling.'

'We'll be fine,' Summer laughed. 'You handled your admirer very well, and the idea of you wearing only a bow on Christmas morning isn't one that entirely repulses me.'

'Good,' he said, raising an eyebrow in a way that made

Summer's legs tingly, 'because I haven't got you anything else for Christmas.'

'I don't want anything else,' she whispered. 'You in a bow, that's me happy.' She didn't mention that that particular daydream also included him wearing a ring by the time the New Year rolled into view.

Summer's feet were throbbing by the time they closed the café doors, and while they'd tried to keep on top of the clearing up while they were working, it looked like a very hungry Tasmanian devil had been trapped inside all afternoon. Despite the chill outside, the café was toasty, and the moment Summer stopped she felt a wave of tiredness wash over her.

'You have a shower,' Mason said. 'I'll get this cleared up.'

Summer shook her head. 'You've been working as hard as me, and you did most of the steering today too. You go.'

'Nope.' He pushed her gently into the living space, where Latte and Archie were snoozing on the sofa, and started to close the door.

'Mason, I—'

'If I get finished in time I'll join you.'

'You don't need to—'

He closed the door, and Summer did as she was told.

She fed the dogs while Mason was getting dressed after his shower, and heard a familiar knock at the bow deck.

Claire waved at her, haloed in the light from the towpath lamps. They were more plentiful than in Willowbeck, with London's nighttime brightness also helping to combat the dark. Summer opened the door.

'You guys ready?' she asked. Her voice was slightly breathless, as if she'd run over from *Water Music*.

'Mason's nearly there, give us a couple of minutes.'

They locked up *Madeleine*, and the three of them stepped off the deck and onto the towpath. Couples and groups of friends strolled past on their way to restaurants, bars or the puppet theatre. The boats themselves were also busy, owners sitting on their decks with hot drinks, wrapped up in coats and blankets, soaking up the atmosphere. Many were adorned with fairy lights and Christmas decorations. One boat had a small, lit display of a reindeer and a donkey on its bow deck, and Summer imagined it was a smaller version of the decorations Jenny had told her about, that would, by now, be up outside the Black Swan.

She and Mason followed Claire along the towpath, and up the steps to the road above. There was a pub on the corner, with old-fashioned lanterns fixed either side of the door, the sign in turquoise and gold stating they were about to enter the Riverside Inn. A couple of people stood outside smoking. Claire pushed open the door and they stepped into a warm fug scented with beer and frying chips, amiable chatter and the clink of glasses surrounding them. It was busy but not heaving, and Summer was relieved that they didn't have to push past bodies to reach the bar or find a table. She had only just stopped feeling hot and bothered; she was ready for a calm, quiet evening with no fuss or stress.

'What can I get you?' Claire asked, leaning on the bar.

Summer and Mason both asked for lager, and Claire ordered them, exchanging banter with the tall barman that suggested they knew each other.

'So how did it go?' she asked, while they were waiting. 'Liking the look of Little Venice so far?'

'It's mad,' Summer said, laughing. 'We were busier this evening than on the hottest days in Willowbeck. Mason's been hit on, I sold some mince pies to Santa Claus, and I'm going to have to do some extra baking before the sun comes up tomorrow if I don't want to use up all of Harry's supplies in one hit.'

'So you're loving it?'

'Yes,' Summer conceded. 'It's brilliant. As long as nobody minds if I stay in bed for a week once we're back in Willowbeck.'

'I don't mind,' Mason whispered in her ear, and she slapped him lightly on the shoulder.

Claire rolled her eyes and handed them their drinks. 'Do you guys want to get a room? Seriously, I've never seen any two people so completely—' She glanced away, as if she couldn't bear to watch them any longer, and then froze.

Summer followed her friend's gaze to a slender woman with milky skin and brunette hair that fell in effortless waves around her shoulders. Her eyes were brown beneath groomed dark brows, her white T-shirt was figure-hugging below a chocolate-coloured cardigan, and her dark jeans clung to long, slim legs. She approached them slowly, a hint of a smile on her full lips, her eyes bright with expectation.

Summer frowned. She didn't know this woman, didn't understand why Claire was staring at her. And then she glanced at Mason, and everything clicked into place.

She remembered the evening Mason had travelled up to Foxburn to see her, not long after she'd met Claire, and Claire had interrupted their dinner. Claire had been a blast from Mason's past, and his shock at being dragged back to an unhappy time in his life had unsettled Summer, because Mason was usually so laid-back and unrufflable. But he hadn't been then, and he wasn't now.

Summer took his pint glass and put it on the bar, because she was sure he was going to drop it. He barely noticed. He was staring at the glamorous woman as if she were a ghost, unreal and unwanted. His face was pale, his eyes wide, and he was frozen in place.

'Mason?' she asked softly, and when he didn't answer she turned to Claire. 'Who's this, Claire?' But Claire didn't need to answer her either because she knew – of course she knew.

The dark-haired woman stopped a couple of feet away from them, her hands at her sides. 'Hi,' she said, in a voice that, while quiet, was unwavering.

'Hello.' Summer reached her hand out, trying to take control of the situation, wanting to show that she was composed and reasonable and not the trembling puddle of uncertainty that she felt inside. 'I'm Summer, are you one of Claire's friends? Do you live in Little Venice?'

'Yes,' she said, shaking Summer's hand. Her long fingers were cool, her grip strong but not crushing. She glanced at Claire, looked away again when she was met with a stony expression.

'I live in a houseboat a little further down the canal,' the woman said. 'Claire and I recently got back in touch. We were friends a while back.' She gave Summer a tight smile and glanced at Mason.

Summer fumbled for Mason's hand. She squeezed it, and felt him move, stand up straight beside her. He cleared his throat and returned the squeeze. Relief rushed through her, his acknowledgement giving her confidence.

'Nice to meet you,' Summer said, trying to focus beyond the thumping of her pulse in her ears. 'You're Tania, aren't you?'

'Yes,' she said simply. 'I am. Hello, Mason, you're looking great.' Her voice lost some of its certainty as she addressed him directly.

'Tania.' His voice was gruff, and Summer's heart ached

for him. How could Claire have let this happen without warning them?

'You weren't supposed to be here,' Claire said, finding her voice, looking to each of them in turn, her eyes wide with panic. 'Tania was – you said you were going away for Christmas.'

'Will you excuse me a moment?' Mason dropped Summer's hand and slipped past them, letting a blast of cold air break through the warmth of the pub as he disappeared outside, the door juddering closed behind him.

'Shit.' Claire pressed her hand to her forehead. 'Sum, I'm so sorry. Tania, I thought you were going to Oxford for the whole of December?'

Tania waved her hand airily at Claire. 'My plans changed, and I didn't think it would be a problem. I just wanted to see him,' she said to Summer. 'Ever since Claire told me about Lisa, about what he had to go through, I've wanted to make everything right between us. I want him to know it's OK, and that I've never forgotten him.'

Summer's legs turned to jelly. Why was Tania telling her this? She didn't need to know that Mason's effortlessly glamorous, confident ex was still thinking about him, the reason he'd left her now neatly packaged away in a plausible – albeit tragic – explanation. The way paved for her to forgive him, and for him to remember why he'd been drawn to her all those years ago.

She nodded dumbly. 'I'll be back in a moment,' she said, keeping her voice as steady as she could. 'Hold onto our drinks, Claire? I think we're going to need them.'

She pushed open the door and stepped into the cold night air. People were hurrying or strolling along the pavements, stopping to look at menus in restaurant windows. She could sense the water close by, the canal a black inky hollow below them, the presence of the coloured narrowboats shifting it away from dangerous darkness, turning it into something much more welcoming. She scanned the roads for Mason, wondering what he would have done, whether he would have gone back to *Madeleine* and the comfort of Archie and Latte, or started walking, his mind a whirlwind of conflicting, unexpected emotion.

Summer crossed the road and gripped the railings. She stared down at the canal and the twinkling lights of the boats, feeling a wave of anger towards Claire. Had she really not known Tania was going to be here? Shouldn't she have warned them it was where she lived, that it might be a possibility? Her friend had looked as upset as she was, but still, she could have prepared them for the worst-case scenario. A short chat would have done it, giving them all the facts when she'd sold them the fairytale proposition of London, a few weeks before Christmas, the magic of Little Venice.

'How about,' she said out loud, trying to expel her fury with words, '"Oh and by the way, guys, there's a chance this trip will also include Mason's ex, who he abandoned because he was grieving for his dead wife, and has been feeling guilty about ever since. So as well as the fun and festivities of Christmas, you're also going to make Mason relive the worst time of his life so, y'know, swings and roundabouts."?'

'When you put it like that, it sounds like a black comedy.'

Summer jumped – she hadn't heard Mason come up beside her, she'd been too intent on her anger and the water below. She flung her arms around him, then leaned back to appraise him. Some of the colour had returned to his cheeks.

'Mason, are you OK? I had no idea.'

His hands were warm on her lower back. 'I know that,' he whispered. 'I'm all right. I just didn't expect to see her here.'

'Me either. What do you want to do?' Summer trailed her finger down his face, trying to smooth out the chink in his jawline, to soothe him in any way she could.

He didn't reply immediately, and she almost made the decision for him, imagined leading him back to *Madeleine*, turning her round and starting the long, slow journey back to Willowbeck.

'I'm going to face her,' he said. 'I can't be given this opportunity and walk away from it – not further than here, anyway. I've wanted the chance to make it right and now, here it is.'

'You should have been given time, you should have known she'd be here.'

'I know now, and I've given myself five minutes to get used to the idea.' He tried a lopsided smile that Summer could tell was an effort, and kissed the end of her nose. 'But what about you? Are – will you be OK with me talking to her? Will you come with me?'

'Of course,' Summer said. *I'll go anywhere with you, for the rest of my life. I'll do everything I can to make you happy.*

He took her hand and they crossed the road, dodging a taxi that came hurtling unexpectedly out of a side road, its yellow light glowing. Mason hesitated for a moment, then pushed the door open, towards a part of his history that Summer didn't think he was ready to deal with, and a woman that she had never thought she'd meet.

Tania.

She knew they had cared about each other, and had often wondered whether, had Mason been a little further forward, starting to emerge from his grief when he'd met her, they would have made things work. It was, perhaps, only a matter of timing that Mason was with her now, instead of Tania. And having seen her for herself, she could understand why they had been together, why Mason had been attracted to her. She pictured the glamorous woman, her silky hair and her expressive brown eyes, the way she had walked, unflinchingly, over to Mason, as if it had been only days since they'd seen each other rather than years.

Suddenly her marriage proposal seemed like an unattainable fantasy, something she'd conjured up in a dream. She was worried that Mason wasn't prepared to see Tania again, to deal with the hurt he'd caused when he walked out on her, but she wasn't ready either.

This was the one thing, the one person, who had the potential to prevent her from marrying the man she loved. What if, once the shock faded, Mason was reminded of all the reasons he had cared about Tania, could see her more clearly than when they'd first met, and realized that he still had feelings for her?

Summer and Mason were making a life for themselves, putting old troubles and complications behind them – Lisa, her mother, painful memories they'd helped each other deal with. She had been hoping to put the cherry on the top of their relationship this New Year's Eve, but now the past was hurtling back towards them, threatening to tear their happiness apart. What had Tania said? *I've never forgotten him.*

Summer gripped Mason's hand tightly, took a deep breath, and followed him inside.

Part Two

Starboard Home

Chapter
9

The atmosphere at the table inside the Riverside Inn was almost as frosty as the early December night. Summer sipped her pint, trying to stay calm, feeling the tension radiating off Claire, sitting beside her. As much as she tried, she couldn't help glancing at her phone, calculating the minutes that Mason and Tania had been gone.

Mason and Tania.

Summer had never expected Tania to come back into Mason's life. Until today, she had been a figure rooted firmly in the past, a woman of almost mythical status. She forced herself to move her phone away from her, unable to stop the sigh from escaping.

Claire put her hand over Summer's. Summer felt a flash of anger but pushed it back down.

'I am so, so sorry, Sum,' Claire said. 'I didn't realize she'd be here. She assured me, when she organized the moorings for us, that she would be gone for the whole month. She said specifically that she didn't want to cause an atmosphere, so I have no idea what she's playing at!'

The remorse on Claire's usually cheerful face changed it completely, and Summer's anger began to fade, replaced by worry at the thought that Tania had misled Claire on purpose. 'I know it's not your fault,' she said quietly. 'But that doesn't make it any easier.'

Claire took a sip of wine. 'Of course it doesn't. God, I had such high hopes for this trip. When I found out we had the opportunity to come to Little Venice for a week, so close to Christmas, and that there would be enough visitor moorings for all of us, I jumped at the chance. And I couldn't imagine being here without you and the canal boat café. I know it's been over a year since we were roving together, and that I manage fine with my band of brothers, but this was too special to miss. And I was going to tell you that Tania had sorted out the moorings for us, but as she'd promised she wouldn't be here, I didn't think it mattered. Especially when you told me Mason was reluctant to come – I didn't want to put him off either.'

They'd spent the last fortnight travelling the British waterways from Willowbeck, Summer and Mason's picturesque fenland village home, after Claire had invited them to join in with the impromptu festive market in London, three weeks before Christmas. Mason had been thrown by the short notice, but after a day or so he'd relented, and Summer had been delighted that she'd have him, and their dogs Latte and Archie, on board her café boat *Madeleine* for five whole weeks. Their excitement upon arriving in Little Venice earlier that day had turned to shock when Tania had been waiting to greet them in the pub.

'I'm sure they won't be gone long,' Summer said, trying to reassure herself more than anyone. Mason had told Tania he was happy to speak to her, and Tania had suggested a late-night coffee shop around the corner. They'd been gone fourteen minutes. 'When did you catch up with her again?'

Claire sighed. 'We lost touch, years ago, after the whole Mason thing happened. But we were down here this spring, just for an overnight, and she came on my boat. She'd recognized it from before, of course, told me she was living here now, had a permanent mooring in Little Venice – I remember thinking she must have sold her soul to be able to afford it. It was a shock to see her, I can tell you.'

'You and me both,' Summer murmured, taking a slow sip of her beer.

'We went for a drink in this very pub,' Claire continued. 'I said that I knew where Mason was, and I told her what he'd told me, that when they met he hadn't long been a liveaboard, and was grieving for his wife; he'd lost everything and was starting again from scratch. I explained that he'd come to realize it was far too soon for him to be in a new relationship, and that he'd decided the best thing for both of them was to walk away. She knows how sorry he is, about how he treated her. I also told her that he was happy now, that he was with you.'

Summer swallowed. 'What did she say?'

'She took it all in, she said she could understand the circumstances, and that it was a relief to know the real reason he'd left.' Claire shook her head. 'I know Mason wanted to get in touch with her, to clear the air between them, but when I mentioned the possibility to Tania she said she needed more time, that when she'd had a chance to mull it over she'd decide whether she wanted to speak to him. I was only in Little Venice that one night, I left the next day and normal life resumed. It was a while before I heard from Tania again, a few text messages, but she didn't mention Mason

119

and I didn't want to push it. I thought when she was ready, she'd ask for his number – whatever. And then she let me know about the moorings, and I realized there was space for all of us. She told me she'd be going away, and I thought that was because she wasn't ready to see him again. Somewhere in the last few weeks she's changed her mind and hasn't bothered to update me.'

It was this fact, more than anything else, that made Summer feel nauseous.

Why had Tania told Claire she was going to leave Little Venice and then done the opposite? She must have known the date they were arriving because she'd booked their moorings. Maybe she'd watched them all cruise up the canal, had perhaps followed Jas or Ryder to the pub, knowing Mason and Claire wouldn't be too far behind. The fact that she hadn't let Claire know her change of plans, so Claire, in turn, could warn Summer and Mason that she'd be there, seemed underhand.

'Why do you think she didn't tell you?' Summer asked, her mouth dry.

'I don't know, Sum,' Claire said, sounding equally unsure. 'Maybe she changed her mind about wanting to see Mason, or maybe her Christmas plans simply fell through? I'm just so sorry. Do you want to – shall we go and find them?'

Summer shook her head, trying not to listen to the whispers of doubt that had started up. She trusted Mason, she knew that he had wanted the chance to speak to Tania, even if these particular circumstances weren't ideal. She couldn't go barging in there and split them up. She had to let it play out.

Ryder put a tray of drinks on the table and handed them

out, flashing a curious glance in Summer's direction. She wasn't sure how much the rest of the roving traders knew about the situation, the history between Mason and Tania, but she wasn't about to do a survey round the table.

'He needs to do this,' Summer said. 'Once he'd told me about Lisa, about why things had ended so abruptly with Tania, he wanted to let her know the truth, to apologize. But not like this, not without time to get his head around seeing her again, and work out what he was going to say. It must be like a thunderbolt.'

'God, Sum.' Claire sighed heavily. 'I know that. If I'd had any idea what she was going to do, I would have warned you, or tried to talk her out of it. I never meant for either of you to meet her like this.'

Summer finished her first drink, and pulled her second towards her. 'Mason talks about Lisa sometimes, but it still isn't easy for him. He's started to open up about their relationship, recalling happier memories, but it's as if he needs to, rather than wants to. I can tell he's not comfortable doing it.' It was easier, somehow, to talk to Claire about Mason, about how *he* might be feeling, than to admit how much Tania's appearance had thrown her.

Claire winced. 'I get that. He's certainly a different creature to the man I knew back then, with the neat hair and meticulous routine, only just learning what it was like to live on the waterways. He was as polished and perfect as his boat, and looking back it was obviously this carefully crafted exterior with a load of shit going on underneath, but because he's so much more relaxed these days, so together, I sometimes forget that he's had all this to deal with.'

'He'll be OK,' Summer said, but it came out as a whisper. 'I'm going to propose to him, you know,' she added. She didn't know why she'd said it, perhaps the need to hold onto something positive when things were suddenly so upside down.

'What?!' Claire's voice was almost a screech, and everyone at the table turned towards her.

'What's going on?' Ryder asked. 'Spill, ladies.'

'Go and find your own gossip,' Claire said, rolling her eyes good-naturedly at him. She turned her body towards Summer, blocking out everyone else. 'Sorry – again. Tell me! This is awesome news.'

'I was going to do it at Christmas,' Summer admitted. 'But then this trip came up, and I knew I'd run out of time to get everything in place. I'm going to ask him on New Year's Eve, hopefully, once we're back in Willowbeck. If it's all – if we're OK, still, by then.'

Claire's eyes widened. 'Why on earth wouldn't you be?'

Summer fidgeted, wondering whether to voice her insecurities. If Harry was here she would let everything come tumbling out, no question, but Claire knew Tania, was friends with her, despite the fact that Tania had kept her in the dark on this occasion.

'Tania's so beautiful,' she said to Claire. 'So . . . composed.'

'Oh God,' Claire said. 'Summer, you have nothing to worry about.' She grabbed both Summer's hands. 'I know this is a shock, and that Tania's appeared out of the blue, but she's in the process of starting her own business, she's settled down here. I don't know if she's seeing anyone because we've not had that discussion, but she's not interested in getting back with Mason. The only possible reason that she's here, tonight, is that she wants to clear the air.'

'How can you be so sure?' Summer's voice was small. She hated herself for sounding so pathetic, but this had knocked her for six.

'Because . . . because she's not, OK? And even if she was, Mason hasn't got eyes for anyone else. That's a hundred per cent, bona fide fact.'

'She said: "I've never forgotten him."'

'What?'

'That's what Tania said. When Mason had walked out and she told me she wanted to talk to him.'

'She might not have forgotten him, but that doesn't mean she wants to pick up where they left off. Mason's so different now, and I'm sure she is. Even if there was the will from either of them – which there isn't – it's just not possible.'

'You sound very confident,' Summer said, trying a chuckle. It sounded rusty.

'That's because I am, Sum. You have absolutely no reason to be concerned. We'll give them another ten minutes and if they haven't reappeared, we'll find them and force them back to the festivities.'

'Sounds like a plan,' Summer said quietly. 'I wasn't expecting it, that's all. Finally facing this . . . figment, this woman I've only ever heard about. I wasn't ready, Claire, and certainly not for her to be so . . . so . . .'

'You can stop that now. Don't you *dare* lose your confidence, Summer Freeman. You're funny and warm and beautiful, and Mason loves you. That's all you need to know. I'm so, so bloody sorry that I wasn't able to prevent this mess, that I've let this week get off to a shitty start. As soon as you come up with a way for me to make it up to you, tell me what it is. But in the meantime, I want to know everything about this proposal. I want to know exactly how you're planning on popping the question, and what your dream wedding looks like.'

* * *

As Summer told her, her nerves began to settle. Claire loved the idea of the banner hanging from Willowbeck's bridge, and asked Summer what Mason's favourite songs were, suggesting that she put together a playlist that *Madeleine* could have going on in the background, and offered to lend her some external speakers and help her set them up.

Summer laughed, as she always did when she was with Claire, her friend's enthusiasm infectious, despite the circumstances. Her glances towards her phone became less frequent – they had been gone thirty-five minutes now – and Summer tried not to picture them leaning towards each other over a table in the café, the windows opaque with condensation, sparks of attraction reigniting between them, like fireflies glowing in the dusk.

Her phone buzzed with a message from Harry, asking if they'd arrived safely. She smiled wryly, picturing her friend's face when she updated her on all that had happened.

She had started to reply when a hand landed gently on her shoulder, fingers tickling her neck. Summer closed her eyes, surprised at the emotion the touch brought, realizing how tense she'd been.

'Mason.' She swivelled round in her chair and then stood. 'Are you OK?'

He nodded. He looked tired, dark shadows under his eyes. 'I'm sorry I was so long,' he said. 'I might head back. Do you want to stay, or . . .'

'I'll come with you,' she said quickly. She couldn't see Tania, and wondered whether she hadn't come back with Mason, but then spotted her long dark hair slipping through the crowd towards the Ladies.

Summer gave Claire a brief hug and waved goodbye to

the others, promising the first round the next evening would be hers, a sentiment that was met with applause, and light heckling from Ryder. She pulled her coat on and did it up, Mason helping her with the stiff top button.

'Do you mind if we don't go back to the boat yet?' Mason asked. 'I could do with clearing my head, and we'll still have time to take Archie and Latte for a walk before bed.'

'If they aren't conked out on the sofa already,' Summer said, smiling gently. 'Do you want me to come, or would you rather be on your own?'

They stepped out into the night. The cold was biting and soothing all at once.

Mason faced her. 'I'd like you to come, unless you're too tired. I want to tell you how it went. I don't want to keep anything from you.' His Adam's apple bobbed, a day's worth of stubble making him look even wearier.

She nodded, relief coursing through her. Maybe there were no fireflies, no sparks. They turned away from the river, along residential streets lined with cars. The air was full of city sounds: shouts, laughter, a distant siren, the underlying hum of traffic. They walked hand in hand, silent except for the occasional direction from Mason.

'I hope you're keeping track of where we're going,' Summer said jokingly, but she meant it. After everything else, she didn't want to get lost on their first night.

'We'll be fine,' Mason murmured. 'Here it is.'

He'd stopped in front of a narrow building squeezed between two others, with a blue awning that looked more suited to a newsagent's than a bar or pub. The windows glowed invitingly beneath a sign that read *Benji's*, a mesh of coloured, twinkling lights covering one of the large panes of glass. Summer followed Mason inside.

It was the smallest, snuggest bar she'd ever been in. It had blue, velvety booths squashed close together and bright mosaics on the walls, the low hum of unobtrusive music in the background. The bar was wide enough for three men standing abreast, and there was a pure white cat sitting at its base, licking its front paw intently.

'How did you know about this place?' Summer asked.

'My editor told me about it,' Mason said, gesturing towards an unoccupied booth in the corner. 'He said it was close to Little Venice, and a bit out of the ordinary. I wasn't sure I'd be able to find it, but . . .' He shrugged, took off his coat and went to the bar.

Summer settled into the comfortable booth and stared at her new surroundings, thinking how surreal the evening had become after the jubilant, busy afternoon serving in the café. To think she had felt threatened by the flirtatious woman in the sparkly hat.

'Here.' Mason slid in opposite her, clinking his wine glass against hers before taking a sip. He was wearing a loose-fitting khaki shirt, the sleeves rolled up to the elbows. Summer caught a whiff of his usual citrus and vanilla scent. He was so familiar to her now, and yet, at this moment, she had no idea what he was about to tell her.

'How did it go?' she asked. 'Are you all right?'

His smile was tired. He reached his hand out and she held it, resting her arm on the table.

'I'm OK,' he said. 'It hasn't been the easiest evening, but I'm glad I spoke to her.' He sipped his wine.

'Did you tell her everything?' Summer asked. 'About Lisa, about becoming a liveaboard?'

He nodded. 'Claire paved the way when they ran into each other a few months ago, so she had some idea. But I

126

wanted her to hear it from me, how I never meant to treat her badly and thought I was doing the opposite when I disappeared, believing it would be best for both of us. That's how screwed up I was.' He sighed. 'I owed it to her to be honest about it all.'

Summer nodded, holding back the question she most wanted to ask. 'And how did she take it?'

'Well. Better than I thought she would, though of course she's had a while to think about it.'

'She forgave you?'

'She said it was water under the bridge.' He laughed gently.

'And how do you feel, now that you've cleared the air? Was it weird, seeing her again?' She drummed her fingers on her knee under the table, hoping Mason wouldn't see how nervous she was.

'Very weird,' he said. 'Good. But . . . it's been so long. And when we were together, I was numb, really. I did care about her, but . . . I've blocked a lot of it out, or my mind has simply refused to let me remember the details. So it felt unbalanced, somehow. As if she'd held a lot more store in our relationship than I had. And tonight, she wanted to hear how things were now, what I'd been up to. She told me about living in Little Venice too, and asked about you, Claire and the other traders.' He looked at the table, his brows knitting together. 'I didn't mean to be so long, but I didn't feel like I could leave.'

'Of course, Mason, it's fine,' Summer said. 'Claire's sorry it turned out this way – apparently Tania had planned to go away for the whole of December. She hadn't expected her to be here.'

Mason looked up at her. 'Tania said she needed to change

her plans, that she can't go and see her family until closer to Christmas. She apologized for springing herself on me – on us, like this.'

Summer nodded, wondering if she believed her. She wanted to, but there was something about Tania's smooth smile, the way she had glided easily towards them through the pub, the look she had given Mason, that was putting her on edge. 'Are you sure you're OK with this?' she asked. 'Do you want to go back to Willowbeck? I'll do whatever's best for you.'

'What's best,' he said, leaning across the table towards her, 'is that we put this behind us now, and enjoy London. I'm not spending two weeks travelling all this way only to turn straight around. I need a few more days at least before we have to tackle all those locks again.'

'You're sure?'

'I'm sure, Summer. It's you, me, *Madeleine* and the dogs against London's Christmas revellers. I've been looking forward to it, and I'm not going to let this put us off course. It wasn't how I'd pictured our first night here, but I'm fine. I've wanted to talk to Tania for a long time. It was a conversation I needed to have, and now it's done. But –' He held her gaze, his dark eyes clouded with concern. 'Are *you* OK? You've been so supportive tonight, looking out for me, giving me time with Tania. But after hearing so much about her, about the history we have, it can't have been easy for you, either.'

Summer swallowed. 'I'm fine,' she said breezily. 'Of course I am. I was worried – angry, on your behalf, but that's all.'

He sighed, let go of her hand and in a moment was round at her side of the table.

'Budge up.' He forced her to scoot along the banquette and sat next to her, his eyes fixing on hers. They had a spark in them, and it was as if he'd come back to life, as if he'd shut the best parts of himself away while he dealt with Tania, and was only now letting them out again. 'Don't worry about Tania,' he said, stroking her hair away from her forehead. 'We've said all that we needed to. We've put the past officially behind us, and if she's there at any point this week – and she told me she might be, while Claire's here – then we'll just get on with it. But I don't want you to worry, about me, or about me with Tania. She is part of my past, and you, Summer, are my future.'

He kissed her. It was soft but passionate, and she pulled him closer, holding onto him tightly. She didn't want to admit to herself – and definitely not to Mason – how much seeing Tania had scared her, how ungrounded she'd felt while the other woman had Mason's full attention. His kiss and his touch were bringing her back to life, too.

'Shall we go and see how Archie and Latte are getting on?' she asked, once the kiss had ended, their faces close, the snug bar seeming to shrink around them. She had a lot of baking to do between now and opening time, but that seemed unimportant now that she'd got Mason back. She hadn't lost him, not literally, but for a couple of hours her whole world had shifted, and she needed to right it again. Mason was the best way of doing that. Luckily, he seemed to agree with her.

'Yes,' he murmured. His fingers traced a line slowly and deliciously down her neck, making her tingle, then he scooted backwards, out of the booth, and held his hand out for her to take. 'Let's go home.'

Chapter 10

Summer dragged herself out of bed before dawn, her limbs stiff and weary after the previous day's cold journey, followed by an afternoon working in the café. Mason was asleep, his curls in disarray on the pillow. She was reminded of Ryder's dig at him, which she'd seen as a compliment. She was more than happy with his Byronic curls, could understand why he'd been propositioned at the hatch yesterday, and why someone like Tania would have been attracted to him. Who wouldn't?

Even their local boatbuilder in Willowbeck, a huge, burly man called Mick, had fuelled Summer's doubts when she was first getting to know Mason by referring to him as Lothario. When she'd got the explanation out of him, it was because everyone – even unapologetically heterosexual men like Mick – could see he was a catch, not because he spent his nights taking scores of different women to bed.

She left Mason sleeping, took the handful of clothes she'd left out the night before, and snuck out of the cabin. She couldn't spend her day ogling her boyfriend; she had to put her focus into the café. It wouldn't be long before the punters started banging on the door for coffee and bacon sandwiches.

She dressed hurriedly, prepared breakfast for Archie and Latte, who were still blinking awake on the sofa, and boiled the kettle. With an instant coffee slowly waking her up, she got to work. She took some of Harry's chocolate and mince pie twists out of the freezer, and prepared the mix for a batch of Christmas brownies with chunks of hazelnut and glacé cherries, and three trays of her festive-flavoured macarons. She'd bought a batch of floury baps from a bakery at their last stop before Little Venice, but would need to find a new supplier while they were here, so she could continue to make bacon rolls.

She opened the door into the café, letting the luxurious smells waft inside, and switched on the coffee machine. The towpath lamps glowed, but the canal was dark. At this hour, even Claire's boat had no lights on, no wintry soundtrack drifting out of the speakers.

Summer stood, clutching her coffee mug, and soaked it all up. There was something mesmerizing about the early morning, the water a black nothing, lapping gently against the sides of the boat. She switched the Christmas tree lights on and they punctuated the dark with soft, rainbow colours. Latte and Archie, fed and watered, pattered into the café, exploring it, checking for any new smells that had appeared since the day before. Summer crouched and stroked her Bichon Frise, and Latte let out a squeak of delight.

'This wasn't a mistake, was it?' she asked her dog. Tania, and the effect the encounter had had on both her and Mason, played on her mind. He had said that it wouldn't ruin their trip, and it was up to her to put it aside, to make the most of being in Little Venice. But Tania was going to socialize with them, and she couldn't imagine there wouldn't be any lingering awkwardness.

Latte looked up at her adoringly, and Summer smiled. 'You're right,' she said, with more conviction than she felt. 'Everything's going to be fine.'

She returned to the kitchen and checked on her bakes. She lined up the next lot of trays, cleared up and filled the dishwasher. Daylight made a slow, sleepy appearance, a streak of lighter sky showing above the buildings, the landscape of Little Venice being revealed as if from behind a theatre curtain. It was cold, the bow deck sparkling with a thick frost, and Summer was relieved to see the water wasn't frozen, however much Mason had told her it would never happen. A man in an orange fluorescent work-suit was gritting the towpath, his breath clouding into the air like smoke.

By the time Mason emerged, Summer had unlocked the hatch and written her menu of Christmas specials on the blackboard.

'You should have woken me,' he said, putting his arms around her. His hair was damp from the shower and water droplets landed on her shoulder.

'You needed the sleep. Now, what do you think – bacon roll and a coffee or tea, three pounds. That's still a bargain in London, isn't it?'

'It's a steal,' Mason said. 'What can I do?'

'Cut open and butter the rolls. You could put the bacon on too, if you like.'

Mason gave her a cheeky smile. 'Have you had any breakfast? Shall we sample them first?'

Summer narrowed her eyes. 'There must be a monumental health risk to having bacon every day.'

'I don't have it *every day*,' Mason protested. Summer stared at him, and his cheeks coloured. 'I'll get started.' He rubbed his hands and disappeared into the kitchen.

She could hear him singing softly to himself as he prepared the rolls, something by Frank Turner, and she felt a stab of guilt that she had been worrying about Tania. She had to remember that, while the circumstances hadn't been ideal, talking to Tania and getting her forgiveness would have lifted a weight off his shoulders. There was nothing, now, stopping them focusing on their future. Summer's heart skipped as she thought of New Year's Eve, the ideas that were swirling around in her head, even more excited now that Claire was on board and was helping her firm them up.

Mason's voice was drowned out as the first chords of 'Don't You Worry' by Lucy Rose drifted out of Claire's speakers, the lights of *Water Music* flicking on. Mason's singing immediately changed to match it, and he popped his head around the kitchen door.

'Your favourite song,' he said. 'It's almost as if Claire's done it specially for you.'

'It's just coincidence. I don't think she knows this is my favourite.'

'But I do,' Mason said. 'I've heard it so often, I could probably recite the lyrics backwards. *Don't you worry, I'm staying here,*' he whispered, and Summer realized how apt the words were right at that moment. She started singing along to crush the lump in her throat, and Mason joined back in, although Lucy Rose's voice was much too high for him, and they quickly descended into laughter. She stopped when she noticed two men in their forties, dressed in smart coats and suit trousers despite it being Sunday, walking towards them on the towpath.

'Coffee and a bacon roll three pounds this morning, if

you're interested?' she called. They were, and Summer waved them towards the hatch.

Sunday in Little Venice was as busy as the Saturday afternoon had been, but Summer thought that everything was moving at a slightly slower pace. The trees that overhung the canal, almost as if they were eavesdropping on the conversations of the liveaboards, were skeletons, the thinnest branches shivering in a light breeze. But the winter scene could never look anything other than festive, because of the brightly coloured narrowboats. Even first thing, there was a couple wrapped in blankets having a loud conversation on their deck, their laughter drifting down the canal. A woman dressed in dark jeans, knee-high burgundy boots and a taupe, woollen coat that looked impossibly soft, walked two miniature schnauzers and a pug down the towpath, her strides long and purposeful, her pets scurrying to keep up.

Behind the trees were large, cream houses, so big that Summer thought many must have been converted into flats, and then beyond them, in the distance, was the shining glass of towering office blocks, the skyline of a more familiar London. Summer could never imagine this towpath being deserted, like it often was in Willowbeck, but today there were strollers rather than rushers, and more laughter, despite the cold that made people stamp their feet in the queue for the hatch, and rub their hands in relief as they opened the bow doors and stepped into the café. Summer always made sure it was either heated or ventilated, depending on the weather.

'Jeez, it's freezing out there,' said a man in a leather jacket with slicked-back hair, looking like he was straight out of a production of *Grease*. He was followed into the café by a woman wearing white jeans and a purple puffa jacket, and two small girls wrapped up like Christmas presents, their scarves and hats bright red against royal blue coats and wellington boots. 'Can we sit at one of these, love?' he asked, pointing at the tables.

'Of course. Have a seat and I'll be over in a moment to take your order.' She watched the family choose a table on the canal side of the boat and dismantle their outdoor apparel, the girls mesmerized by the water and what they could see in it. 'Duck,' 'leaf,' 'boat,' they shouted, pointing things out in turn.

'Now girls, what have I said about sound levels?' the mum asked.

'Ssshhhh,' said the younger girl, pressing her finger to her lips.

'Exactly. When we're out with other people, they don't always want to hear our conversations.'

'But what if they're fun?' asked the older girl.

'They might be having their own fun conversations. Let's have a look at the menu, see what cakes they do.'

This seemed to placate them and Summer popped her head into the kitchen, where Mason was lining up more rolls, buttering them and laying them on a tray, his movements methodical. The crackle and smell of bacon was overwhelming, and Summer put her hand on her stomach.

Mason looked up. 'I told you to have one. Did you get any breakfast?'

She shook her head. 'We've got a family in the café now.'

'You see to them, and I'll prepare you a deluxe bacon sandwich. A Mason Causey speciality.'

'What makes it so special?'

He looked at her aghast, as if the answer was obvious. 'I'm making it!'

Laughing, she left him to it.

The busyness continued, the café filled and emptied, filled and emptied, and by the end of the day the floor was a mass of muddy footprints, exacerbated by a short, sharp rain shower that had darkened the skies around three o'clock and acted as a precursor for nightfall. The crowds dispersed noticeably earlier than they had the day before, and Summer made the decision to close at four o'clock, allowing her time to replenish her stock before whatever evening activity Claire had organized for them all.

She got a text confirming that plans were to go back to the Riverside Inn, and Summer was good to her word, getting the first round in. There was no sign of Tania, and for that she was thankful. The conversation was much more relaxed, and she sat between Mason and Jas on a long bench upholstered in maroon fabric, her back to the wall.

There were no wooded copses with fairy lights – an unlikely find in London and far too cold at this time of year anyway – and Summer was comforted by how straightforward it felt. But then, halfway through the evening, the door burst open and all conversation was drowned out by a rendition of 'We Three Kings' as a group of men and women, dressed as elves in red and green costumes, and hats with bells on the end, bustled into the pub. They stood in the middle of the space, forcing the drinking customers to move back around the edges, and continued to sing their carol with gusto.

'Oh good Lord,' Ralph said, leaning in closer so Summer could hear him. 'What a way to ruin a quiet Sunday drink.'

Summer laughed. 'It's Christmas! And I think they're quite good, don't you?'

'Collecting for some charity no doubt,' Doug added.

Summer rolled her eyes. 'What's wrong with that? It's the season of giving and goodwill, and that doesn't just mean buying your friends and family expensive presents that they don't really want. This,' she said, gesturing towards the group, 'is what Christmas is – or *should be* – all about.'

She gave a triumphant smile which faded when she realized one of the elves had noticed her pointing, and was waggling her finger, beckoning her forwards, her cheeks rosy in the warmth of the pub and her fur-lined jacket.

Summer shook her head and sipped her drink, but as the carol singers came to the end of their current song, the beckoning elf approached her. 'Come and join us for a few,' she said. 'The more the merrier.'

'Oh nooooo,' Summer said, laughing nervously. 'I can't sing. You don't want me.'

'No discrimination here, not even for the vocally challenged. Come on, everyone knows the words to "Jingle Bells."'

The other elves were moving through the pub, trying to encourage other reluctant punters into the impromptu singsong. She saw the tall, bearded man behind the bar shrug his shoulders genially and lift the hatch.

'Yeah, go on, Summer,' Ryder said, giving her a wicked grin. 'Join in.'

'I'm not—'

'What was that you were saying about it being the season of giving and goodwill?' He raised an eyebrow. 'You can't be a spoilsport now.'

'I can,' she said, then realized how petulant that sounded. 'Mason, tell them. Nobody wants to hear me sing.'

Mason gave her a soft, quick kiss. 'You'll be wonderful,' he said. 'I'm so proud of you.'

'Mason!' she squeaked, watching as he tried not to descend into laughter. 'You traitor.'

'I've heard you singing in the shower,' he said. 'Have confidence in yourself.'

Summer thought about folding her arms and refusing to budge, but the female elf was still standing next to their table, watching her expectantly, and she didn't want to be the bah humbug member of the party. She sighed and hauled herself to her feet.

'I'm Milly,' the elf said.

'I'm Summer. It's . . . lovely to meet you. Do you do this kind of thing often?'

Milly chuckled. 'We're actually part of the cast of the pantomime that's playing in the Canal Café Theatre. The run starts tomorrow night – we've just had our final dress rehearsal and thought we'd come out and do a bit of publicity.'

'Which pantomime are you doing?' Summer glanced at the other elves, still encouraging members of the pub crowd to join them. She counted them – there were seven. 'Ah,' she said. 'So you're not actually elves, you're dwarves. Which one are you?'

'I'm Happy, and tonight, at least, we're a bit of a hybrid. These outfits are Christmas elves – the director would have a fit if we brought our performance costumes to the pub the night before opening.'

'That's very sensible,' Summer said. 'You don't want to meet Snow White tomorrow smelling of beer.' She grinned, and was pulled into the huddle in the middle of the pub. Milly was standing next to her on one side, and a very tall, burly man wearing a rugby shirt was on the other.

A male elf with a loud, tenor voice, called out: '"Away in

138

a Manger". Three, two, one,' and they launched into the first line of the carol.

Summer felt her cheeks redden, and focused on her Converse sneakers and the floorboards beneath them. When she did glance up, she saw that her friends were grinning at her, Claire's face pinched as she tried to hold in her laughter, Jas swaying side to side in time to the music. Ryder gave her an over-enthusiastic thumbs up, and when she caught Mason's eye, he mouthed 'I love you'.

After that, Summer let herself loosen up, and once she and the group of motley Christmas elves had been through 'Jingle Bells', 'Silent Night' and a very raucous version of 'We Wish You a Merry Christmas' which had far too much emphasis – as always – on the "wish", the pub was filled with enthusiastic clapping.

Summer gave an awkward bow, and shook Milly's hand. 'Good luck with the pantomime.'

'Thank you,' she said. 'It was lovely to sing with you, Summer.'

'You too,' she replied honestly. 'And Merry Christmas!'

She raced back to her table where her friends gave her an extra, embarrassingly long round of applause, and Ryder pushed a fresh drink in front of her.

'Here you go, Dopey, you've earned it.'

'Ha ha,' Summer said dryly, accepting the drink.

Mason put his arm around her and pulled her close. 'You were wonderful,' he said.

'I bet you couldn't even hear me over that guy.' She pointed at the tall man who had been standing next to her, and who had unleashed an impressive baritone when they'd started singing. He probably led the chanting at rugby matches.

'That doesn't matter,' Mason said. 'You were by far my

favourite Christmas elf – dwarf – whatever they were supposed to be.'

'A bit of a hybrid, apparently,' Summer said. 'It was fun, though. And not *that* unexpected.'

Mason raised a questioning eyebrow.

Summer laughed. 'We're with this lot,' she said, gesturing to Claire, Ryder and the others. 'Nothing's ever straightforward when they're around.'

That night, sleep came to her much more easily, and with her baking done and her lie-in longer, she bounced out of bed on Monday morning ready to face whatever Little Venice had to offer her.

Unfortunately, that turned out to be Tania.

Despite the reassurances Mason had given her, she felt a churn of anxiety when the glamorous woman walked into the café mid-morning. There was a temporary lull in custom, which meant she didn't even have an excuse to serve her quickly and keep conversation at a minimum. It was as if she knew, Summer thought, or was controlling everyone's behaviour, making them avoid the café at the precise moment she appeared, like a baddie in an X-Men film.

She was wearing a fitted, caramel coat over pale jeans and tan boots, delicate gold studs in her ears offsetting her subtle, shimmery makeup. She looked like a mirage, and Summer was frozen to the spot.

'Hi,' she said, in her bold, even voice. 'When we were talking the other night, Mason told me all about your café. I thought I'd come and sample some of the macarons. It's very pretty,' she added, glancing around her.

'Thank you,' Summer said. 'Take a seat. What can I get you to drink? How many macarons?'

'Oh, a selection, you choose. And a latte with skimmed milk.'

'No problem.' Summer waited for Tania to sit down, but she didn't.

'These are great,' she said instead, picking up a carving of a sleigh adorned with gifts, one of Norman's more elaborate creations.

'They're made by Norman, one of our neighbours in Willowbeck. He's not that interested in making money from them, but he would be doing them regardless, and I think the world should know about his talent – our little corner of the world, at least. He's slowly come round to the idea that me selling them for him is a good thing, and he's made some of these specifically for Little Venice.' She smiled, but Tania didn't, intent on examining the other models.

Summer busied herself making Tania's latte, wondering if she should get Mason, who had taken the lull as an opportunity to spend time working on his new article. He wanted to write about their trip, the wildlife they'd encountered in London and on the journey, but with the cold weather it had so far been sparse, and Summer had seen him staring at the blank page of his notepad.

'I'm sorry our introduction wasn't great,' Summer said, filling the void left by Tania's silence with an apology she didn't need to give.

'No problem,' Tania replied, failing to acknowledge the way she had sprung her presence on them. 'It was great to see Mason again after all this time. I can't deny—' she stopped, gave Summer a quick smile as she accepted her latte. 'You do know about me and Mason, don't you? How it ended?'

'I do,' Summer said, bristling at the assumption he'd kept her in the dark. 'He's told me everything.'

Tania gave her a quick, businesslike nod. 'It was good to talk it through, to set things straight. And have a chance to catch up, too. It was surprising how easy it felt, how much of a connection there still is, after all this time.' She smiled wistfully, and Summer's stomach knotted.

'Right,' she said. 'I'm glad you had that chance, and I know Mason has wanted to apologize to you, to put everything that happened behind him. It's important that you were both able to say all you needed to.' She kept her voice strong, controlled, hoping that Tania would get the message.

Tania gave her a quick, amused look, and Summer felt instantly smaller. She drew in a long breath, wiped her hands down her apron and started putting macarons on a plate.

'We have some new festive flavours,' she said. 'I'd love to know which one's your favourite. Will you excuse me for a moment?' She handed the plate to Tania, waited while she picked a table and then hurried through the kitchen to the living space. Mason had his notepad on his lap, his head in his hands. She loved the way he wrote out his articles free-hand first, often sitting on the deck of *The Sandpiper* to immerse himself in the nature he was writing about.

'Mason?'

'My mind is a blank,' he said, groaning.

'You've had a lot to deal with over the last couple of days.'

'That's no excuse for this,' he said, waving his hand at the pad. Summer took it from him, squinting as she tried to decipher his handwriting, which wasn't so much scruffy as it was too joined-up. Words ran together, some letters were indistinguishable from each other – the thoughts spilling from his brain on to the page.

Slowly, her eyes took it in: *Article no. 14. It's understandable to think that the only wildlife about at this time of year is a handful of robins and a few brazen foxes, but if you take the time to look out of your window, or slow down on the post-Christmas lunch walk, what's really out there?* She smiled. She loved the opening line. She wanted to help him with it, but now wasn't the time.

'Mason, Tania's here. She's come to sample some macarons.' She raised her eyebrows when he looked up, his frown deepening.

'That's all?'

'Supposedly. She said you'd mentioned the café, and she wanted to come and check it out. I didn't know if you'd want to see her, or . . .?'

He sighed, and pushed himself up to standing. 'I'll come and say hello.'

'Great.' Summer went back into the café, relieved to see an old couple hovering by the hatch, change purses out in anticipation.

'Mason,' Tania said. Summer could hear the change in her voice, the warmth that she'd held back until he appeared, the flirtation in it. She wondered how Tania had the nerve to be so forward in front of her, what she thought she would achieve by telling Summer that she and Mason still had a connection.

Summer smiled at the old couple, but it was through gritted teeth.

'Hi, Tania, how are you?' Mason asked.

'Good thanks, great. How's it going in the café? Have you had a chance to see the sights of London yet?'

'The café's been busy, so we've not been out and about that much, but we've taken Archie and Latte to Regent's Park and Primrose Hill. The views from there are stunning.'

'Oh yes, your Bichon Frise. She sounds adorable.'

143

'She's Summer's dog,' Mason said. 'Though that means they're both ours, really, which I know Summer's delighted about. Archie can be a bit on the disobedient side.'

Summer gave the old couple their drinks and their change, and turned away from the hatch. 'Archie's only badly behaved with you, he's a sweetheart with me.'

Mason inhaled sharply. 'That's not true. Last week he almost drowned himself under your watch!'

'That's because you were opening the lock, and I was steering. He was trying to get to you! And I seem to remember it was you who'd tied them onto the deck, your knots that didn't prevent him jumping in the canal.'

Mason folded his arms, his stern expression failing against a grin. 'You could have checked them.'

'I didn't think I needed to.' She paused. 'OK, I suppose I should have realized that nothing's foolproof where you and Archie are concerned.'

Their eyes locked, and Summer returned his smile.

'I need to get going,' Tania said, frowning at her phone and shoving it deep into her pocket. She put her plate and mug on the counter and gave Summer a smile that could have frozen the canal. 'See you soon, I hope?' As she passed Mason she reached her hand out and brushed her fingers against his, her words directed only at him.

'Bye,' Summer said to Tania's retreating back, glad she hadn't pointed out the mistletoe the two of them had been standing beneath. Her heart sank as Mason stared incredulously at Tania, then ran his hand through his hair as if shaking off her touch. He looked disconcerted, and Summer could already feel the exhaustion at having to deal with her own insecurities – her constant wavering between worrying his ex was after him again, and reminding herself that

144

Mason would never be unfaithful to her, however hard Tania tried.

'I had a look at the Winter Wonderland website,' she said, changing the subject. 'It allows dogs, but they say that it isn't the best place for them, because it's so busy and noisy, so I think we should take them for a long walk before we go tomorrow. I don't want to risk Latte or Archie getting squashed, or lost when they *somehow* manage to slip their leads.'

'Unfair,' he said, but the word didn't have any weight behind it. 'Lunchtime's coming up, do you want me to stay out here?'

She did, but the café was still quiet. 'That article won't write itself. I'll call you if I need you.'

'Now this,' Summer said the following evening, staring up at the attractions, the lights and whooshes and screams invading her senses, 'is what London at Christmas is all about!'

'I feel twenty years too old,' Mason shouted, as they stood in front of waltzers adorned with a light system that was more frantic than festive.

'Me too,' Summer said. 'Let's wind the years back.'

She waved to Claire and Jas; they'd arranged to meet up in the Belgian Bar in a couple of hours, and her friends were soon lost in the crowds.

She dragged Mason into one of the seats, waited until the security bar was brought down over them, and then snuggled into him, closing her eyes as the music ramped up, its rhythm getting faster and faster in time with the ride. It was years since she'd been to an amusement park, so long since she'd smelt the overwhelmingly sweet scent of candy floss and butter popcorn mingled together. She felt giddy, reckless, and leaned over to kiss Mason despite the pull of the ride stealing control of her body. She got his chin and he laughed, burying his head into her neck, his nose squashed against her as the direction changed again.

They went on the Ferris Wheel, drinking in the view, the city twinkling in the darkness, the gold and red of headlights and taillights marking the larger roads, the cold air numbing their lips. Mason bought her a white fluffy hat with pink-tinged ears from one of the market stalls, and they drank mulled wine and shared a bag of roasted chestnuts. When they approached the ice rink, it was Mason's turn to pull her forward. Summer laughed, until she realized he was serious.

'Come on, polar bear,' he said, tugging the ears of her hat, 'it'll be fun.'

'Can you skate?' It had never crossed her mind to ask him before now.

'A bit,' he admitted, sheepishly. 'We lived close to an ice rink when I was younger, and I went there with friends quite often, not just at Christmas.'

'OK then,' Summer said. She could put aside her fear of falling over and having her fingers sliced off for him. They finished their chestnuts as they stood in the queue, and then were given the heavy, solid boots with lethal-looking blades on the bottoms. They changed into them on benches that weren't quite dry, the laces rough against her cold hands. She remembered going skating with Ben as a child, the way he had zoomed fearlessly around the rink while she had clung onto the edge for dear life, her brother completing about twenty laps to every one of hers.

They walked over the thick rubber matting together, and then Mason stepped onto the ice and turned, the movement quick and expert. Summer's mouth fell open. 'How often did you say you went?'

'Come on,' he said softly, holding out his hands. She ached to be able to cling onto the wall, to have at least half of her body pressed against it so if she did lose her footing she could simply slide down to the compact ice, away from the other skaters. But Mason wasn't having any of it. She took his hands, squeezing them tightly, and stepped out onto the ice, feeling the immediate loss of grip, so that her foot slid forwards and Mason's arms were around her in a flash, holding her firmly.

'I can't,' she murmured into his shoulder.

'Yes, you can.' He put his hands on her waist this time, and skated slowly backwards, his movements small and controlled, allowing Summer to test out her legs on the ice. She was sure she looked like a baby giraffe taking its first steps, but with Mason's hands to steady her, the warmth in his eyes, she began to feel more confident. As they made their way slowly around the rink, she held onto his elbows, and then his hands, so he was no longer supporting her waist, so she was further from him, more independent. He was still skating backwards, and she shook her head, smiling.

'You're a pro.'

'Far from it. But it's like riding a bike, it all comes back to you.'

'I wish it didn't for me,' Summer said. 'I remember clutching onto the sides and flinching whenever someone whooshed past me.'

'And look at you now. But we can stop any time you want.'

'No, I want to do this.' And she did.

She wanted to be here, the air thick with a cold, clean freshness that wasn't due just to the ice; the dark of the winter's night high above, the rides flashing, whizzing and blaring around them, trapping them in a festive cocoon. There was a giant Christmas tree at one end of the rink, its lights white against decorations in gold, pink, blue and silver. It was glitzy but tasteful, and being there, on the ice, made Summer feel like she was in a Christmas film. *Elf*, or *Serendipity*. Oh, how she loved the ending of *Serendipity*, the deserted ice rink, the snow, the glove floating down to land on John Cusack. She closed her eyes and the air whipped around her as someone sailed past, clipping the heel of her boot and catching her off balance. She squealed as the momentum twisted her away from Mason.

'Whoa!' He grabbed her waist and pulled her into him before she landed on the ice, as someone yelled 'Sorry' in their direction, already halfway round the rink. 'Are you OK?' he asked. They were pressed together, his nose millimetres from hers, his eyes wide with concern.

'I'm OK,' she said, thinking that this was much better than *Serendipity*, because how could she have coped with meeting Mason, spending a day falling for him, and then having to pass all those years apart, never knowing where he was?

'Do you want to get off the ice?'

She shook her head. 'No, I'm starting to enjoy myself. But there's something that would help me enjoy it even more.'

'Anything,' he said, solemnly, and then watched in horror as she took her fluffy-eared hat off and, while Mason was holding tightly onto her, used both hands to pull it down over his wayward hair, his curls sticking out beneath it.

'You have to skate with this on,' she said, only just managing to say it before laughter took over. He looked ridiculous and cross and utterly gorgeous.

'Oh I do, do I?' He spun them both round, making her

squeal again, and then they began their slow, steady progress over the ice, Mason skating backwards, holding onto her, never letting go, never breaking eye contact, wearing the fluffy hat in a way that only he could. As they skated, London sparkled and sang around them, and Summer lost herself in it, deciding that in this moment, everything was as it should be. Even if she did look like a baby giraffe skating with a curly-haired polar bear.

Chapter 11

When Summer woke on Thursday morning, their penultimate day in Little Venice, Mason wasn't beside her. And then, as she began to emerge from the fug of slumber, she heard banging. Her stomach knotted with a familiar tension, one that came from nearly two years of being a liveaboard, her senses – and worry – tuned to all the things that could go wrong on the boat, especially in the cold.

She thought of Norman and Valerie in Willowbeck, and hoped that Jenny and Dennis were on hand to help them should they need it. Sliding out of bed and pulling a hoody over her pyjamas, she followed the bangs and thumps, past the tiny bathroom to where the engine was housed, in front of the stern deck. She found her boyfriend, clad in only his boxer shorts, peering at parts of the engine Summer didn't entirely understand.

'What's wrong?' she asked, and Mason jumped, cracking his head against the engine casing.

'Fuck,' he muttered, rubbing his temple.

Summer winced and squeezed his shoulder. 'Sorry, I didn't mean to startle you. Is everything OK?'

He turned, his smile a half-grimace. 'It's making a funny noise. Stating the obvious, I know, but I'm worried that one of the pipes is blocked somewhere. Have you seen the weather this morning?'

Summer shook her head, anxiety prickling down her spine. 'Frozen?'

'Not the river, but – it's getting colder, and I think we need to be prepared.' There was an uncharacteristic wariness in his voice, and Summer knew that he was worried. 'The last thing we want is for the pipes to freeze and then crack, or for the heating to break down. Mick's given me a few tips, so I'm checking it over. Go back to bed for a bit.'

'Why don't you have any clothes on? Never mind the river being frozen, your extremities will fall off!'

Mason laughed. 'I'm safe, don't worry. To give her credit, *Madeleine*'s heating is efficient, and the fact that she's still cosy this morning means the worst hasn't happened – yet. But I'm not happy with this banging.'

'Maybe it's a ghost,' Summer said, widening her eyes dramatically.

'That,' Mason said, turning to the toolbox on the floor, 'would be a harder problem to solve. I'll be a while, get back under the duvet.' He put a screwdriver between his teeth and turned back to the engine.

Summer ignored his suggestion and went to make tea. She returned with a steaming mug, one of his tattier jumpers – not that she ever minded staring at his body, but she didn't want to add any more drama to their trip by failing to prevent him from catching hypothermia – and two very curious dogs, who would no doubt hinder rather than help him.

Realizing that hovering behind him would be about as helpful as Archie and Latte's contributions, she left him to it, checking the kitchen appliances and the café, ensuring everything was working, and also that the doors and windows hadn't frozen solid. She'd been getting more live-aboard-savvy since she'd been in her café, but that didn't mean she could diagnose every unusual sound her house-boat made, and she was grateful that Mason was prepared to take on that role, however un-feminist that sentiment was.

As the sun climbed higher in the sky, the extent of the frost was revealed, its sharpness diluting the colours of Little Venice as everything was given a white, shimmering coat. The hot drinks machine would be working hard today, and she was glad she had extra bacon.

Once Mason appeared, declaring everything seemed to be without issue, rubbing his forehead either because of the perplexing sounds that he hadn't diagnosed, or because he was still smarting from knocking his head, she showered and started her fifth full day in the café. She winced at the cold air that sliced at her when she opened the hatch, and knew she would have to balance being welcoming at the takeaway counter with keeping the café's interior snug enough for people to want to sit inside.

Mason took control behind the counter, serving customers with a charm that made Summer feel both proud and lustful. She'd never imagined that 'hot café owner' would be on her list of romantic fantasies – the fact that he was a nature photographer, that he was talented and caring in equal measure was more than attractive enough for her – but as she looked at him, a white apron with red trim over his scruffy blue jumper, a dusting of icing sugar on his cheek and his hair as badly behaved as usual, she felt overcome with love.

Once they made it back to Willowbeck she wouldn't have long to organize her proposal, and there was no way she could start working on the sign she wanted to secure to the bridge when they were both living on the same boat, so she would have to fit it in between Christmas and New Year. Perhaps she could keep it in a back room in the pub if Jenny and Dennis would let her, and then find a way of disappearing intermittently to paint it so Mason didn't get suspicious. Maybe the reserve would have a sudden influx of a rare breed of winter goose that would keep him occupied?

As she was musing on this, wondering which god she needed to pray to to make it a reality, dress-down Santa Claus came into the café.

'So I see he hasn't been stolen away, then?' he asked, his round face breaking into a grin.

'Sorry?' she asked, trying to recall their previous encounter.

'Your man – you've survived London so far. He hasn't been whisked away by another fawning customer.'

Summer couldn't help smiling in return. 'Not quite,' she said dryly, her mind unhelpfully replaying the moment Tania had walked towards them in the pub.

'And has it been eventful, like I said it would be?'

'No wild swimmers so far – the plummeting temperatures have probably seen to that – but it's definitely had its moments.'

'The weather's supposed to get worse over the next few days. There's talk of it failing to get much above freezing until after the weekend.'

'Really?' Mason joined their conversation, sending a couple

of older women away clutching chocolate twists, their footing cautious as they navigated the gritted towpath.

'Yes, young man,' Santa Claus said. 'I've heard rumours the river could freeze. It might be a repeat of 1963, when the Thames last froze over, or the frost fairs of the nineteenth century. You could have an ice rink outside your door any day now. Are you good at skating?' He looked to Mason and then her, and Summer got a funny feeling in her chest.

Was he another Valerie? Did he somehow know about their visit to Winter Wonderland? Were the rumours he'd heard actually premonitions? She wondered if Mason was as unnerved as she was by his pertinent question, but he seemed unconcerned.

'Funny you should mention that,' he said. 'We went to Winter Wonderland the night before last, and tried out the ice rink. I haven't been for years, but—'

'But he's a natural,' Summer finished. 'He put all my wobbling to shame. I felt in very safe hands.'

'Good you've got some practice in, then. Any mince pies today?'

'Sure,' Mason said. He pulled the plate out and asked the man how many he wanted, before putting them in a paper bag.

'You thought they were OK, then?' Summer asked, giving the closest table an extra, unnecessary wipe down.

'The best mince pies in all of London, and I've been around a bit, believe me.' Dress-down Santa tapped the side of his nose, and Summer tried not to laugh hysterically. She found herself checking to see if there was a sleigh on the towpath, reindeer stomping their hooves impatiently, or a pair of red braces peeking out from beneath his tan-coloured jacket.

Once he'd left clutching his treats, Summer shook her head. 'Is it just me, or was that a bit weird?'

'What's that?' Mason asked. He was rearranging the remaining mince pies into a more attractive pattern on the plate.

'Him. The whole – y'know, mentioning ice skating when we were only doing it two days ago, saying he'd been around a bit when it came to mince pies. How he looked . . .' Her words trailed off as Mason stared at her. She could see he was trying hard not to laugh.

'Summer . . .'

'Don't you think it's a bit strange? All a bit—'

'*Miracle on 34th Street?*'

'Perhaps.'

He walked over and planted a kiss on her head. 'He's a slightly large, jolly man with white hair, who likes mince pies. And it's not unusual to go ice skating in December.'

'What if his predictions about the weather are right?' she asked, almost pleading. Mason was making perfect sense, but she couldn't quite let it go.

'It's bloody freezing,' he said. 'Either it's going to warm up, or it's going to get colder. He has a fifty per cent chance of being right.'

'It could stay consistently at this temperature,' she argued, her protestations getting weaker.

'It has to change eventually, and that's what we'll remember. Let's keep our fingers crossed that he isn't Father Christmas, doesn't know about the weather in advance and we're not going to end up getting stuck in Little Venice. I'm having a great time, but I can only stand so many late nights out followed by early mornings in the café. I'm starting to feel old.' He stretched his arms up to the ceiling, his shoulder making a cracking noise as if to prove his point, and twisted his neck from side to side.

'Mason Causey, you are the least old person I know. I mean, obviously there's Tommy, and—'

'And you,' he said, amusement dancing in his eyes. 'You're younger than me.'

'You know what I mean. You're full of energy.'

'And Archie and Latte,' Mason continued. 'Pretty sure if either of them were thirty-six years old we'd be entering them into the *Guinness Book of World Records*.'

She hit him with a tea towel. 'You know what I mean! I was being figurative, not literal.'

'About the age thing, or about Father Christmas making a visit to *Madeleine*? Maybe I should write about the magic of Christmas instead, because I've encountered bugger all wildlife so far.' He sighed, running his hand over his jaw.

Summer heard the door open behind her. 'Why don't we visit London Zoo before we go back to Willowbeck? That would add some spice to your *Nature Today* article, especially if you didn't mention where exactly it was you encountered the gorillas and meerkats.'

Mason stood in the middle of the café, shaking his head slowly. Laughing, Summer went to tell the young couple that had just come in about the daily specials.

Summer and Mason reunited with the other roving traders that evening, after Summer had triple-checked with Mason that he didn't want to stay at home in his slippers and curl up in front of Netflix. She wondered if he regretted the decision as Ryder announced he was taking them to a 'special little bar he knew' about a ten-minute walk from the canal. When they arrived, they discovered the exterior brickwork had been painted black, the bar's name, Rose Garden, glowing in red neon lettering above the door.

'*Rose Garden?*' Mason whispered to Summer. 'It looks like a strip club.'

She giggled. 'This is Ryder, remember. He'd never bring us to a straightforward pub. When I was roving it was always wooded glades and abandoned bandstands. If it's his choice, it's never ordinary.'

Mason gave an unimpressed grunt as he held the door open for her. They stepped into a foyer that was so low-lit Summer thought the bar must be closed, but as the room opened up she could see that there were already people occupying booths. Ryder's chosen watering hole was a compact square space, the décor and furnishings black with sharp streaks of colour – geometric prints on the walls spotlit from below, a neon yellow strip above the bar, white glowing cats' eyes around a polished wooden square that Summer assumed was a dance floor, though she couldn't imagine more than ten moving bodies fitting on it at the same time. It was achingly modern, not Ryder's usual style at all. She wondered if they'd be served their drinks out of teapots.

Mason scanned the menu, his eyebrows rising. 'All hopes of a pint are out of the window, then.'

'This, you wonderful people, is my treat,' Ryder said, flinging his arms wide. 'I was sourcing some cocktail mixers for a client several aeons ago, and they introduced me to this sumptuous little cavern. They do the most spectacular cocktails. My good friend Nate will be mixing up a storm for us.' He led them to a large booth with a reserved sign on the polished black table, and went to sort out their drinks.

'Have you been here before?' Summer asked Claire and Jas. They both nodded, their smiles echoing Summer's earlier comment that this was typical Ryder. Doug and Ralph seemed relaxed enough, going through the cocktail menu as if they knew it intimately. Ralph was wearing a midnight-blue velvet jacket, and Summer, in a grey wool dress over black leggings and sparkly ballet pumps, felt distinctly underdressed. Even Mason, wearing a smart black shirt and dark Levis, looked more suited to the London bar.

'Temperatures are meant to dip tonight,' Jas said, looking at his phone and nodding. 'Wood burners working extra hard for the rest of the week, ladies and gentlemen. Keep those fires burning!'

Summer saluted, and pushed away a niggle about the banging noises in her engine.

Ryder returned with three jugs of cocktails adorned with umbrellas. One jug looked like it was full of Coke, the liquid in another was a peach colour, and the third was lurid blue, reminding Summer of the alco-pops she used to drink in her late teens.

'Long Island Iced Tea, Sex on the Beach and, just for us, a concoction Nate has dreamt up called Canal Boat Christmas. Take your pick.'

Mason and Summer both threw caution to the wind and tried the ice-blue Canal Boat Christmas, Ryder adding straws to their full glasses with a flourish.

'Cheers,' Claire said, raising her Sex on the Beach, and they clinked glasses.

Summer took a sip and winced. It was strong, and tasted of aniseed and lemon juice. 'Sambuca?' she asked Ryder, but he gave her an innocent shrug, his eyes flashing. Summer put her glass down, knowing she should take it slowly. If

Ryder was in charge, then there was no guessing what was in it – it could be full of absinthe for all she knew.

She began to settle into her surroundings, adjusting to the gloom, the bar busy but not packed, the music not too loud that they couldn't hear each other.

A figure appeared in the doorway. Summer squinted, waiting for recognition to hit her. When it did, she sighed inwardly.

Tania approached the table. She was wearing skintight black trousers, a sequined rose-pink top and towering, nude heels. 'Room for a little one?' she asked.

'Of course, the more the merrier.' Ryder steered her to his side of the table, and started to introduce her to the cocktails as if they were friends of his. Summer and Mason exchanged a glance, his smile reassuring.

Summer vowed not to feel insecure. She turned to Claire. 'Where will you be for Christmas? Where are you off to after London?'

'I'm heading back to Wales,' Claire said, crunching one of her ice cubes. 'I've not been back for a couple of years, so it's about time. I'll leave the boat moored up and get the train. It'll be weird travelling by railway instead of waterway.'

'I bet your family will be pleased to see you.'

Claire made a noncommittal noise. 'We'll see. How about you? Back in Willowbeck I assume, getting ready for the big question.' She whispered the words, checking that Mason was engrossed in his conversation with Jas.

'I won't have much time when we get back to sort it out,' Summer said. 'And I have to get the tone right. Mason's not showy, but he doesn't mind a bit of fuss, and I'm sure he'd like it if I included the other residents of Willowbeck. It feels like such a close community now; we're all friends. I was thinking a New Year's party could work, though it'll be a damp squib for everyone if he turns me down just before the fireworks.'

'Oh hush,' Claire said, 'he's potty about you. If he says no I'll eat my new Lorde LP.' Summer laughed, and lowered her voice further. 'Tania popped by the café the other day. She changes temperature depending on whether she's talking to me or Mason.'

Claire shook her head, her eyes sliding in Tania's direction. 'You're imagining it, Sum. The air is cleared, the past has been put to bed. I hope you don't mind that she's come this evening, she said she wanted to spend time with us while we were still here. Maybe I should have mentioned it.'

'No, it's fine. Mason said she might be making another appearance before we left.'

'Then why are you gripping the table so tightly?' Claire asked gently. 'You have to get over it, Summer. I know it's not easy, and God knows I've only contributed to the stress of the whole situation, but you and Mason are as solid as *Madeleine*'s hull. He's not going anywhere, and if you can't do it before then, make sure that when you put a ring on it on New Year's Eve, you stop this nonsense and look towards the future.' She poured herself more cocktail, her eyes widening. 'Ooh, I know, tomorrow evening let's go into the city, just you and me, and we can look for a few things to make the proposal more special. Are you planning on getting him a ring?'

'I was, but I have no idea where to start.'

'We'll do it together. Mason won't mind being abandoned for a bit of shopping, will he?'

'He'll probably relish the quiet,' Summer admitted.

160

As the evening wore on and the cocktails kept coming, Summer felt everything grow hazy. People swapped seats, Tania slid in next to Mason, blocking him in, and Summer tried extra hard to be casual, smiling nonchalantly when he gave her an apologetic look and leaning into Ralph as they discussed their respective Christmas plans. Jas got his camera out and blinded everyone with the flash, apologized and then did it again, no doubt taking photos for his blog. Tania turned her head away, her usually calm features creased into a frown until Jas put the camera back in his smart satchel.

The chatter and laughter grew, the bar filled up and, at some point during the evening, a black curtain was drawn back to reveal a large screen and state-of-the-art karaoke machine, the whole thing surrounded by glowing lights like a dressing-room mirror.

All the faces, bar Claire and Ralph's, turned to Ryder in horror.

'You didn't,' Jas said.

Ryder lounged back on the sofa, his leg crossed at the knee. 'First one to do Whitney Houston gets a free drink on me.'

'You've been plying us with free drinks all night,' Doug said, 'probably so we wouldn't walk out when this happened.'

'I was inspired by Summer's *bashful* performance the other night. And who doesn't love a bit of karaoke?' Five hands went up, and Mason looked as if he was in physical pain. 'Fine,' Ryder said, shrugging. 'But give it half an hour and you'll be climbing over me to get to the stage.'

Summer wasn't convinced, and she wasn't sure anyone else was either, especially when a man from the opposite side of the bar lurched to the stage and started a shaky rendition of 'Wonderwall'.

'As a connoisseur of music,' Summer whispered to Claire, 'you can't possibly approve of this?'

'I embrace all music,' Claire said. 'My particular favourite for this kind of occasion is "Build Me Up Buttercup". You should join in!'

Summer laughed. 'I don't think so. I've done enough singing in public for one week.' She turned as Mason sat beside her and poured them both another drink. 'I didn't expect this,' she whispered, leaning in close.

'You'd warned me about storytelling, but I had no idea this was on the cards.'

'There was categorically no karaoke when I was roving before. There were folk songs, but they were fun, intimate, no audience outside the group, and definitely no Queen renditions.' Mr Wonderwall had finished, and a young woman started to perform a Beyoncé song, her voice in tune, but not quite powerful enough to pull it off. 'You're not up for it, then?' she asked.

Mason rubbed his jaw. 'Not even with another jug of Canal Boat Christmas inside me. When can we escape?'

The answer turned out to be not soon enough, and Claire managed to pull both of them up to join in with The Foundations song, the cocktails working their magic on Summer so that when Claire asked her for the fifth time, she jumped eagerly out of her seat. Mason, she was sure, only succumbed to Claire's entreaties so that he wouldn't be forced to perform something else on his own.

Their rendition received resounding applause from the whole bar, especially Ryder who, Summer noticed, had avoided singing all evening. She wasn't surprised that he had got away with it, and was shocked into silence when, as the evening was drawing to a close, he sauntered to the stage, dragging Tania by the hand, and they gave a confident, if not entirely tuneful performance of 'Somethin' Stupid'. The catcalls and whoops from their group almost drowned out the singing, but Ryder, pushing his floppy blond hair back from his face, was entirely unflustered. Tania seemed, to Summer's biased, not entirely sober eye, as if she relished being the centre of attention.

It was after two in the morning when they left the bar, and as they walked home in the freezing air Summer decided, through her drunken haze, that it had been one of the most entertaining nights she'd had in a while. Her flat pumps with their grippy soles had been the right decision, but Claire and Tania weren't so lucky, and Claire skidded on the slippery pavement, Doug and Jas catching her just before she fell.

Tania was firmly clamped to Ryder's side, and while Summer was wondering whether Claire minded, how strong her feelings really were for the most enigmatic member of their group and why she refused to confide in her about it, they slunk up beside her without her noticing.

'We haven't had a chance to chat all evening,' Tania said smoothly. 'It's been great fun. I had no idea Ryder was a karaoke hound.' She placed a hand, fingers splayed, against his chest. It was both sexy and territorial, and confusion clouded Summer's already misty thoughts. Was Tania after Mason, or Ryder, or was she imagining it all?

'Me either,' Summer replied. 'He's full of surprises.'

'That,' Tania said, 'is most definitely true.' She grinned at Summer, her eyes sparkling, and Summer had the sense that it was genuine, a conspiratorial glance between friends.

'Ladies, ladies.' Ryder's protest was lazy. 'I only ever aim to please.'

'Yourself,' Summer added quickly, and they all burst out laughing, Ryder included.

Quiet descended for a moment, punctuated by the sound of their footsteps.

'It's been lovely to spend time with you,' Tania said. 'And I'm sorry, Summer, if our introduction was awkward. I didn't mean to cause you, or Mason, any discomfort.'

Summer was so surprised by her apology that she took a few seconds to reply. 'That's fine,' she mumbled, self-conscious that Ryder was listening intently to everything.

'I'm so pleased we had a chance to talk things through. It feels like a fresh start. Thank you for letting me borrow your boyfriend for a bit.'

Summer almost tripped as she stared at Tania, wondering why she was suddenly being friendly, whether this was actually another, more veiled attempt to wind her up. But then Tania whispered something in Ryder's ear, making him laugh, and Summer knew their chat was over. She left them to it, her heart pounding in her ears as she caught up with Mason.

He took her bare hand and slipped it, along with his gloved one, inside his coat pocket.

'Where are your gloves?' he asked.

'On the bed, I think. I got them out, but then Latte distracted me.'

'Here.' He took a glove off and gave it to her.

'No, you keep them.'

'Wear it.' He paused, pulling it onto her left hand, then put her right one back in his pocket.

London was by no means quiet, but they were walking

through pockets of sleepy, residential side roads where only streetlights glowed, past alleys that were disconcertingly dark, slinking cats and darting foxes occasionally crossing their path. The thick frost gave everything an ethereal quality, entirely in contrast with drunken revellers, shouting incoherently in the distance, their fervour increasing as Christmas got closer.

Summer replayed the evening's events in her mind, and giggled. 'You did karaoke.' Saying it out loud made her giggle harder.

'Not one of my finest moments,' he admitted, steering her round a bus stop. 'You and Claire carried it.'

'Shush with your flattery. Singing's not my strong point. Claire's amazing though, she's got music running through her veins, and you—'

'Managed to murder The Foundations' greatest hit. I think we need a rule that what happens in London, stays in London.'

'I'm happy with that, but I'm not sure Ryder will agree – he was filming our performance.'

Mason looked at her aghast, and almost walked into Jas. They had reached the canal, Jas and the others standing on the pavement looking down at the sleepy boats with their colourful Christmas lights.

'Holy fuck,' Claire whispered.

'Oh shit,' Jas echoed.

'What?' Mason asked. 'What is it? Why have we stopped?'

'Look,' Claire said, standing aside to let Summer and Mason see what had brought them to a sudden halt.

Summer stared. Her first thought was that the canal had never looked prettier, everything twinkling in a dreamlike way. Her second was that there was something clearly very wrong about the nighttime scene in front of them. 'Oh,' she heard herself say. 'Wow.'

'Crap,' Mason murmured, his hand squeezing hers as they stared down at the beautiful, and definitely frozen, canal. 'Santa Claus was right.'

Chapter 12

They made their way gingerly down the steps, clutching onto handrails and each other, their chattering silenced in the wake of such an unexpected, trip-changing event.

'The canal is frozen,' Ralph said, shaking his head. 'The canal is actually frozen. In London.'

'Unprecedented,' Doug agreed. 'When's the last time this happened?'

'No idea,' Jas said, testing the towpath for slipperiness, then taking one of Claire's arms while Ralph took the other. 'These shoes were not meant for ice, Claire.'

'God, I know that now,' she said, clinging onto the two men gratefully. 'And if there was ever a time not to fall into the canal, this is it. I don't want anyone here to test out how thick the ice is, OK?'

'What do you take us for?' Ryder murmured, helping Tania down the steps. Even he seemed shell-shocked by the discovery, one that would undoubtedly halt their journey out of Little Venice the following day, all of them at the mercy of the weather.

Breaking the ice, Summer remembered her mum telling her years ago, was a fool's errand. It would damage the boats, as well as being hard work, dangerous and entirely pointless. The ice on the canal could continue for miles. The only thing to be done was to sit it out. And as long as they couldn't vacate their visitor moorings, then nobody else could come and take their places, either.

'It looks like we've at least one more day of trading,' Claire said, as Jas and Ralph deposited her on the deck of *Water Music*. 'I guess we make the most of it, and keep an eye on the weather forecast. Night.'

They all said their goodnights. Ryder stood on the towpath with Tania having a low, whispered conversation, and Summer and Mason left them to it, stepping carefully onto *Madeleine's* bow deck. Summer felt more sober than she had five minutes ago, and a headache was thrumming behind her eyes, warning of tomorrow's hangover. She rubbed her forehead, and Mason paused to kiss it before unlocking the door. He had to wrestle with it, the ice creeping into the lock and along the doorjamb, and his expression was pensive as they made their way through the darkened café. Summer stopped to cuddle Archie and Latte who were blinking up at them, disturbed from their slumber as she switched on the lights, and they took off their coats.

'You OK?' Mason asked. 'Glass of water?'

'I'll get it. Why did I think trusting Ryder's cocktails – or his choice of entertainment – would be a good idea?'

'Hey, it was a good night, wasn't it? We survived karaoke, and if you drink a pint of water now, tomorrow won't feel so horrible.'

'But it will still be frozen,' Summer said, as Mason gently guided her through to the cabin, tickling Archie under the chin as he passed. 'We'll be trapped here.'

'Trapped? Is that how you feel?' He sounded confused, concerned, but when she didn't answer he disappeared, and Summer cleaned her teeth, peeled off her clothes and climbed under the covers. Mason returned with two glasses of water and sat on the side of the bed, refusing to budge until she'd drunk hers, then went back and refilled it.

He slipped under the covers, his feet colder than hers, and wrapped his arm around her, pulling her against his bare chest. She rubbed his feet with her own, trying to warm him up.

'Do you feel trapped here?' he asked again. 'Haven't you enjoyed it? I know Tania's appearance has made things more complicated, but . . .'

'Little Venice is wonderful,' she said. 'Meeting people in the café, skating with you, new territory for the dogs to explore, the pubs – even karaoke tonight. But it's like all holidays, you enjoy it, and then you love going home again. This week's been fun, but we were only going to make it back to Willowbeck just in time for Christmas to begin with, and I haven't even sorted out when I'm going to see Dad and Ben.' She wondered whether she was prepared to compromise her proposal plans, do something much simpler on New Year's Eve, or if she should delay it again. The thought made her sad.

'The ice could melt tomorrow,' Mason said. 'We could set off a day late, cruise earlier in the mornings, longer into the evenings, and still make it back in time. I know what you mean about home, though.'

'I miss Valerie and Norman, Dennis and Jenny,' she said, aware she was rambling, her words slurring slightly. 'I miss the robin that lands on the hatch shelf and chirps at me, I miss my regular customers and the way Mike and Harvey

169

tease Archie from the roof of *Cosmic*. And I miss *The Sandpiper*. Your bed's so much more comfortable than this one.' She knew she sounded morose, but she couldn't reveal the main reason she was upset, that her plans to propose to him were being delayed again, this time by – of all unlikely things – a frozen canal.

'We'll get back to all that,' Mason said softly, his kisses feathery in her hair. 'And if we're stuck here for a couple more days, then the best thing to do is embrace it. The cold won't stop the customers, even if it's stopped the canal. And Latte loves Regent's Park. We can take her and Archie for another walk there before we go. In a couple of days, we'll be on our way back to Willowbeck. Now, get some sleep.' He kissed her gently and Summer responded, comforted by his words, his calm, the way that he could dispel any worry, however big it seemed. Her eyes didn't need much encouragement to close, and she fell asleep with Mason's feet still entwined with hers.

When she woke the following morning, the world was light, but not bright. She peeled the curtain back, preparing to wince, and found that, even with her tender head, she didn't need to. There was no sun, just a sky full of dull, grey cloud. The smells were the next thing she noticed: coffee and bacon and something fruity and comforting. Her stomach growled, insisting on some stodge to soak up the remaining alcohol in her system, and she picked up her phone, staring at the screen, trying to take in what she was seeing. It was half past ten!

She jumped out of bed and raced through to the kitchen. Bacon was sizzling slowly on the hob, and the fruity scent turned out to be blueberry muffins, rising and browning in the oven. Shape-wise they were slightly haphazard, but they looked and smelled delicious. She tiptoed to the café doorway and peered around the frame. Mason was standing at the hatch, serving a customer, and three of the tables inside were occupied. The others were covered in used crockery and crumbs, and a similar scene of dirty cups and glasses, scattered coffee grains, surrounded the coffee machine. He turned away from the hatch and pushed his hair back from his forehead. His face was flushed, his apron covered in telltale smudges: butter, chocolate, icing sugar.

'Mason,' she called, and an old couple at one of the tables turned in her direction. The old lady gave her an amused smile, and she glanced down at her penguin pyjamas, the heat rushing to her cheeks.

'Summer.' Mason planted a firm, hurried kiss on her lips. 'How are you feeling?' He took a tray and began piling up the empty crockery, a latte glass wobbling precariously.

'Why didn't you wake me?'

'Because you needed to sleep,' he whispered, approaching her with the full tray. 'I've got this. Sort of.' He gave her a lopsided smile, and Summer had to resist the urge to snog his face off in the café doorway.

'You're amazing,' she said. 'Have I ever told you that?'

'I'm covered in milk,' he said. 'I had an accident with the frother on the coffee machine. At least five people saw me get a face full of semi-skimmed.'

'Give me five minutes,' Summer said, turning away from him.

Mason grabbed her hand. 'You sure you're OK?'

'I am,' she said. 'I'm sorry I was so miserable last night. You're right, we should treat this as a bonus. I'm going to embrace it.'

*　*　*

They worked as a team while the surface of the water stayed steadfastly frozen beneath a gunmetal sky. The pavements were heavily gritted, and signs had been put up on the towpath warning people of the dangers of going near the canal.

'They need to be more careful,' Mason said, drying his hands on a tea towel and frowning as two teenage boys had a friendly tussle at the edge of the towpath. 'If they fall on the ice and go through . . .' He shook his head and pressed his hands into the counter.

One of the outcomes of Lisa's death, and the circumstances surrounding it, was Mason's heightened awareness of danger. She knew that if one of those boys – or anyone else for that matter – fell into the canal, through the ice, then he would try to save them. She had seen it first hand, and while it was another reason she loved him so much, it also scared her. She had almost lost him once, and she didn't know what she'd do if he gave his life saving someone else's.

'It'll thaw soon,' she said, with more confidence than she felt. It was so cold, the word bitter not doing it justice, and she found herself constantly patting the walls, windows and ceiling of *Madeleine*, whispering a mantra, asking her boat to stay strong through the worst and get them safely back to Willowbeck. The engine hadn't repeated its banging noises of the other morning, so maybe Mason's tinkering had worked, but she couldn't entirely banish her unease. But Londoners weren't going to let a bit of cold stop them – it hadn't snowed, after all – and so the café's hot drinks, breakfast butties and warm pastries were more welcome than ever.

They closed around six, the combination of sub-zero temperatures and darkness sending people scurrying indoors, and even though Summer could feel the weariness in her legs, the ache in her head from a late night and too much to drink, she wasn't going to cancel her shopping trip with Claire.

'Stay safe, stay warm,' Mason said, pulling the polar bear hat low over her ears and smiling with approval.

'The boys are going to the pub about eight,' she said, 'and Claire and I will aim to get there at nine-ish.'

'I'll spend a couple of hours on my article,' he said. 'But I'll be there later. Don't buy the whole of Harrods.'

'As if. There's only so much we can fit on two narrowboats. I've been working it out.' She gave him an angelic smile and he waved her off from the bow deck.

She watched as he bent to stroke the dogs and then turned the café lights off, disappearing inside the snug living space. She wondered how much he missed *The Sandpiper*, with its space and its elegance, its clean lines. She loved *Madeleine* – her mum's legacy – but this week had made her realize how much smaller it was, how it was more a café now than a home.

Claire met her on the towpath and they got the bus to Oxford Street, pointing out the Christmas lights and trees to each other, the elaborate displays in shop windows. They got off outside Selfridges and wandered through the departments, stroking fabrics, ogling Kate Spade handbags and sequined notebooks, towering patent heels and brooches that cost more than Summer's boat.

'I'm not going to find Mason a ring here,' she murmured, peering into a glass cabinet.

'I know, but you have to come, don't you? It's bloody magnificent. Look!' Claire found a beautiful blue scarf with silvery swallows dotted over it. The price tag surprised Summer, and when Claire was distracted by the scented candles, the smell of too many subtle scents overpowering on top of each other, she took one off the stand – it would be her Christmas present to Claire.

As she did, her eye caught another scarf. There was only one of this particular design left, and it was nestled between two others so that she'd almost missed it. It was cream, with stylized cupcakes and coffee mugs printed on it, the colour palette pale pinks and reds with the occasional hint of blue. Subtle shimmers of gold transported it from fun to special, and the fabric was impossibly soft against her fingers. Her first thought was how much it reminded her of the designs she had painted on *Madeleine*'s exterior the previous summer, and the second was that her mum would love it. She would have unwrapped the classy, Selfridges tissue paper and gasped in delight, then fixed Summer with that wicked, gleeful look that said she knew her daughter had been far too generous, but she was going to accept the gift and cherish it anyway. It would have looked stunning against her mum's blonde hair, the glinting gold complementing her perfectly.

Summer still hadn't got used to the fact that she didn't need to buy her mum a Christmas present any more, that Maddy would never see this scarf, or what Summer had made of the café, or listen, greedy for every detail as she told her about the moment she asked Mason to marry her. She wouldn't sob with delight as her daughter walked down the aisle, or throw too much confetti over them when they kissed. Her mum would have loved Mason, she knew, and would have teased him affectionately about everything, his hair and his job and his dog, while telling Summer in private that he was wonderful.

Summer closed her eyes, trying to swallow the lump in her throat. She stood and faced the scarves for a moment longer before finding the cash desk to pay for Claire's present.

They braved the cold, and Claire led her away from the wide, bustling pavements of Oxford Street and down the side roads, where smaller, independent shops glowed invitingly.

'How about this?' Claire asked, stopping in front of a jeweller's, its window display understated, only a couple of silver holly leaves proving they knew what season it was.

'It looks a bit pricey.'

'Go inside, Summer. Stop stalling!' She almost pushed her forward, and they stood in the doorway, the eyes of the very tall, suited shop assistant swivelling towards them.

'What can I help you with?' he asked, his tone much warmer than his stance suggested.

'Do you have rings, for men?' Summer asked, forcing the words out.

'Of course, madam, this way.' He ushered them towards a cabinet against the far wall.

'Thank you.'

The range was small, and while some of the rings were far beyond Summer's price range, there were a few that weren't, and one in particular that caught her eye.

'Do you know his size?' Claire asked.

Summer nodded. This bit, she was prepared for. 'I got some of my old rings out a few weeks ago, when we were still in Willowbeck. I said I needed to sort through them, and I got Mason to put them on – on all his fingers, in the pretence that I could decide which ones to keep. Most only went up to his first knuckle, but he has long, slim fingers, so a couple of my thumb rings fitted him. This,' she said, pulling out a thick silver band with swirls that looked like waves, 'fitted his ring finger perfectly.'

'And he didn't suspect a thing?' Claire asked.

'Nope.' Summer smiled at the memory. 'He just sighed good-naturedly when I told him he had to be a jewellery model. He didn't seem remotely suspicious.'

'Good old Mason,' Claire murmured. 'Which one's caught your eye?' She brought her face level with Summer's, and Summer pointed at the ring she was transfixed by. It looked like brushed silver, with a silhouette of a tree etched into it.

'That one's cobalt with a matt finish,' said the assistant, hovering close by. 'Not many men go for diamonds, understandably, but the tree detail is unusual. It's from one of our independent jewellers. They carve the shape in with a tiny chisel, and then blacken it so it will stand out against the metal.'

'Do you have different sizes?' Summer asked.

'Of course. Do you know what you need?'

She held out her thumb ring. He took it and ducked down behind the counter.

Claire's grin was wide. 'Summer, it's perfect. Oh my God, he'll love it!'

'I think so too.' She hugged her friend, giddy with excitement. 'Thank you for bringing me here. I never knew I'd find something so . . . so totally Mason!'

'Serendipity,' Claire said. Summer couldn't disagree.

They made it to the Riverside Inn at half-past nine, their bellies full of Wagamamas, the boxed ring tucked safely inside Summer's handbag. It was Friday night, and the pub was packed. They wove through the throng of bodies and found their friends close to the window, two tables pulled together, a sea of empty glasses covering them. It seemed none of them were suffering with hangovers after their cocktail experience the previous night, or else they were self-medicating with hair of the dog. Summer waved at Jas and Doug, dumped her shopping bags under the table and flopped happily into a chair, her gaze taking in the rest of the scene. Mason was chatting to Ralph, and Tania and Ryder sat against the wall, their faces angled towards each other. She was wearing a figure-hugging raspberry jumper, her full, smiling lips painted to match.

Summer smiled brightly when Mason spotted her, and he said something to Ralph and slid off the bench, coming round to kiss her.

'You're freezing,' he said. 'Let me get you a drink. Mulled wine?'

'Sure. Claire?'

'Sounds good to me.'

She followed him to the bar, pushing her elbows out to make it through the scrum.

'How was late-night shopping?' he asked.

'Productive, and fun. I'm ready for Christmas.' She'd been able to pick up most of the things she'd been looking for, unsurprising considering where they'd been. As well as several smaller, silly gifts, she'd bought Mason a folio to keep all the copies of his magazines in, a record of his achievements bound in impossibly soft leather. Everything was stored on his computer, of course, but this was special – like the framed photos he had dotted around *The Sandpiper*. She hoped he'd like it, hoped he'd love the ring. Hoped, hoped, hoped . . .

'Wow,' he laughed, 'you're ready?'

'Perhaps a bit over-prepared – it's easy to get carried away. But if we're travelling right up until Christmas Day . . .'

He nodded, distracted by the barman asking for his order.

'How's your evening been?' she asked brightly.

'I've made progress on my article,' he said. 'Not as much as I'd hoped, but some. Archie and Latte demanded a long walk, but it gave me time to think, to decide how I'd frame it.'

'That's great,' she said. 'Can I read it later?'

'I'd love you to.'

She led the way back to the table, clearing a path, Mason clutching the drinks behind her. Claire patted the seat next to hers and Summer landed on it, her throbbing feet immediately grateful. Mason put their drinks down and took the seat next to Summer, resting his arm along the back of her chair.

'You're a star, Mason,' Claire said, holding her drink up.

'Sounds like you've had a good night,' Mason replied. 'Are you completely sorted for Christmas now too?'

'Oh God no,' Claire laughed. 'I got one thing. But it's been a successful evening all round, hasn't it, Summer?' She gave her a pointed look and Summer tried not to blush.

'I need to get moving on mine.' Mason ran his hand through his hair. 'I don't want to run out of time.'

'If you need any help with Summer's gift, just let me know.' Claire said, grinning.

'Thanks, Claire, I might—'

'Mason,' Tania said, appearing behind them, her hand on his shoulder. 'Can I chat to you for a second?'

Mason frowned, glanced up at her. 'I'm just catching up with—'

'It won't take long,' she cooed. 'I need your advice about something.'

Mason didn't reply immediately, but leaned into Summer, kissing her cheek, whispering in her ear. 'Do you mind?'

Summer forced a smile, shook her head. 'Of course not.'

Mason squeezed her hand, held it for a moment longer than necessary and then followed Tania round to the other side of the table.

Summer watched them go, then picked up her glass and took a tentative sip. The wine was hot and spiced and exactly what she needed.

'Summer,' Claire said, a warning in her voice. 'Don't you dare.'

'I'm not doing anything,' she said calmly. 'I'm not thinking anything, not wondering anything, not imagining anything. I'm just drinking my drink, taking a load off.'

'You've just bought him the most stunning ring,' Claire whispered.

'I know, and I can't wait to give it to him. I want Mason to be happy, and I would never stop him from being friends with anyone.'

'But?' Claire asked softly.

'But,' Summer echoed. 'It's not the easiest thing, watching them. And Tania's been . . . she's said some predatory things, as if she still wants to be with him. And why is she here in the first place, when she told you she was going to be away?'

She swallowed, panic rising inside her at the returning swell of emotion. It was only exhaustion, she told herself, that dog-tired feeling the evening after the night before, the hangover screaming at her to go to bed and sleep it into oblivion. And the fact that they couldn't go back to Willowbeck yet, their plans suddenly off-kilter, the thought of missing Christmas Day in her sleepy, fenland village, missing out on a drink at the pub, seeing Jenny and Dennis's display of glowing penguins and reindeer, not enough time to prepare everything in exactly the way she wanted for her proposal. And then there was the scarf, the reminder that her mum wasn't there to see her living her life, happy and successful and in love.

She wiped frantically at her eyes, dipping her head, hoping nobody would notice.

'Summer,' Claire said, 'God. I didn't realize—'

Summer blinked. 'Don't let Mason see me like this, he'll think it's because of Tania.' 'Is it not?' Claire asked softly. She put her arm around Summer's shoulders and pushed their shopping bags securely underneath the table, towards Jas's feet. He glanced at them, and nodded his understanding as Claire led Summer towards the door.

Shivering outside, because the inside of the pub was too busy to find a quiet corner, Summer told Claire everything, releasing her words, along with her sobs, into the inky black sky. The force of her emotion surprised her; she was happy, on the verge of something monumental, but she'd let the doubts niggle at her constantly since Tania had appeared, and she'd kept them from Mason after that first night in Benji's snug bar, trying not to let her insecurities get the better of her.

And it wasn't just Tania, she told Claire. It was because she cared so deeply for Mason, because she didn't have her mum to guide her, because there were so many ways it could go wrong.

'I was even worried when I saw how concerned Mason was about a couple of boys playing close to the frozen canal.' She laughed at her own ridiculousness as her tears continued to fall, the tissue Claire had given her sodden. 'I thought he was preparing to go in after them if they fell. I'm so scared of losing him, either to Tania or to some horrendous accident, or simply that he'll say no. But I know it's irrational, I know he loves me. Why am I being like this?'

'It's human nature,' Claire said. 'You've dealt with so much loss – both of you have. Your mum, Lisa, the fire last summer. It's entirely understandable that you're worried about it when you're about to take this step. Tania being here has raked up the past, and your mum's not far from your thoughts because you wish she was here to see you do this. It's pre-proposal nerves, Sum, and I'm glad you've told me, stopped keeping it to yourself. Hopefully you can see that you don't need to be worried. Not. At. All.'

Summer sniffed, feeling better after Claire's reassurance and noisily purging her fears. She owed her friend more than one drink for putting up with her in this state. 'If I'm like this before the proposal, imagine what I'll be like leading up to the wedding!'

'Oh God, total Bridezilla. Glad I'll be roving. Harry can deal with it.' She took out another tissue and wiped under Summer's eyes. 'Can't have you going back in looking like I've assaulted you with Midnight-Black Perfect Lash.'

'You won't tell Mason any of this?'

'Of course not, but I think you should. Obviously not the proposal bit, the root of it, but be honest about Tania, and about your mum – you talk to him about her, don't you?'

'I do,' Summer said quietly.

'So be as honest as you can without spoiling the surprise. And whenever you start to worry, think of that ring with its fancy cobalt and its etched tree, and Mason's reaction when you open the box in front of him. Honestly, Sum, the fact you found that ring means you're meant to be together. It's a sign.'

'Thanks, Claire, I don't know where I'd be without you.'

'Still in Willowbeck with none of this stress or frozen-canal malarkey, that's where. Now, shall we go in? I'm freezing my tits off out here.'

When they went back inside, Tania was deep in conversation with Doug, and Mason was sitting in Summer's chair, talking distractedly to Jas. He shot up when they reappeared.

'Are you OK? Where did you go?' He put his hands on her arms, his dark eyes latching onto hers, and Summer drank in his concern, biting back the urge to tell him everything, including her New Year plans.

'Outside,' Claire said. 'Sorry, I was feeling a bit faint – it's hot in here, and I needed some fresh air. Summer came with me.'

Mason's brows lowered in confusion. He looked carefully at Claire, and then Summer. 'How do you feel now? Come and sit down. Do you want some water?'

There was shuffling as they moved chairs around, and Summer found herself between Claire and Mason for the rest of the evening. She wasn't sure if Mason believed Claire's story – she couldn't imagine her eyes didn't still have the telltale signs of her outburst – but he seemed to take it at face value, and she tried to heed her friend's advice and stop worrying.

When they got back to *Madeleine* and the neat cabin with its warm winter duvet, Summer almost cried with relief.

'You look exhausted,' Mason said. 'Are you sure you're OK? Was Claire . . .' he hesitated, clearly uncomfortable calling her out in a lie.

'I'm fine,' she said quietly. 'And Claire was taking the fall for me, she didn't feel faint. I got a bit overwhelmed, and needed to get out of the pub for a moment. But it's tiredness, mainly, too many cocktails last night. I found a scarf in Selfridges, and it reminded me of Mum; it would have been perfect for her Christmas present.'

'Oh, Summer.' He wrapped her up, his hug strong and

warm and all-consuming, as if he wanted to protect her from the world. She took deep breaths, refusing to give in to more tears. He kissed her forehead, stroked her hair, and Summer blocked out everything except the feel of being in his arms, the sensation of his lips, his fingers, touching her. And despite her tiredness, her body began to wake up. She lifted her head up and he brought his lips down onto hers, his kiss familiar and intoxicating. As their movements became more urgent, as they discarded their coats and she slid his jumper over his head, felt the tug as he unbuttoned her jeans, she realized this was what she needed; to be lost in him. She wanted to feel nothing else but Mason.

When she woke the next morning, she reached an arm out to find that Mason's side of the bed was empty. It was still fairly early, and there were no tantalizing smells coming from the kitchen. Pulling her hoody over her pyjamas, Summer moved blearily through the boat, noticing that the canal was still very much frozen. Latte was asleep, her small body a cotton wool ball, but Archie was pacing, his tail wagging sporadically, as if he wasn't sure whether he was happy or not.

'What is it?' she asked him, crouching, trying to ignore the knot that was tightening her stomach. 'Where's he gone, Archie?'

Her phone didn't have any answers, the screen resolutely clear of notifications.

Dazed and unthinking, she switched on the kettle. Valerie always told her things would be better with a cup of tea, and she was sure they would, that Mason had just nipped out to check on one of the other boats, called on by Jas or Doug to a potential problem, and Summer had slept through the commotion. But then she saw the note, scribbled hastily on one of her order pads in blue Biro. She recognized Mason's untidy handwriting.

Had to go – fighting – urgent!! Be in touch v soon. I LOVE YOU. M. Xxx

She should have been reassured, especially by the last words. But she didn't understand what it meant, didn't understand the references – who was fighting? Was there something he needed to clear up with Tania from last night that he'd failed to mention? She couldn't make sense of it, why he'd had to leave without waking her. She tried his phone but it went straight through to voicemail. Little Venice was still and quiet outside, not even ripples on the water to comfort her. Standing in the empty café in her pyjamas, holding onto Mason's note as if it was only a matter of time before it revealed its secrets, Summer had no idea what to do next.

Chapter 13

The urge to shut down the café and go and find Mason was strong, but Summer knew she had to be rational. It wasn't a kidnapping, there were no signs that the note had been written under duress – and Summer had watched enough episodes of *CSI New York* in her pre-boat days to know what that looked like. Mason had gone off to do something important; she just had to wait for him to come back. She showered and fed the dogs, spending longer than usual with them, trying to calm Archie who was still restless, letting out the occasional, high-pitched bark, which was unusual for him.

Early morning sunshine spilled through every window, setting off the gold and silver shimmer of her bunting, making a mockery of the Christmas tree lights. The frozen canal sparkled, the towpath glistened, and Summer felt suddenly, overwhelmingly, Christmassy. So they would be here a few days more than planned – that was fine. She'd told Mason she was going to embrace it, and that's what she intended to do. She pushed the niggling worries about his unexpected disappearance to the back of her mind – he would explain what the fighting meant when she saw him.

The coffee machine hummed, the cold air that blasted through the hatch removed the last of her sleepiness, and Summer was about to put on some Christmas carols when she realized it wouldn't be long before *Water Music* did that for her. She baked macarons and scones with chunks of cranberry, the delicious smells filling the café. She took vases out of a cupboard and put one on every table, a sprig of mistletoe, which she'd bought the previous evening with Claire, inside each one.

'You open, love?' someone called. 'Only my hands are fit to fall off.'

Summer raced to the hatch to greet her customer. The man looked to be in his forties, the fluorescent orange of his jacket and trousers making her eyes smart. He had thick gloves on, a beanie hat pulled low over his forehead, but he was still stamping his feet, jiggling up and down, his warm clothing no match for the cold.

'Why don't you come in for a few moments and warm yourself up?'

'Can't leave me cart, love,' he said, indicating behind him with a quick move of his head.

Summer peered round him, and saw the gritting cart on the towpath. 'Nobody will steal it, surely. We can keep an eye on it.'

'People nick anything that's not tied down, even if they've no use for it. Coffee and a bacon sarnie would do me the world, though. I'll do me little ice dance out here in the meantime.' He grinned, and Summer laughed and went to check on the bacon she had sizzling on the hob.

'How much do you have to grit?' she asked, while the

186

coffee machine spurted its way through making the Americano he'd asked for. 'And do you have to cross over, do the other side of the towpath?'

He shook his head. 'Nah, my patch is up for a couple of miles thataways,' he pointed down the way they'd cruised in, 'and then just into the Paddington Basin. Been busy last few days. Usually it's litter picking, now it's anti-slip.'

'Pretty important on a towpath,' Summer said, pouring milk into the top of his coffee. 'Slipping over on the ice is bad enough, but when there's a canal close by, it's even more dangerous.'

'Ain't that the truth.'

'What time do you have to start?' Summer asked, thinking how cold and dark and generally unappealing it would be before dawn, having to get out of bed and walk the streets alone, shaking salt onto the towpath.

'About four thirty,' he said. 'Any later and you're missing the first commuters. Not that this place ever truly sleeps, mind. Just this morning I saw a bloke hot-footing it down thataways about five o'clock,' he thumbed to his right, 'paying no attention to the fact that I was coming towards him, and where he'd come from hadn't been gritted yet. I called out for him to slow down, but he was excited about something, that much was clear. Told me he had to go after a woman, that he couldn't wait, but I'm not sure what bird would be up and eager to see anyone that time of the morning.'

Summer felt a twinge in her stomach. 'Sounds crazy,' she said unconvincingly. 'What did he look like, this man?'

'Why? You missing one, love?' His grin lasted only a second, then he became much more serious. When she looked closely, she saw that he had very blue eyes. 'Oh, right. Well, y'know, he was fairly well rugged up, dark coat, boots – I remember seeing them because I was worried about him slipping, y'know, but his boots were sturdy. Had the stupidest hat on, though. I wondered if he had a screw loose, to be honest.'

'Stupid hat?' Summer asked weakly. If Mason had left early, in the dark, desperate to sort something out with Tania, then maybe he hadn't had time to find his own hat.

'Yeah,' the man said, as Summer passed him the bag with his bacon sandwich in, and he nodded his thanks at her. 'He was wearing a white hat with ears, kinda like some deranged polar bear.'

'Calm down, Summer. Tell me everything, again, from the beginning.' Claire blew the froth on her latte, creating a little hole in it. Summer stared at the drink, wondering how she'd got herself in this mess. If they'd only stayed in Willowbeck, if she hadn't had grand ideas about coming to Little Venice, about showing Mason how life had been for her with Claire, Ryder and Jas.

'I woke up and Mason was gone, and then I found this in the kitchen.' She smoothed out the note on the counter, and Claire ran her finger over it, as if tracing his handwriting.

'Right,' she said, frowning. 'And then this council guy said he'd seen someone leaving early, racing on the slippery path, and that he'd told him he was going after a *woman*?'

Summer nodded. 'And it had to be Mason.'

'Because of your polar bear hat?' She raised her eyebrows.

'It's just like him, grabbing the first relevant thing he sees, and it would have been dark. If he didn't want to wake me . . .'

'You're sure this guy said he'd said he was going after a woman?'

'Yes. I'm sure.'

'There's clearly some mistake,' Claire blustered, but Summer could see the tension in her shoulders. 'Maybe he was going shopping, and said he was going after something *for* a woman; maybe there's a thing he wants to get you for Christmas, and it's going to be sold out, or—'

'At five in the morning?'

'Yeah, but Sum,' Claire picked up a chocolate-log-flavoured macaron and popped it in her mouth, waited a few seconds until she could speak again, 'if he was going after a woman – which is the most ridiculous thing I've ever heard, by the way – why would he do *that* at five in the morning?'

'Because Tania texted him, because he's realized he still cares for her, because she wanted to speak to him last night and it's all clicked back into place. I know she still likes him, she's been dropping the least subtle hints ever since we met her. Oh God, Claire, what am I going to do?' She pressed the heels of her hands into her eyes, and felt Claire gently clasp her wrists and pull them back out again.

'We're not going to jump to any conclusions, not until we've seen Mason and got the story from him. Did you guys have a fight last night? Did you tell him everything you told me outside the pub?'

'No,' Summer said. 'I didn't tell him everything. I told him about Mum, but not Tania, not – not anything about that. But we definitely didn't have a fight.' She wondered how she could even be considering that he'd gone to see Tania after the previous night, but right now nothing made sense.

'Oh, Summer,' Claire said. 'You need to be honest with him. If you don't tell him how insecure you're feeling about Tania, he'll—'

'Rush off to see her at five in the morning?'

'I can't believe that's what's happened,' Claire said, shaking her head. 'I just can't.'

'What other woman is there?' Summer asked, and then seriously considered the question herself. His parents were up in Northumberland, and he wasn't that close to them, so it wasn't likely to be his mum – unless something bad had happened. For a few moments she considered the possibility that it was to do with Lisa: perhaps there was somewhere nearby that had been important to them both. It would make sense – his past had been stirred up by seeing Tania again – but she couldn't imagine him rushing off so early. And what about what he'd said to the gritting man? What could the 'fighting' in his message mean? Unless there was someone else she was unaware of, all thoughts led back to Tania.

Claire too, it seemed, was stumped. She picked her phone up, pressed the screen then held it to her ear. 'She's not answering,' she said after a while. 'Not that that means anything. She's friendly when she wants to be, and not so much when she doesn't.'

'Tell me about it,' Summer said.

Claire put a cinnamon macaron in her mouth, her eyes not leaving Summer's face. Latte and Archie were at her feet, the café was empty – it was still only half past eight – and Summer felt a sudden weariness, an aching in her bones, in her mind, as well as anger and frustration at herself.

'You don't really think Mason's gone bed-hopping from you to Tania, do you?' Claire asked. 'I mean, Sum, the idea is ludicrous.'

Summer leaned her elbows on the counter. 'I'm just so confused. Seeing her here, when for so long she's been a spectre in Mason's past, has been so strange. She was part of the reason Mason and I took so long to admit our feelings

190

for each other. I was worried what kind of a man he was when he was prepared to treat her like that. Until I knew the truth, I felt sorry for her, because I was imagining how hard it would be, being close to Mason and then losing him suddenly. But I don't believe that, however much she still wanted him, he would get back with her. Or if he did, if he decided that he loved her after all, I know he'd tell me first. He's too honest to be a cheater.'

'So if you think all that,' Claire said, 'if your feelings around Tania are pure discomfort, and you know Mason wouldn't cheat on you, then what's the problem?'

'This is,' Summer said, waving the note. 'What is the fighting reference about? And the gritting man saying Mason told him that he was going after a woman? I don't know what the answer is.'

'If it was me, I'd be more concerned that he was prepared to go out in public in your polar bear hat. That certainly shows dedication to his cause, whatever that might be. Look, I'll go and ask the others, see if anyone saw him or if he mentioned anything in the pub while we were shopping. You stay put – he'll probably be back in an hour's time with an explanation so straightforward you'll be laughing before he's finished giving it to you.'

'Thanks, Claire.' Her friend dropped to her knees and gave Archie, and then Latte, an enthusiastic hug. The dogs responded with their usual tail-wagging ecstasy, and then Claire strode out of the café and down the freshly gritted towpath, her phone clamped once more to her ear.

'Where is he, Archie? Where's he run off to?'

Archie looked up at her, panting slightly, and barked.

'That's not helpful,' she said, 'but I appreciate you trying.'

While the café was quiet, Summer called Valerie and

then Harry, giving Valerie a glossed-over version of Little Venice that didn't include Tania, or Mason's vanishing act. She should have known, however, that she wasn't going to get away with it.

'Are you OK, Summer? Only you sound slightly strained. London's not getting on top of you, is it?'

'No Valerie, London is wonderful. It's vibrant and buzzy. The river freezing was unexpected, of course, but I'm sure we'll be able to leave in a couple of days. And in the meantime, business is definitely booming.' She laughed, but could feel the weight of Valerie's silence.

'Take care of yourself, Summer,' the older woman said. 'I want you back safe and sound in Willowbeck. And don't forget that things are quite often not what you think. When you see hooves, look for a horse, not a zebra.'

With that cryptic statement she rang off, and Summer was left staring at the phone.

To Harry, she told everything. She leaned on the counter, her voice a low whisper, Harry content to wait while Summer broke off to serve customers, though for early on a Saturday it was fairly quiet.

Harry was shocked that Tania was there, and that Summer hadn't told her before now. She, like Claire, agreed there must be a straightforward explanation for Mason's disappearance, though she couldn't come up with an answer that entirely reassured Summer.

'You can get anything in London, can't you? He's probably off sorting out your Christmas present, something unique. Fighting through the crowds, maybe?' she said, trying to decipher the words. 'Whatever it is, you have to tell me as soon as he turns up.'

'What are you up to today?' Summer asked, desperate to

change the subject and stop the thoughts circling inside her head, if only for a few minutes.

'I'm taking Tommy Christmas shopping, so he can get Greg's present. And possibly mine – I'll have to avert my eyes at that point.'

'While giving him the money to pay for it?'

Harry laughed. 'Yes, there's that too. It'll be fun. I don't mind a bit of Christmas shopping chaos. I bet it's epic in London.'

'It is – Selfridges was nuts!'

Harry sighed longingly, and after a final reassurance from her friend, Summer thanked her and they ended the call.

In between customers, Summer made the tables shine until they gleamed. She was frustrated with herself for fearing the worst, and it wasn't as if she and Mason were tied together. Of course he could go off on his own. It was just the words in the note, and the story from the man in his fluorescent work outfit that were niggling at her. When a young family came in, she put all her energy into making the two boys spectacular hot chocolates, with cream and marshmallows and crumbled macarons on top.

'Oh wow,' the mum said as she approached, 'what do you think of those, boys?'

Their eyes lit up like diamonds, the younger one gasping until Summer feared he might explode.

'I wish I'd gone for one of those now,' their dad said, looking impressed.

'There's still time to change your mind,' Summer said, grinning.

'Oh I don't think . . .' He patted his stomach, then exchanged a glance with his wife. 'Yeah, go on then. Two more of those please.'

His wife nodded her agreement. 'We'll need the energy for Winter Wonderland.'

'Oh, is that where you're off to? I went a few days ago, it's fab.'

'James is desperate to go on the ice rink, aren't you?'

The boy nodded, his nose already covered in cream.

'It's magical,' Summer said, 'very festive. Very fast, too! I'll go and make your new drinks, cancel the coffees.'

As the family put their coats on she wished them a great time, and had just finished clearing the detritus on their table, the splodges of melted cream and marshmallows, when Claire came back into the café, followed by dress-down Santa. She did a quick mental stocktake, relieved when she remembered she had a whole tub of freshly baked mince pies in the kitchen.

Santa stood patiently behind Claire, but she waved him forward. 'What can I get you?'

'Ten pies this time, please. I'm taking advantage of your semi-permanent status here. You off as soon as the canal gets its act together?'

'We are,' Summer said. 'Though God knows when that'll be. Everyone says a couple of days, but then it wasn't ever expected to freeze in the first place, was it?'

'Someone up there's going for extra Christmassy! Can I get a gingerbread latte too? It's so cold out there, I need the sugar.'

'Coming right up.' She turned to the coffee machine.

'So,' Claire started, not bothering to be discreet. 'I asked everyone and nobody has a clue where Mason's gone, no hints last night in the pub, and I went up to Tania's boat, she's not there, no sign of anyone.' She huffed. 'I mentioned the note, the fighting part, and what the gritter said. We're all drawing a blank. Jas said he'd check things out online, do a search on social media around this area, but I don't know if it'll bring anything up. Still, it's early; he'll likely be back soon. Doesn't he always have one of your bacon sarnies?'

'He does,' Summer said. She felt an irrational pang of sadness that he might miss it.

'I like a good puzzle,' Santa Claus said softly. 'Is this your fella? The one who was flirted at by the woman in the sparkles?'

'That's him.' Summer wondered why she wasn't bothered by his nosiness. But she'd enjoyed his visits, his friendliness, and she realized she felt entirely comfortable talking to him about it. 'He left before I woke up this morning, scribbled down something about fighting.' She took the note that had, by now, collected a couple of coffee splatters, and handed it to him.

He stared at it, his white brows furrowing. 'In my job,' he said, 'communication is very important.'

Summer imagined him collecting the lists of children and toys from his elves, wondering at the possible mix-ups when someone had asked for a Furby and got a Barbie instead. She shook the ridiculous thought away.

'If you don't communicate properly, then all manner of things can go wrong,' he continued. 'You don't know what the fighting might mean, who he's angry with?' He peered at it closely over his half-moon glasses.

'Mason doesn't get angry with anyone,' Summer said quietly.

'And the guy Summer spoke to earlier,' Claire interjected, 'told her that the man he'd seen – which we know was Mason – had said he was off to see a woman, and that he was excited about it, or something.' She leaned towards Santa conspiratorially, as if they were working on a case and he was the expert profiler.

He held a hand up. 'No "or somethings". It's very important that we know exactly what the man said. Can you remember?'

'Uhm.' Summer closed her eyes, thinking back. '*He* said that *Mason* said he was "going after a woman" but that he wasn't sure what bird would be waiting that early in the morning.'

'Hmmm.' Santa ran his hands over his lips, staring at the note and then peering out of the window.

Claire and Summer exchanged a glance, Claire's lips twitching with amusement.

'Your fella,' he continued, 'he said something to me, that first day you were here.'

'Oh?' Summer tried to remember. 'What was that?'

He sighed, shook his head. 'Are you sure it's "fighting"? His handwriting's pretty appalling, and if he was rushing, in the dark . . .'

'What else, though?' Claire asked.

'And the man you talked to definitely said that Mason used the word "woman", not another word he just interpreted as meaning woman?'

'Such as?' Claire asked.

'Bird,' Summer blurted. 'Bird – he used the word bird. What if Mason had said bird, not woman? And – and the fighting could be sighting. Sighting! Bird sighting!' The revelation hit her like lightning. She whooped, and Archie and Latte added their own barking voices. Santa Claus laughed, a big belly laugh, and Claire raised her fists in triumph, so that when Jas walked into the café clutching his tablet aloft,

Summer wasn't surprised that he froze mid-sentence, his eyes widening in alarm.

'Sorry, Jas,' she said, 'we've just figured something out about Mason. We think we know why he went, even if we don't know where.'

'Ah, I think I can help you with that part,' Jas said. 'If you promise not to scream at me?'

'No screaming, Brownie's honour. What have you found?'

Jas put his iPad on the counter and waited for them all to peer in. 'I looked at Twitter this morning. I had to do a couple of searches, for the London area and also hashtags, different nature organizations – not everyone gets as excited about this stuff as your man, Summer, but a hen harrier sighting in Battersea Park is definitely not an everyday occurrence. I reckon that's what Mason's gone after, polar bear hat and all.'

Summer stared at Claire. 'You told them he was wearing my polar bear hat?'

Claire shrugged. 'That's how we knew it was Mason the council guy had seen, it's an integral part of the story.'

'Besides,' Jas said, slightly apologetically, 'if he was wearing it, then he can't be that embarrassed about it.'

'Is the harrier still in the park – it's a bird of prey, isn't it?' Summer asked, changing the subject.

Jas glanced at his screen. 'Yup, as of four minutes ago. It's kind of like a buzzard, but much less common. It's been travelling up the line of the Thames since yesterday afternoon, and Battersea's where it's at now. Why? Aren't you going to wait for him to come back?'

'Yeah, Sum,' Claire added. 'Surely now you know he's OK, that he's not gone after . . . something else, you can wait here.'

'No I can't,' Summer said, shrugging off her apron. 'I thought he'd gone to see Tania. The fact that I believed, even for a second, that he might have done that, means I need to talk to him, to apologize. I've been letting Tania get to me, letting her intimidate me ever since we arrived, and I need to be honest with him about that – about everything. I need to go now.'

'And if he's more focused on the bird of prey than you?'

'Then I'll wait it out, but I have to find him.'

Claire nodded decisively. 'Do it. And don't close the café. We'll take over the reins until you're back. Me and Jas.'

'You will?' Summer asked.

'We will?' Jas echoed.

'Yup. *Water Music* was jam packed yesterday, and I really need to sort it out before I open again, put everything back in its rightful place. Besides, coffee and bacon sandwiches will be in much higher demand than LPs on a day like today. You can leave it in our safe hands.'

'Archie and Latte too?' Summer asked, knowing she was pushing her luck. 'I'm not sure how popular I'll be if I turn up to a rare bird sighting with a couple of dogs that could easily scare it away.'

'We'll get them to help,' Claire said, grinning.

Summer laughed. 'Good luck with that!'

She collected her coat, gloves and scarf from the cabin, and picked up Mason's beanie hat at the last moment. It was freezing outside.

'Go and find your mad, bird-watching boyfriend, Summer.'

'I will. Thanks so much, Claire, Jas, thank you for all your help, San—' she stopped herself just in time, though from his knowing grin, the cheerful, semi-regular customer must have known what she was about to say. He had, after all, solved their puzzle for them.

She pushed open the doors of the café and stood on the bow deck, inhaling air that felt like pure ice. As she went to shut the door behind her, she heard Jas say:

'She's only going because she wants to get that hat off him, right? What grown man races about London after birds of prey, wearing a fluffy, polar bear hat with ears?'

My man, Summer thought, grinning widely as she stepped carefully off the deck and onto the towpath, feeling the roughness of the salt beneath her boots.

Chapter 14

At first Summer thought she could walk to Battersea Park, find her way through the London streets, but checking the route on her phone told her it would take over an hour, and that wasn't taking the ice-covered pavements into account. She memorized the journey – tube first, then bus, then a short walk, and, with her phone tucked inside her bag and her hands inside gloves, she made her way to the Underground station. The tube was full of shoppers and revellers, the mood more jubilant than she would have expected, perhaps because it was actually warm in the packed carriages, the ice and biting December wind only a memory for those few, brief stops.

When Summer emerged back outside, she was assaulted with it once more. The sky was blue, the clouds had dispersed to allow the sun in, but its warmth couldn't cut through the chill of the wind, the feeling that, as she stood and waited for the bus, her skin was being covered in tiny ice-crystals, slowly freezing her anxious expression into place.

The bus was a double-decker, and Summer climbed to

the top, drinking in the sights as they drove through Chelsea, towards the river. It had been several years since she'd been to London, and while lots of things had changed, shiny new buildings bursting up towards the sky, so much was familiar and, at this particular moment, comforting.

The journey would take her close to an hour – she'd been going thirty-five minutes already – and she had no idea if Mason would still be there when she arrived. She tried his phone again, but it had been going straight to voicemail ever since she'd discovered him gone. If he had been sitting there for hours, waiting for the movement – or return – of a harrier, then he was likely to be frozen as solid as the statue of the Buddha that, she had seen from the pictures on her phone, looked out over the river from its seat in the park.

Finally, the bus drove across Battersea Bridge, the Thames stretching out below them, wide and churning. It was blue-brown beneath the winter sun, dotted with tour boats and the occasional industrial barge. It was, of course, far too big to be frozen, unlike their little canal, but Summer remembered dress-down Santa telling them that it had frozen over as recently as the 1960s. She wondered how much of London would come to a standstill if that happened again. Above them, aeroplanes left puffy trails in the blue sky, and even those seemed to wink with an extra layer of sparkle.

The bus's electronic announcer told her they had arrived at the Battersea Park stop and, walking the last part of her journey, Summer stepped into the park, suddenly with no idea where to go. She studied the signs for the boating lake, the children's zoo, the mini golf course, but she wasn't going to find one announcing the arrival of a large bird of prey. She went onto Twitter, scanning her timeline, searching for 'hen harrier' and 'Battersea' and coming up blank. It wasn't her favourite social media platform; she kept her Facebook page for the café much more up to date, and so was nowhere near as expert as Jas, or even Mason, who posted infrequently but used it to search for wildlife news.

'Can I help at all? Only you seem rather perplexed.' She started at the voice, and looked up from her phone.

An elderly gentleman wearing a bottle-green anorak, his tall frame leaning on a walking stick, gave her a warm smile. His face was thin, his gaze direct behind large, gold-rimmed glasses.

'Uhm, thank you. I heard there was a hen harrier spotted here? I don't know if – maybe it's moved on . . . but—'

'Oh it's here all right,' he said. 'Or at least its admirers are. A whole cluster of them, down towards the peace pagoda. Do you know where that is?'

Her smile was pure relief. 'No, could you tell me?'

'That way, dear. Follow the main path, and the signs will soon point you right. I hope you don't mind me remarking, but you don't exactly fit the twitcher stereotype. But maybe you're from a newspaper? Some might say that a hen harrier sighting in such an unlikely place was some sort of Christmas gift, a sign of something.' He narrowed his eyes, his smile brief but not unfriendly.

'A sign of what?' she asked.

'Who knows? It's a strange occurrence, that's all, and some-thing reporters will no doubt make the most of.'

'My boyfriend's a nature journalist,' Summer said. 'That's why I'm here – I'm looking for him.'

'He'll be in the throng then, I'm sure. Good luck to you.' He held out his hand and she took it, clasping his bony fingers.

'And to you!' She started walking in the direction he'd told her, and soon came across the signs for the pagoda.

The park was beautiful, and full of interest. There were so many different areas; some formal, some fun, activities for children and families, quiet spaces for walking and thinking. Summer tried not to get distracted as she made her way to the pagoda. As she got nearer, she saw what she was looking for. Not a large, brown bird with owl-like markings round its eyes (she had looked it up on the bus), but a group of bodies, indistinguishable with their backs to her in black, navy and green jackets, lenses angled up towards the mature trees fringing the park, looking over the Thames. She scanned them for a white hat with ears, and then, failing that, looked for Mason's dark curls.

It didn't take her long to find them; he was one of the few who didn't have something to keep the heat from escaping out of the top of his head.

She paused for a moment, chewing her lip.

She wasn't worried about the harrier – if it hadn't been disturbed by a whole crowd of gawping people, then it was unlikely to be disturbed by her approach – but about what Mason would say when she revealed her fears to him. She tiptoed slowly towards them, noticing a few people lingering on the path, clearly wondering what was going on. The watchers were being watched. The idea, along with the relief at finding her boyfriend, made her smile.

She walked quietly up, crouched down behind him and placed a hand gently on his back. She felt him flinch, his head whipping round. His eyes widened when he saw her, and a grin spread slowly across his face. The end of his nose was red with cold and his lips were pale, worryingly close to blue, but he looked happy.

'Summer,' he whispered, wrapping an arm around her and pulling her against him. 'What are you doing here?'

'I came to find you,' she said, matching her volume to his. 'You're like a block of ice. How long have you been sitting here?'

'A few hours. The hen harrier is in a tree up there,' he pointed. 'Brian, from the London Ornithological Society, says it's likely to leave any time now, and then that'll be it.'

'What do you mean "it"? Haven't you seen it yet?'

'Nope. Brian thinks it's a visitor from Europe, that it would usually stay in the farmland or heathland close to the Kent coast over the winter, and has somehow gone off course – you'd never ordinarily see one anywhere close to here – and headed further down the Thames in confusion. It's stayed in the trees overnight, but is likely to be off any moment, back along the river and out on its original route. It's a once-in-a-lifetime chance, Summer. Here, at least. I'm glad you'll get to see it.'

'Me too,' she said, biting her lip. 'Oh, and – here.' She took his beanie hat out of her pocket and pulled it down over his head. 'I'd rather you didn't get hypothermia. Rumour has it you left wearing the polar bear.'

He gave her a sheepish look, and took the white fluffy hat out of his pocket. 'It's more suited to you. And a few of the guys here thought it might scare the harrier off prematurely if I kept wearing it.'

Summer sucked in her laughter. 'Seriously? They thought you looked like a real polar bear?'

Mason held her gaze, his expression solemn. 'Some of them are very particular,' he said, his whisper dropping down so she could barely hear him.

She nodded and tapped the side of her nose, trying desperately not to laugh.

'Ooop, what's that?' a voice said. 'That her?' There was an

excited rustling, all the heads craned upwards and Summer found herself doing the same. Despite the lack of leaves, the tangle of branches still made it hard to see what was up there. They stared for a few moments, until a wood pigeon came flapping out of the tree, squawking.

'Is she really up there?' Summer whispered.

'Supposedly,' Mason said. 'You need a lot of patience for this sort of thing.'

'I have very little patience when it's below zero.' Summer bounced up and down, wondering how long it would take her knees to freeze into position.

'There's a café in the park if you want a hot drink?'

'I'm fine,' she said. 'Sorry, I shouldn't moan.'

'You can moan all you want,' Mason said, 'but do it quietly to me or the particular people will start to grumble.' He flashed her a grin, and they went back to looking up at a tangle of branches, the blue sky peeping through beyond.

Summer didn't know how long they stayed there, in relative quiet, while the day ticked forward and people went about their lives. She dared not look at her watch, tried not to think about Claire and Jas running her café, Latte and Archie causing as much havoc as possible with neither of their masters to be seen. The cold was working its way into her bones, so she had no idea what Mason must be feeling like – if he could feel anything at all.

Eventually, when Summer had decided that becoming a statue in one of the prettiest parks in London wouldn't be such a bad existence, someone shouted 'There!' and there was a flurry of movement, of lenses angling and cameras snapping.

'Where?' Summer asked, suddenly frantic that she might miss it.

Mason put his arm around her waist and pointed, and Summer watched as a huge bird – a dog-sized, brown bird – seemed to drop out of the sky, floating on a wingspan that looked impossibly wide, its breast pale, its tail and the underside of its wings bands of brown and cream, like the icing on a French Napoleon cake. There were gasps and coos, a multitude of photos taken. Mason snapped several with his Leica, but his face was transfixed, his eyes not leaving the bird as it swooped down towards the river and then rose, up and up, beyond the trees and into the blue, soaring along the line of the Thames, out towards the estuary and the Kent countryside.

Everyone watched it go, watched long after it had become a dot, and then nothing, just the blue, cloudless sky.

'Wow,' Summer said, slightly breathless.

'Could you believe her wingspan?' Mason asked, his voice fast with excitement. 'She was incredible.'

'Beautiful,' Summer agreed. 'Have you ever seen one before?'

'Never. *Never.*' He kissed her full on the lips. 'I'm so pleased you were here to see her too. I'm sorry I left so early. I brought my phone, but when I tried to text you I realized it had run out of battery. How did you know where to come?'

'Long story,' Summer said. 'Could we go and find somewhere, to talk?'

He frowned, his pale lips pursing in confusion. 'Sure. Give me a second to say goodbye to Brian.'

Summer pushed herself creakily up to standing, and held out her hands for Mason to grab. He rose slowly to his feet, wincing as he unfolded himself from the position he had been in for hours. He stamped his feet a few times, and then approached a man with red cheeks and flyaway brown hair, wearing a North Face jacket. She turned away, drinking in the beauty of the Buddha in the peace pagoda, its golden body glowing in the sun. She felt cold to her core, and wondered how long it would take them both to warm up.

'Where do you want to go?' Mason asked, rubbing his hands together. 'I could do with a hot drink.'

'A hot bath might be more useful.'

'True,' he laughed. 'Don't know where we're going to find one of those, though. Shall we settle for the bus?'

He took her hand and they strolled through the park, then found the bus that took them halfway back to Little Venice. Summer was reluctant to open up to him in such a public place, so she kept the chatter light, focusing on the hen harrier, asking Mason questions about its usual habitat, why it had ended up somewhere so unlikely. He didn't have the answers to everything, but he spoke with such animation and excitement that Summer found herself being infected by it.

'So you won't struggle with your article now, then?'

Mason grinned. 'I'll struggle to stick to the word limit. And look.' He showed her his photos. One was blurry, the first focusing on the tree branch in front instead of the hen harrier behind, but the other four were stunning, capturing the bird mid-flight, its tail towards the lens as it rose higher in the sky.

'They're brilliant, Mason. The whole thing. I'm glad I came to find you.'

'Why did you? Did you really want to see the harrier?'

'I wanted to see you,' she said quietly.

'OK.' Mason sounded perplexed. 'I would never have been gone that long, and I was going to ask Brian if I could call you on his phone before I left.'

'I'm not angry, Mason. But I – let's wait until we're off the bus.' She felt a sudden rush of nerves. She should have told him as they were walking through the park, not waited and made him anxious, building it up into a big thing. Maybe it was, the fact that she'd been worried he'd gone to see Tania, but she didn't want it to be. Would her admission spell the end for them, Mason seeing it as a sign that she didn't trust him? Her palms prickled with sweat, despite the cold.

The bus pulled up to their stop, and instead of heading to the tube station, they wended their way off the main road and down a side street, choosing a small patisserie that was busy and cheerful, but not packed to the rafters. Summer found a table at the back of the café, hidden away under a spiral staircase that led up to the first floor. She waited while Mason ordered coffee and Danishes, returning to the table with steaming mugs and a plate of flaky, appetizing pastry.

'I think we're due a sugar and caffeine fix,' he said. She could see he was nervous, taking longer than usual to arrange everything on the table, pulling off his coat and shrugging it over the back of the chair before sitting down. He ran a hand through his hair, gave her a quick smile. The tips of his ears were red, she noticed.

'Mason, I—'

'What did you—'

They spoke at the same time, both apologized, both waited for the other so that silence hung limply over the table.

Summer closed her eyes and took a deep breath. 'I was worried you'd gone to find Tania,' she said. 'When I woke up and you were gone. I found the note, and I—'

'What?' Mason asked softly. 'Why?'

'The note,' she repeated. 'I thought it said something about fighting, and then I spoke to the man who'd been gritting the towpath, he said he'd seen someone at five a.m., in a polar bear hat, and that they'd been excited about going after a woman. I tried to think of something that would make sense, but . . .'

'I never said that.'

'I know. You said bird, he interpreted it as woman. I got so confused. But it doesn't make up for the fact that I thought you'd gone to see Tania, that you'd had some epiphany after spending time with her, that your feelings . . .'

He grabbed her hand with both of his. They were freezing, despite the gloves he'd been wearing in the park. 'I don't have feelings for Tania any more.' He said the words quietly, but firmly. 'I'm not sure how much I ever really did, how much of it was me looking for comfort after Lisa's death. It's been good to clear the air with her – it was a shock seeing her at first, but now I've done it, I'm glad. But as for my feelings for her, they're . . . they're nothing, Summer. Someone I was close to once, someone I treated badly. That's where it ends. I promise.'

'I'm so sorry,' she said, a lump wedging in her throat. 'I'm sorry I couldn't believe that, and put my worries aside. I'm sorry I thought, even for a second, that you might have gone to her. She was so confident, and some of the things she said made me feel like – like she still had feelings for you, and that she could take you from me if she wanted to.' She focused on her coffee, afraid to look up, to see disappointment on his face, or anger, or worse – a look that signified they were over, that she'd gone too far. But she forced herself, and what she found was sadness, incomprehension, his brows lowered. He stroked her palm with his thumb.

'I love you, Summer. Nobody else. I didn't realize how much seeing her would affect you, and I'm sorry if I contributed to that. I know I spent too long with her that first evening, that I should have been more forceful when she wanted to speak to me last night.' He raked a hand through his hair. 'God. I'm sorry I've done this, Summer, and that I didn't realize how you were feeling in the first place. I've left you to get on with the café, I—'

'You didn't leave me! You've helped me constantly, you took control when I was hungover. You've been brilliant, Mason. And I think that's why I was worried. Tania got to see what you're like now, she had the opportunity for her feelings to resurface, and she's so glamorous, so confident and together.'

'Summer,' Mason chided gently. 'Do you need me to list all the reasons I love you? To me, you're everything – don't compare yourself to anyone else. There isn't another Summer Freeman, and she's the only woman I care about. Please, *please* don't ever think I would abandon you, go running off at the crack of dawn into the arms of another woman. Birds – yes. Women – no. And always assume, if I'm not in touch, that it's because I've forgotten to charge my phone, or left it behind it altogether. Organization's not exactly my strong point.' He raised an eyebrow and Summer grinned, elation filling her up like a helium balloon, her fears suddenly ridiculous in the warm coffee shop with Mason sitting opposite her.

'I love you so much, Mason. I couldn't bear the thought that I might lose you, but I'm so sorry I didn't—'

'No more apologies,' Mason interrupted. 'They're officially banned for the rest of the day. From you, anyway.'

Summer nodded. 'How did you know there was this rare bird of prey in London?'

Mason sighed. 'I couldn't sleep last night. I was thinking

about you and your mum, about . . .' He shook his head. 'My head was full of stuff, anyway. I ended up browsing Twitter, which on my feed is a load of wildlife geeks and charities, and a couple of people tweeted that they thought they'd seen a huge bird going into the trees yesterday evening. I saw there'd been sightings from the estuary down to Battersea during the afternoon, and on balance it looked like it was worth checking out. I got up at five, walked to Battersea—'

'God, Mason. How have you not frozen to death by now?'

'My fingers might take a couple of days to thaw out, but I had a good hat to keep me warm. Got a few funny looks from other early risers, though I've no idea why.' He shook his head, feigning confusion, and Summer laughed. 'Did you shut the café to come and find me?'

'Nope. Claire and Jas are in charge. They're looking after Archie and Latte, too.'

'They are?'

'That was the plan when I left, anyway. We should head back soon and rescue them.'

'In a little while,' Mason said, smiling in a way that made her insides flip in happiness. 'But first, share this with me.' He pulled the cinnamon whirl in half, pastry and icing sugar going everywhere, including into Mason's coffee. As he swore under his breath, Summer wrapped her ankle around his under the table.

She checked herself for any niggle of worry, any lingering thoughts about Tania and her designs on Mason, and found that he had completely wiped them all. As usual, he had taken hold of her concerns and smothered them with love and logic. She watched him try to rescue the flakes of pastry from his

211

jeans, and knew that despite the occasional calamity, his failure to charge his phone or control his dog, she had found a good man, one of the best. Men like Mason, she reasoned, were probably as rare as a hen harrier in London.

Chapter 15

Summer and Mason arrived back in Little Venice after lunch. The sky was still clear, the air still freezing. They stopped for a moment, looking down at the canal, all the boats exactly as they had been a couple of days ago, most now twinkling with Christmas lights and decorations. The river remained a frozen plateau, though Summer thought, if she looked carefully, she could see cracks starting to appear. The beautiful blue bridge looked serene, arching over everything, shimmering in its frosty jacket.

'How long do you think it's going to last?' Summer asked.

'I'm not sure,' Mason said. 'I've never experienced anything like this, apart from the odd, brief frozen patch when I was cruising. But that never lasted more than twenty-four hours. It can't go on for much longer, but even a day or so more, and we'll be travelling on Christmas Day. Not to mention that the disruption here will put the whole canal network off kilter for a while.' He sighed.

'So we're not going to make it back to Willowbeck for Christmas, whatever happens?'

'Not unless we leave *Madeleine* here and get the train back, and I don't think we want to do that, do we?'

Summer shook her head. 'I couldn't leave her down here. It wouldn't feel right, even if Claire and Jas were looking after her. In Willowbeck it's different, we know *The Sandpiper* is safe there.'

'Do you want to go and see how they've got on?'

'Yes,' she said, pushing away her trepidation. It had only been a few hours, what could have happened?

The first thing she noticed as she opened the café door was that Latte and Archie were sitting on chairs at one of the tables, licking clean the plates that had been left there. Other than that, the café was empty. Empty, but only recently. Every table was a mass of dirty crockery, and there was a distinct smell of burning coming from the kitchen. The coffee machine was steaming angrily and part of the Christmas bunting had been pulled down from above the counter. Summer stared at Mason, and his wide-eyed expression reflected her shock back at her.

'Hello?' she called tentatively. 'Claire, Jas?'

'Oh my God,' came the instant response. 'You have to save us!' Claire appeared in the doorway, her dark hair pushed back from her sweating, red-cheeked face, her apron – Summer's apron – looking like she had massacred a whole tray of chocolate muffins. 'What's happened?' Summer couldn't be angry. Claire and Jas had been doing her a huge favour, while she went running all over London after Mason and his bird of prey.

'What hasn't happened?' Claire said, huffing. 'First, a whole team of rugby players came in, demanding cream teas. And then a busload of school children, and then, would you believe, these aliens came down in their spaceship . . .' She shook her head, exasperated.

'What Claire's trying to say,' Jas said from behind her, oven glove over one arm, wiping sweat off his forehead with the other, 'is that neither of us have any idea how to run a café, and it's been a bit full on.'

Claire nodded, her expression forlorn. 'Yes. Exactly that. And your dog, Mason,' she jabbed him in the ribs as she spoke.

'Ouch!'

'Too right. He's a bloody nightmare! Gets into everything. Doesn't behave at all. What method are you using, the *Inbetweeners* dog handling manual?'

'He's mischievous,' Mason said defensively.

'Summer, it's been crazy busy. I hope we've not ruined the reputation of your café permanently, I think we served most customers what they asked for, and were relatively cheery, at least at the beginning. Give me music nerds searching for the forty-fifth-anniversary gold vinyl of *Ziggy Stardust* any day.'

Summer laughed, hugging her friend. She smelt of coffee and sugar, her perfume musky underneath. 'Thank you for looking after it, and the dogs. I appreciate it, and there's no lasting damage.'

'I think there might be to this batch of scones,' Jas said, pointing at the blackened hulks sitting on the tray he was holding.

'You too, Jas,' Summer said. 'We can get this place ship-shape in no time.'

'You're sure?' Claire's sigh was one of pure relief.

'You go. I'll sort it out.'

'And me,' Mason added.

'Nope. You have an article to write about the great hen harrier of Battersea Park.'

'All of this is my fault,' he said, sweeping his arms wide. 'I'm not leaving you to do it alone.'

'You found it then,' Jas said, grinning.

'I did.' He ran his hand through his curls, and they fell back haphazardly around his face. Summer thought he looked tired, but that was unsurprising considering how early he'd got up, and how many hours he'd spent sitting motionless in the cold. 'Not sure I went about it the right way, though.' He flicked a glance at Summer.

'Everything's good,' Summer confirmed. 'Really good.'

Claire gave them a weary smile. 'Excellent news. Sorted. Right, I'm going to go and have a small, sugar-infused breakdown, and I'll see you later.'

'Bye, guys.' Jas waved a laconic hand and handed Summer the oven glove on the way out.

'Thank you again, I owe you.'

Once they were gone, Summer and Mason surveyed the café, and then burst out laughing.

'No rest for the wicked,' Mason said ruefully.

The weather stayed at a consistent below-freezing for the next few days. Summer put all thoughts of getting back to Willowbeck aside, knowing they were entirely in the hands of the winter gods and that there wasn't anything she could do about it. She focused on the café, put back together in a couple of hours by her and Mason after Claire and Jas's very kind, but somewhat haphazard, intervention, and on her boyfriend and their pets. They took Archie and Latte to Regent's Park and further afield, one of them taking the longer, daytime walks while the other worked in the café, and then both of them rugging up in the evenings, once darkness had fallen and London was a blur of noise and cheer, taxi lights and Christmas trees in windows, to walk them together.

Summer felt so much happier since her mad dash to find Mason, her confession about her doubts around Tania, his heartfelt reassurance and apology. She had noticed small changes in him, too. How he couldn't walk past her without kissing her, how she would find him looking at her when she was distracted, smiling when she caught his eye, his fingers pressed thoughtfully to his lips. He seemed more attentive but also slightly nervous somehow, as if he thought he'd had a close call, had almost lost her. That was so far from the truth, but the whole episode had brought about a subtle change in their relationship. She felt even closer to him, if that was possible.

'The weather looks like it's going to break in the next couple of days,' he said, scrolling through his phone as she emerged from the shower on Tuesday evening, after a full-on day in the café. She was thankful that Mason had been thoughtful enough to keep his shower quick, and leave her enough hot water. Claire had invited them out, saying that Ryder had found them somewhere a little different for the evening's entertainment. Of course it was going to be different – it was Ryder, after all – but Summer prayed that it wasn't more karaoke.

'That's good.' Summer watched as droplets of water fell from his damp hair onto the collar of his navy shirt. 'But we're too late to make it back to Willowbeck, aren't we?'

'I think so. It's less than two weeks until Christmas, and I have no idea how easy it's going to be to travel after days of the boats being displaced by the ice. I wonder if—' he stopped.

'If what?'

'If we should stay here until after Christmas, start the journey to Willowbeck on Boxing Day? Otherwise, who knows where we'll end up. We could be in a position where there are no moorings available close by, and we have to spend Christmas Day cruising. What do you think? I know it's not ideal, but it's probably best to make the decision now.'

Summer sat beside him on the bed. 'You're probably right,' she said. 'But is that even possible? We've already well outstayed our seven-day mooring here.'

'I spoke to Claire. Because this is so unprecedented, they've left our spots open for the time being.'

'What about the people who were due to have them after us?'

Mason shrugged. 'The whole canal system is so up in the air, nothing can be guaranteed. The local river trust says that because of that, we can stay here until the river's thawed and someone else arrives to take our place. I suggest we take that offer, and if nobody else needs the mooring, start back home after Christmas Day in Little Venice.' He put his hand on her knee. 'But what do you think? I know how much you want to see Valerie again, and Dennis and Jenny.'

'There's always Skype,' Summer said. 'But you can't Skype *The Sandpiper*.'

Mason laughed. 'True. But Valerie's keeping an eye on her for me. It's not what we planned, but would you be happy with that?'

Summer smiled. 'There are worse places to be on Christmas Day than Little Venice, and as long as I've got you and Archie and Latte, and we're not stuck in some temporary mooring next to a waste disposal—'

'Which could very well happen.'

'Then I think you're right. Christmas in London it is!'

'Sure?'

'Sure.' She hoped it wasn't a sign, someone up high telling her that proposing to Mason was a bad idea. They wouldn't be back in Willowbeck until after the New Year now, so it would have to be delayed yet again. Since the events of a few days ago, Summer was even more sure that she wanted to marry him. Maybe she'd still do it, wherever they were on New Year's Eve, whichever part of the Grand Union Canal they had reached. It didn't have to be a big, flashy occasion, and she had the ring now. What was stopping her?

'Good.' Mason's voice was loud, bringing her back to the moment. 'Christmas in Little Venice. It's settled.' He gave her a grin that could have melted the ice – why hadn't she thought of that before? – then left her to get dressed while he went to give Archie and Latte their dinner.

That evening, Summer found herself standing, along with the others, outside an old, abandoned-looking warehouse. It was tall and made of dirty red bricks, with small windows like hundreds of piggy little eyes. Ryder led them to the side of the building, down a dark alleyway. Summer could picture it in the opening scenes of a serial killer film, and wondered how close they were to the haunts of Jack the Ripper.

'Where the fuck is he taking us?' Mason whispered, his usual consternation at Ryder's antics for once not making her laugh.

'To be slowly tortured and killed?'

'Quite possibly.'

Ryder started climbing a black metal fire escape stuck to the outside of the building, and there was an obvious pause from everyone below.

'Oh, come on, guys,' he said. 'This is legit, I promise!' She couldn't see them in the dull light of the alleyway, but Summer knew his eyes would be twinkling.

Ralph was first to ascend, followed by Doug and Claire, then Summer dragging Mason, and Jas taking up the rear. Once through the heavy metal door, they followed Ryder along several corridors with black walls, until they emerged into a huge room that, in complete contrast, was painted white – the walls and ceiling, even the floorboards. The lighting was low, there were benches around the edge of the room and a few modern-looking curved armchairs. Large cushions in red, blue and yellow were dotted about on the floor, which still left an expansive, empty space in the middle of the room. They were the only ones in there, apart from a tall woman with red curls standing behind a well-stocked bar.

'What is this place?' Jas asked.

'It's all ours for the night,' Ryder said, walking backwards, arms wide. 'Our own space in London. What do you think?'

'Have you kidnapped it?' Doug asked. 'Why did we come up the fire escape?'

Ryder laughed, tapping the side of his nose. 'It's incredible, right?'

Uncertainty seemed to be the overriding emotion as everyone gazed around them, unsure why this few people needed such a big space to themselves. Summer wouldn't be dancing, that was for sure – there would be absolutely nowhere to hide.

'Drinks, people.' Ryder clapped his hands impatiently. 'And then . . . storytelling. I've missed our sessions, pubs and clubs are far too loud. This place is perfect.'

Once they all had a drink – Mason overjoyed to discover that there was ale on tap – they settled themselves in a makeshift circle around a small table, and from somewhere, the lights were turned down even lower, the room plunged into an approximation of a séance setting.

'Who's going to start us off?' Ryder asked, leaning back on his cushion.

Summer stayed quiet. When she'd taken part before, all those months ago, the crowd had been much bigger, full of people she didn't know, and so it had felt more anonymous. She was strangely embarrassed at the thought of spinning a yarn about ghosts – or anything else for that matter – in front of a small group of close friends.

'I'll go,' Jas said. 'I've got a goody.'

'Jas, my man. Start us off.'

Jas settled himself on his seat, opened his mouth and then paused, his eyes lingering on each of them in turn. It built the anticipation, Summer knew. She was already itching to hear what he had to say.

He started speaking, his voice smooth and steady. 'Imagine if someone you thought you knew turned out to be hiding a dark secret. Imagine if they'd been lying to you about who they were the entire time. A beautiful woman with long dark hair, milky skin, deep, chocolate eyes. She's confident and fun, sometimes a little flirty.' He raised an eyebrow, glancing at Ryder and then Mason. 'She encourages a friend of hers to make a trip, to travel across country and to bring all her friends, make a week of it. It's nearly Christmas, the canal looks stunning at this time of year and no, there's absolutely no chance of it freezing over, trapping them all.'

There was a smattering of laughter at this, and Summer could see that everyone – mostly everyone – was enjoying this bizarre tale. Claire, however, looked on edge. Summer tried to catch her eye, but her friend ignored her.

Jas continued.

'It all seems innocent enough. She joins them for drinks, visits their boats, maybe even buys some of the gifts they're selling. She's friendly – perhaps a little too friendly in some cases, but it's nice to reconnect with old friends, especially at this time of year. There are some photos taken in a club one night. A blogger puts them on his blog, talks about his trip to London, the latest adventures of a man, his boat and his dog. Lots of the comments he's read before, followers checking in, recounting their own stories, it's standard stuff. But then one person notices the woman, comments that he's seen her before somewhere, and asks what the blogger knows about her. The blogger knows very little. He says as much, and the matter is dropped for a day or two.

'But then this person comments again, saying they can't ignore it any longer. They're a liveaboard too, though in a different part of the country. He knows who this woman is, in fact she got to know a friend of his, made out she was interested in him and then accused him of selling stolen goods. She took his friend's boat apart, then called in the police, who arrested him. She is, he suggests, working under-cover on England's waterways, and that any close acquaintance with her should not be taken at face value.

'The blogger is unnerved, but not entirely convinced. He doesn't know this commenter personally, and it could be a case of sour grapes, of bitterness from this man whose friend was targeted, or someone simply winding him up. He trusts his friends, but wonders if they really know that much about the woman that has appeared in their lives quite suddenly, inviting them down to London, turning up when she was supposed to be visiting family elsewhere. The blogger wonders what he should do; he is unsure.

Who is weaving him the story? This woman, who he has spent evenings with, or the follower, one of thousands who comment on his blog, who he doesn't know from Adam? And if this man's story is true, and his friend was arrested, doesn't that mean he must have been guilty of selling stolen goods? It's a quandary, and one he has no idea how to solve.'

Jas sat back, taking a long, slow sip of his drink.

Nobody applauded.

Summer felt a shudder run down her spine. She looked at Mason. He was frowning, his fingers pressed to his lips.

Ryder grinned, unable to hide his delight at the turn of events. 'Well, well, well,' he said, his voice thick with smugness.

'Jas,' Claire said, 'what the fuck? You're talking about Tania, right? This is all true?'

Jas shrugged, looking suddenly sheepish. 'I don't know, that's the thing. But that's what someone on my blog said. That his friend was investigated by her last year, that she's undercover, looking for anything illegal on the waterways. He could be stirring, could just be causing trouble, but I – what do you think? You've known her longer than any of us.'

Claire opened her mouth, glanced at Mason. 'God, I – I don't know. She worked for the Canal and River Trust when I first knew her a few years ago, but as a licensing officer, nothing like this. Since we've been reacquainted, she hasn't mentioned anything. Come to think of it, when I asked her what she did she dodged the question, said something vague about starting up her own business.'

'You think she'd have a better cover story if she was *under*cover,' Ralph said.

'So she's been investigating us?' Doug asked. 'What on earth for?'

Claire turned to Mason. 'She's not said anything to you, has she?'

Mason rubbed his forehead. 'No, nothing that would tie in to what Jas is saying. She mentioned this new business, like you said, but only told me it was at the very early stages, and didn't go into any detail. I honestly had no idea, but then, until we arrived here, I hadn't seen her for years either.'

'Why would she be investigating us, though?' Doug asked again. 'And was it just opportunistic, because we were here, or was it planned?'

There were noncommittal murmurs round the room, and Ryder went to replenish everyone's drinks. Summer knew he'd be loving this, everyone getting tied up in knots. She tried to recall the conversations she'd had with Tania, and remembered telling her about selling Norman's carvings. The profit Norman made on them would be tiny, and she'd never spoken to him about registering with the tax office, leaving it up to him how he ran that side of things. But would tax issues fall into her remit? Were those the kind of illegalities Tania was worried about? She realized she was chewing her fingernail and sat on her hands to stop herself.

'She invited us down here,' Claire said, her voice unusually small. 'She phoned me up and suggested we could have a week selling our stuff in Little Venice. She'd already booked us the moorings. At the time I thought she was just being enthusiastic, happy that she could help. She said she wouldn't be here herself this week; that she'd be in Oxford for the whole of December. Then she turned up on that first night, but I didn't see anything suspicious in it. I just assumed her plans had changed, or that she'd decided she wanted to see Mason again after all.' She shook her head. 'God, what a fool I am.'

'We don't know that this is true. As Jas says, his reader could be stirring the pot.' Ralph put his palms flat on the table.

'But now I think about it, it seems weird,' Claire said. 'And the first time I saw her again, when she appeared on my boat in the spring, she was happy to see me, sure, but she asked a lot about all you guys, the other boats I was travelling with.'

Ryder sauntered over from the bar, putting drinks on the table. 'She invited herself back to my boat the other night. When the canal froze over.'

Everyone stared at him.

He shrugged. 'She said she'd love to see it, even though I told her the best she'd get was a sleeping bag on the floor.'

'Or a four-star hotel room,' Jas said, resurrecting the joke that while Ryder claimed to live a simple, uncomplicated life there were rumours that he didn't actually sleep on board cabin-less *The Wanderer's Rest* at all, but found a luxurious hotel every night. This time, nobody laughed.

'She still went with you?' Doug asked.

'Yeah, she did. And then the moment we were on the boat, she became as coy as you like, despite some world-class flirting in the bar. She wandered round, saying it was such an unusual boat, asking me about my business, what kind of things I sold.'

'And what did you tell her?' Summer asked. Ryder's business had never been easy to pin down, and she'd always thought he was opportunistic, selling whatever was going, whatever he thought he could make a profit on. She had no idea if that stretched to illegal goods, though.

'I told her the truth,' Ryder said. 'That I trade in anything and everything. Whatever comes my way, and seems right at the time. I don't hold a lot of stock, and my sources are varied, depending on where along the waterways we happen to be. She left soon after that, the air no longer charged with sex.' He raised a laconic eyebrow. 'Now everything's beginning to make sense. Asking how much profit I make and what I spend it on didn't seem like great foreplay at the time. She wanted to find out if my merchandise was dodgy, and left frustrated in more than one sense.'

'Holy shit,' Claire spat. 'What a sneaky, sneaky cow. Drawing us in like that, inviting us down here, making total fools of us while she checked out how above board we are. Like a viper.'

'Steady on,' Doug said.

'It could all be a misunderstanding,' Ralph agreed.

'It does feel like it's all slotting into place, though,' Jas said quietly. Summer felt sorry for him, for the fact that he'd unleashed this on them all, but it was the right thing to do. She wondered how Mason felt, discovering that Tania had been tricking them. He was keeping quiet, sipping his drink, watching the drama unfold.

'So, begs the question,' Ryder said, leaning back on one elbow. 'What are we going to do about it?'

'Confront her,' Claire replied immediately. 'Tomorrow night, at the pub. Find out the truth. Nobody's been challenged, so she clearly hasn't found out anything bad about any of us – not that there's anything *to* find.'

'Maybe she's biding her time?' Doug suggested.

'Not any longer.' Claire shook her head. 'Not now we know what she's up to.'

The storytelling session limped on for a while, but it was clear nobody was in the mood and they finished early. When Jas started walking towards the fire escape, Ryder called him back.

'Come on, we can go out via the main stairs. This way.'

'What?' Summer asked. 'What do you mean "main stairs"? What about the crazy fire escape you brought us up earlier?'

'Oh that,' Ryder dismissed her confused look with a wave. 'This is their function room; I hired it out for us tonight. Technically we shouldn't have been using the fire escape – it was just to add a sense of drama to proceedings.'

'Yeah well,' Ralph said, patting Ryder on the shoulder. 'I think it was Jas who managed that on this occasion, don't you?'

'What are you thinking?' Summer asked Mason as they took Archie and Latte for a quick walk before bed. The towpath was glittering once more, the break in the weather Mason had predicted showing no signs of materializing, and the dogs yipped and snuffled at lampposts and hedges, the scents of other animals harder to pick up in the cold.

'I'm thinking that I don't know Tania well enough to be surprised. I want to know why she's been investigating us, if she's found anything illegal in any of the businesses, though from the indignation tonight, it doesn't sound like anyone's worried. Not even Ryder seemed bothered, but maybe that's because he thinks he's invincible.'

'So you don't feel let down by her?'

'I don't feel enough for her to be let down by her. We've laid our demons to rest. If she's making a living this way then good for her. But I wish she hadn't targeted our friends, I'm angry on Claire's behalf because she thought Tania was trying to build bridges, and to use their old relationship as a way to get closer to an investigation is cynical.'

'What about her flirting with you, though? The way she behaved in the café? Maybe that was part of it, pretending to still have feelings for you as an excuse for hanging around. That – as well as her friendship with Claire, it just all seems so false.'

Mason put his arm around her shoulders, pulling her close. 'It looks like she's going to get her comeuppance though. Maybe we should get some popcorn in for the boxing match tomorrow night?' He grimaced. 'I was lucky that by the time Claire knew I'd walked out on Tania all those years ago, me and *The Sandpiper* were far, far away. I wouldn't like to be on the receiving end of her anger, that's for sure.'

'No,' Summer agreed. Genuine, white-hot anger from Claire would not be pretty. 'Neither would I.'

Chapter 16

The following evening, after she'd shut down the café, and while Mason was working on his article, Summer took Archie and Latte for a long walk. It might have been her imagination, but she didn't think the air was quite so biting as it had been, her lips and nose not going numb quite so quickly. The parks closed around dusk, but the dogs were happy enough trotting along the towpath; there was enough to keep their senses occupied, and Mason had tired them out earlier by spending a couple of hours with them in Regent's Park, at one point – he'd told her – threatening Archie with becoming a zoo exhibit when he dug someone's ancient towel out of the bushes and refused to let it go. Summer could picture Mason and his dog having a tug-of-war in the middle of one of London's most popular parks, and the image brought a smile to her face.

But this walk was for her more than the dogs. So much had happened since they'd arrived in London; their week-long, Christmas selling spree had been a lot less straightforward than she had imagined it would be, and she wondered if, had she had an inkling of all that was ahead, she would have agreed to come at all. But then she thought of Mason and the harrier sighting, their conversation in the patisserie as they tried to thaw out, and knew she wouldn't change anything. Archie wrapped his lead around a lamppost chasing a leaf skeleton, and Summer crouched, unwinding it carefully while he waited, Latte snuffling her nose into Summer's hand, looking for a treat. Summer took a couple out of her pocket and gave them each one. They kept walking.

She loved looking at the other narrowboats moored up to the towpath, their different names and paintwork, the snippets of liveaboard home life she could see through portholes and windows when the curtains hadn't yet been drawn.

There was a cream boat with pale green trim called *Ulysses*, that had the most subtle white fairy lights trailed along the roof. There was *Dorothy*, painted with horizontal rainbow stripes. She wondered if they had a Toto on board, or if the wooden floor running throughout the cabin was painted to look like yellow brick. There was a *Kingfisher* and a *Windcheater* and a *Fair Maiden*, and there was a boat that, earlier in their trip, had been covered with plants – along the roof as well as on both decks. Now, with such freezing weather, all the plants were probably inside. In elaborate grass-green script on a pale yellow background was written *The Flower Shop on the Canal*.

She knew whose boat was next. It was painted a duck-egg blue with fuchsia trim, and was called *Persephone*. She wondered why Tania had picked that name, or if she'd simply bought it like that, and hadn't wanted to go through the rigmarole of renaming it, as Summer had done with her café. Or perhaps, she thought uncharitably, Tania liked having a boat named after the queen of the underworld. Archie and

Latte were straining at their leashes, unhappy with Summer's dawdling, and she picked up her pace.

Summer almost felt sorry for Tania.

She was meeting them in the pub later – Claire had sent her a text earlier that day simply saying: It's on! So Mason would get his boxing match, though she knew he was being flippant, and felt as uneasy about the whole thing as she did. Tania had been a thorn in her side ever since they'd arrived in Little Venice; a thorn created by her fears that Mason's past would come back to haunt them, by her own insecurities, and by Tania's intimidating behaviour, the suggestion that, if she felt inclined, Mason could still be hers for the taking.

He had put her fears to rest, but Tania certainly hadn't made the trip easy. And if what Jas had said was true, and she'd been friendly with them all simply to try and nail one of them for illegal practices, if her flirting with Mason had been part of her cover, didn't she have a right to be angry with her, as Claire was? But she didn't feel angry, she just felt weary. She wanted everything Tania-shaped to be put behind them, so they could get on with their lives. Despite the feelings she'd had about Mason's ex when she'd first reappeared, Summer wasn't looking forward to the showdown at all.

The pub was busy, the air thick with the smell of beer and cold, the musty scent of pine needles, as if one of the punters had spent the whole day wrestling a giant Christmas tree. Summer felt a pang of regret. She'd had such grand ideas about how they would decorate *The Sandpiper*, where the tree would go and the glittery paper chains would hang. Tomorrow she was going to give *Madeleine* – her living space rather than the café – similar treatment, but it was so much more cramped in there, she would have to work hard to make sure it didn't look cluttered.

She followed Mason to the bar and pulled out her purse to pay once he'd ordered the drinks, then they both carried them over to the table. Everyone was there except for Claire and Tania.

'Where's Claire?' Summer blurted.

'She's doing her warm-up,' Ryder said. 'Getting herself psyched.'

'Don't joke.' Summer gave him a condescending look.

'We're not sure,' Jas said. 'She's not technically late yet, but seeing as she set this up I would have thought she'd be here early. Unless she's changed her mind.'

'It's not entirely necessary, though, is it?' She sat down next to Mason. 'Confronting her in front of everyone.'

'I think it is,' Doug said, his words contradicting his mild manner. 'If she's been investigating us then fine, but to make out she was rebuilding her friendship with Claire, to set her sights first on Mason, and then Ryder, all to find out if any of us are dodgy, that's a pretty callous thing to do.'

'But she's undercover,' Summer said. 'How else was she supposed to do it?'

'Not like that.' Ralph agreed with his friend. 'No need to make it personal. She could have posed as a Mystery Shopper – anything.'

'But she already knew Claire and Mason,' Summer protested. 'Anonymity would never have worked.'

'I just think that . . .' Doug started, his words faltering as his gaze lifted behind Summer's head.

'Evening, lads and lady,' Claire said. 'You all OK for a drink? Tania's at the bar.'

Everyone murmured their assent, Doug staring at the table as if he'd been caught with his hand in the cookie jar.

'Are you really going to do this?' Summer asked as Claire sat down.

'Oh yeah,' Claire said, her eyes glinting. 'I most certainly am.'

Tania was wearing a black jumper with lace detailing on the sleeves. Her lips were a pale, shimmering pink. She assessed the table, put down two large glasses of red wine, and slid along the bench so she was next to Ryder.

'Hi, guys,' she said. 'How are you coping with your extended stay in Little Venice?'

'Oh yeah, loving it,' Ralph said.

Doug nodded and pushed his glasses further up his nose.

'It's a blast,' Ryder said laconically, resting his arm along the back of the bench behind her.

'The weather's supposed to break tomorrow, that's what I've heard.' She held up her wine glass, clinked it against Claire's. 'Will you be off straight away?'

'We'll see,' Claire said, her voice clipped. 'We don't know how much of the canal has been frozen, what impact it's going to have on our journeys out of here. Damaged boats, people trying to get places in time for Christmas. The waterways are going to be a nightmare for a while yet, so it might be best to stay put for the next few days, at least.'

'Of course,' Tania said. 'How about you two?' She looked at Mason, then Summer. 'Are you returning to Willowbeck as soon as possible?'

Summer resisted the urge to put her arm around Mason's shoulders.

'We're going to play it by ear too,' Mason said. 'Though

there's no chance of us making it home before Christmas Day now, not even if the waterways are clear, so we'll probably stay here rather than risk getting stuck somewhere less than ideal on the way back.'

'Sensible plan,' Tania said. 'Christmas in London will be wonderful.'

'What are you doing for Christmas?' Jas asked.

'Oh.' She waved a dismissive hand. 'I've got my mum in Oxford, I'm going to get the train up next week.'

'Sounds good,' Jas said.

The table fell silent, and Summer could almost taste the tension, chew it down and spit it out. Something had to give. Claire was staring at Tania, running her fingers up and down her wine glass as if she was Blofeld and the glass was the white, Persian cat. She didn't know what she was expecting – some Scooby-Doo-type reveal, something dramatic and angry. Her friend's approach was entirely unexpected.

Claire leaned forward, so that Summer got a whiff of her strong, musky perfume. 'Have you been investigating us, Tania?' she asked.

The silence round the table took on a different quality. Everyone's eyes turned towards Tania, except for Doug, who continued to stare at the table, and Ryder, who was looking at Claire with his usual, undisguised amusement.

Summer watched Tania closely, her face impassive for a moment, and then she dipped her head and looked up again, a smile playing across her lips.

'Investigating you for what?' she asked. No outrage, no real surprise, but she was going to see whether they had any proof before admitting it.

'I don't know,' Claire said loudly. 'Stolen goods, other illegalities. We're not dodgy, Tania, we're legitimate traders.'

'I know that,' Tania said, her voice rising to match Claire's.

Mason squeezed Summer's thigh under the table.

'You do? So what have you been doing here, then? Luring us down to Little Venice, playing Mrs Oh-So-Nice so you could get your teeth into us. I mean, what the fuck, Tania? I thought we were friends.'

'We are,' Tania said. 'We were.'

Claire's eyes widened. 'Were?' she whispered.

'It's been over five years since we were close, Claire. You can't rebuild something like that so quickly.'

'You can if it's genuine,' Claire said. 'And I thought it was. When you walked onto my boat in the spring, I was delighted.'

'I was pleased to see you too,' Tania said, 'of course I was. But it also gave me the opportunity I'd been looking for.'

'Which was?' Mason asked.

'To look into something that's been on the action list for a while. Ryder's business.'

The man in question raised a single eyebrow.

'Ryder?' Claire repeated.

'Ryder and *The Wanderer's Rest* have been one of my department head's targets for months. We knew you all spent a lot of time together, travelling up and down the canals, so when you turned up in Little Venice I knew it was time to be more proactive.'

'What, exactly, are you investigating?' Ryder asked.

'Whether your irregular business is a cover for something else. There's no consistency. One week it's designer trainers, the next it's fishing tackle, then it's tablet computers. All in small quantities, often to order, but with no real plan around what you sell or when you sell it. It's exactly the kind of thing we look out for.'

'What can I say? I'm a fixer. I'm spontaneous. I go where I'm needed, bring in what's required.'

'There have been lots of rumours and accusations about Ryder Holdings.'

'Accusations?'

'Of drug dealing. Illegal substances passing hands, your other stock used to hide what's really going on.' Tania folded her arms.

Ryder stared at her, his lips parted. For once, he was speechless.

'You think Ryder deals drugs?' Claire asked, incredulous.

'Not a fucking chance,' Jas said, angrier than Summer had ever seen him.

'So the whole thing,' Claire continued, 'meeting up with me again, staying in touch on the phone, inviting us to Little Venice, sorting out our moorings for us, it was all so you could investigate Ryder for something as ludicrous as *dealing drugs?*'

Tania pressed her lips together, gave a little nod.

Summer exhaled, like a balloon with a hole in it. She hadn't realized she'd been holding her breath. 'That's the most ridiculous thing I've ever heard.'

Tania looked her right in the eye. 'It's my job. I feel bad that it blurred a couple of lines, but Claire and I were never going to be bosom buddies again. We've both moved on.'

'And what about Mason?' Summer continued. 'Flirting with him, coming to the café, was that all part of it too?' She felt Mason's grip on her thigh tighten. She slipped her hand under the table and laid it over his.

Tania's smile flickered. 'It was good to see Mason again, to have the past explained – that was very personal, not part of my work, and I'm pleased it happened. But I had to be convincing, and it would make sense for my feelings for Mason to be rekindled now I know the truth.'

Claire sighed harshly. 'So were you after him again, or was that part of this crazy fucking plan? Drugs, Tania, really? Maybe you should take a closer look at your sources next time.'

Tania smoothed her hair over her shoulder. 'I've just been doing my job, Claire. I can't go into detail about it.'

Summer chewed her lip.

'Well, it's over,' Doug said firmly. 'We know now, you've admitted it. You'll have to stop investigating him.'

'I'm done. He's no longer under investigation.'

'What?' Several voices spoke at once.

'And so . . . so what did you find?' Claire blustered.

'Nothing. Despite outward appearances, all of Ryder's business dealings have been legitimate. Unconventional, granted, but no proof of any illegal substances changing hands, or even being present. We've been investigating him for months, keeping tabs on where you've been, sending in officers to see if they could uncover anything.

'Everything we found was above board. But I wanted to spend a few days with him myself, get onto his boat, do some more digging to be absolutely sure. It makes no sense to me, Ryder,' she said, turning to him. 'If you put more effort in, you'd make a lot more money. It all seems so haphazard; you can appreciate why we thought there was something else going on. I don't understand why there needs to be this air of subterfuge, this mysterious way of going about things.'

Ryder stared at her, his face a shocked mask. When he spoke, his voice was so forlorn that Summer had to stop herself from laughing. 'Then you don't understand me at all.'

'Were you ever going to tell us, if we hadn't found out?

Or would your project on Ryder have gone unmentioned?' Claire asked, through gritted teeth.

'No need to tell you,' Tania said. 'Nothing to report. But I knew you'd figured it out, so I thought I'd better turn up tonight and give you an explanation.'

'Not a very satisfactory one,' Jas said. 'You've used your friendship with Claire to manipulate us, and now that's over you're going to swan off into the sunset?'

'Would you rather I'd found something on him?' Tania laughed softly. 'I can only say I'm sorry that I've hurt some of you, but this is what I do, working undercover, getting to the truth. If I'd spotted Claire's boat back then, and done nothing knowing full well that Ryder was one of our targets, I would have been failing at my job.'

'Yeah, but what about friendship?' Ralph asked. 'Don't you mind failing at that?'

'I should leave you to it,' Tania said, rising.

'So that's it?' Claire asked, standing with her.

'What else do you want me to say? I've enjoyed spending time with you all, getting to know you again, Claire, seeing you, Mason.'

He sipped his pint, and didn't reply.

'Have a lovely Christmas, all of you,' she said. 'And if you're ever in Little Venice again I'd like to come for a drink – no agenda this time.'

'Yeah right.' Claire folded her arms as Tania slid out from behind the table and, giving a final, easy wave, her head held high, walked through the crowd towards the door.

Claire sat heavily, tears in her eyes. 'God. She used us all. Ryder, I am so, so sorry. I can't believe she thought you were dealing drugs.'

'Don't worry about me,' Ryder said breezily, but Summer

could see it had rattled him. His skin was even paler than usual, his blue eyes wide with shock. He reached his arm across the table, placed his hand on top of Claire's.

'We're sorry, Claire, Ryder,' Jas said. 'It was a shitty thing to do – to both of you.'

'You don't need her, you've got all of us!' Ralph raised his voice at the end, trying to inject levity into it.

'What do you want to drink?' Doug asked. 'Stiff whisky? Brandy? Tequila?' He rose and went to the bar, not waiting for an answer.

'Look how much trouble I've caused,' Claire said through her tears. She wiped her cheeks. 'I brought you down here for this wonderful Christmassy week, ended up exposing you and Mason to Tania and messing things up for you – and then it turned out her friendship wasn't even legitimate, and what I was actually doing was allowing my best mate to be investigated for fucking *drugs*.'

'Quite impressive, when you think about it,' Ralph said.

Claire laughed, despite herself. 'I am an awful judge of character.'

'Hey, thanks!' Jas said, grinning.

'Are you all right, Mason?' Claire asked.

'I'm OK.'

'You've been very quiet,' Summer murmured.

'It's a lot to take in. You handled it well, Claire, considering how she's treated you. You too, Ryder.'

Claire sniffed loudly, her tears drying on her cheeks. 'What about you?'

Mason shook his head. 'This isn't about me,' he said. 'It just proves that I don't know her any more – that none of us do. I think the best thing we can do is put Tania firmly in the past, and start looking forward to Christmas.' He

239

rubbed Summer's thigh, and treated them all to one of his blistering smiles.

'I'll drink to that,' Doug said, placing a tray of glasses on the table; the amber liquid inside smelt like brandy. Everyone picked one up and they clinked glasses.

'You going to be all right?' Summer asked Claire, once the comforting liquid had burnt down her throat.

'Yeah,' Claire said. 'I've still got you guys, right? I'll get over it.'

Ryder cleared his throat loudly. 'She has, however, managed to completely ruin my life.'

'I'm sorry,' Summer said sincerely. 'It must have been horrible to discover you were under suspicion for something like that.'

'I wasn't worried for a second,' Ralph said. 'You're far too soft to operate in those dangerous circles.'

Ryder rolled his eyes. 'That is *not* the point!'

'What is it then?' Jas asked. 'You – rightly – got off scot-free. She has at least proved that the ambiguous Ryder is in fact an honest, respectable trader who just happens to sell stuff in the most convoluted way possible.'

'And how exactly am I supposed to continue doing that, now that I've been outed as a fair trader?'

Everyone stared at him. Summer replayed his words in her head, and then laughed. 'You're annoyed because you *weren't* found to have been doing anything dodgy?'

'Of course,' he said, folding his arms. 'What the fuck did she think she was doing, sweeping in like that, ruining my reputation? I mean, *obviously* I don't deal drugs, but she could have left the rest of it alone! She wouldn't even let me seduce her, for God's sake.'

Claire shook her head, and voiced what everyone else was

thinking. 'Do you know what, Ryder, you really are something else.'

'Good. Glad you still think so. That's what I'm going to have to count on after this embarrassing debacle. Maybe I should dye my hair black, start wearing guy-liner.'

'You'd look like an ageing Goth,' Jas said.

'Paint over the name on my boat, so it's completely anonymous?'

'Everyone can spot your boat a mile off, even without the name,' Doug said. 'And if you're still at the helm . . .'

'True, true.' He rubbed his chin. 'Come on lads and lasses, help me out here. How am I going to come back from this? I need to keep my enigmatic nature intact.'

'Don't worry about it, Ryder,' Claire said. 'It's over, the whole thing. And I, for one, am glad. In a few more days, we'll be able to leave Little Venice and Tania behind, and everything will go back to normal. Fingers crossed she was right about the weather breaking.'

As she said that someone walked over to the table next to theirs, exclaiming loudly. His coat was shiny, and he shook water droplets out of his hair.

'It's raining,' Doug said. 'It's got warmer, it's actually raining.'

There were collective sighs of relief around the table.

Mason kissed Summer. 'We can start our journey back to Willowbeck on the twenty-seventh. Boxing Day, if you'd prefer?'

'I would,' Summer said. 'Let's have a magical Christmas in Little Venice, and then go home.'

The mood visibly lifted, and Jas went to the bar.

'We've still not solved my dilemma,' Ryder said. 'I cannot cruise out of London with my mystique ruined.'

'You do know that's a Marvel character, don't you?' Doug asked.

'Whatever. I'm going to need some serious help. How can I recover my ambiguity? I feel like I need to go big, do something crazy for the New Year. It can be my resolution.'

'I've got a great idea,' Mason said. 'Something that will help with your image, get people to understand exactly what you're all about.'

'OK,' Ryder said, narrowing his eyes. 'But I don't *want* them to understand what I'm about. That's the whole point.'

'It's a new look. Nothing too drastic, but it will have a real impact.'

'What is it?' Claire asked, her tears dry, her face open and excited as Summer was used to.

'Yeah Mason, what is it?' Doug asked.

'Paint your boat yellow,' Mason said, his expression solemn. 'And then write *Ryder's Independent Trading Co.* on the side. You could always add your most common destinations too. Willowbeck, Little Venice, Peckham. Is there a canal that runs through Peckham, does anyone know?'

'Brilliant idea,' Ralph said. 'Yes, Ryder. Go for it.'

'It's so innovative.' Doug shook his head in wonder.

'It's genius,' Jas said, replacing empty glasses with full ones.

'It is?' Ryder looked from one face to the next, as everyone tried to hold in their laughter.

Summer was grinning. She wished that Mason had actually done it – painted Ryder's boat yellow and added the slogan that adorned the Trotters' three-wheeler in *Only Fools and Horses*, instead of just suggesting it.

Summer could almost see the cogs working as Ryder tried to figure out the joke. And then, the penny dropped. He threw a beer mat at Mason's head, and the table descended into laughter. After the confused, uncomfortable silence of earlier, it was very welcome, and even Ryder didn't seem to mind having a joke made at his expense.

This, Summer knew, was the real group of friends. They might not always travel together, they might make mistakes every now and then, but when it came to the important things, they wouldn't let each other down. That was one of the joys of living on the waterways – your friends would always have your back. And, Summer knew from past experience, that was completely invaluable.

Chapter 17

It was Christmas Eve. They had made it. Summer wasn't quite sure why it felt so momentous to have reached Christmas Eve with their boat still afloat, but as she lay next to Mason, listening to someone singing 'O Holy Night' badly from the towpath, she felt happiness swoop through her stomach and up into her chest. Mason breathed deeply and rolled over, and then his body tensed and he was awake, sitting bolt upright before Summer could grab hold of him.

'What day is it?' he asked warily.

'Christmas Eve. Were you having a bad dream?'

'No.' He blinked sleep out of his eyes and lay back down on the pillows. 'A deep sleep, that's all. It took me a moment to orientate myself.'

'We're in Little Venice,' she said, laughing softly. 'We have been for three weeks. And tomorrow is Christmas Day.'

'It is, isn't it?' He smiled up at the ceiling. 'It's been quite eventful, all things considered. Are you looking forward to going home?'

'Yes,' Summer said. 'I can't wait to see Willowbeck again.

But in a way I'm glad we've ended up here for Christmas Day. Little Venice is such a beautiful place, we've been so lucky to come here, despite all the . . . complications. We'll probably have lots of Christmases in Willowbeck, so this one will always stand out. Valerie and Norman are fine, Dennis and Jenny are putting on a Black Swan Christmas which they're both going to, and we'll see everyone in a couple of weeks, anyway.'

Over the last few days the temperature had risen, the ice on the surface of the canal had thawed, and things were slowly starting to get back to normal. Ryder and Jas had heard word of disaster areas along some stretches of the waterway. Not everywhere had frozen over, but many of the narrower parts had, and there were several places that were blocked, with narrowboats trying to get to their Christmas destinations as soon as the river was passable. They'd advised that staying put until at least Boxing Day would give the routes a chance to clear.

'And *The Sandpiper*,' Mason added. 'I hope a bird hasn't got in while we've been away. Or a squirrel! Bloody hell.' He ran a hand through his hair, looking momentarily traumatized.

'It's fine.' Summer wrapped her arms around him. 'Valerie did a recce yesterday. Everything is spick-and-span, no squirrel gnawings or bird poo. She's waiting for you with open arms.'

'Waiting for *us*,' Mason corrected. 'She's your home too, you know.'

'We're a two-home family, get us!' Summer laughed.

'And a two-fractious-dog family soon if we don't feed them and take them for their morning ablutions.'

'Mmmmm.' Summer snuggled into him. 'But we could

have a bit longer in bed, surely? We don't have anything to do today. We've got all the food in for tomorrow, and we're not opening the café.'

They'd made the decision to close their boats on Christmas Eve and Christmas Day. They'd worked so hard in the run-up – Summer was making brandy butter macarons in her sleep – and thought that the last-minute, mad-dash shoppers wouldn't be as likely to stroll along the towpath today anyway, they'd be fighting the scrums in Tesco's and Oxford Street. Summer was looking forward to a lazy day, soaking up the Christmas atmosphere in London, finding somewhere to go for a mulled wine and a mince pie.

Mason sat up again. 'I do actually have a few things to do.'

'Oh?' Summer felt a wave of disappointment. 'What?'

'Well,' he laughed awkwardly. 'I might not have been quite as organized as you have, with . . . certain things.'

'You know I don't need anything for Christmas, Mason. Other than you.'

He cupped her chin and kissed her. 'It's all under control, but I'll need to pop out at some point. Come on, those dogs won't wait forever.'

They had just finished a breakfast of bacon sandwiches with cranberry sauce when there was a loud banging on the door. Summer frowned at Mason, but he made no move to get up.

'I hope that's not somebody asking why the café isn't open,' she muttered, but when she stepped through the kitchen door she saw it was Claire, wearing a long maroon duffle coat and black woolly hat.

'Hello! Happy Christmas Eve,' she said, inviting Claire onto the boat.

'You too. And guess what we're doing today?'

Summer looked at her blankly.

'We're going to the zoo!' She clapped her hands like an excited schoolgirl.

'We are?' Summer glanced behind her as Mason appeared in the doorway.

'Yup, you and me, baby. Claire's taking you to the zoo, today, the zoo, today, the zoo, today, Claire's taking you—'

'Are they even open on Christmas Eve?'

'They are. I checked. Come on, get your coat.'

'I'm, uh—' She looked to Mason for help, but he just grinned at her.

'It's a great idea, and it'll allow me to do what I need to, maybe finish off that article and get it to my editor before the end of the day.'

'I thought you finished it yesterday?'

'I've got a couple of last bits to tinker with. It's an important piece, it will probably be seen by a lot more people than usual – online at least – so I want to make sure it's perfect.'

'There you go then,' Claire said. 'Winning all round.'

Summer went to put her coat on, slightly dazed at the turn of events. She couldn't imagine that London Zoo was the most Christmassy place in the capital, or that they would sell mulled wine, but if Claire was desperate to go and Mason was happy to have her out of the way while he finished things off, then she couldn't complain. She knew what it was like to feel unprepared for Christmas, and she wanted Mason to be as relaxed as possible before they started their long journey back to Willowbeck. And it wasn't like the trip had been remotely predictable. After the events of the last few weeks, she could definitely cope with an impromptu trip to the zoo.

* * *

The festive spirit in the zoo took Summer by surprise. Claire insisted they see the penguins first, and Summer squealed with delight when she saw they had their own little Christmas tree in their enclosure, close to the water's edge. There were red, green and gold baubles hanging from the trees down the zoo's main walkways, and Christmas songs, Wham and Slade and Mariah Carey filtered out of speakers attached to every café and eatery.

There was a lot to see, and even though it was no longer as cold as it had been, they spent a lot of time in the living rainforest, their hats and scarves coming off as they soaked in the tropical atmosphere. As they walked over to see the lions, Claire slipped her arm through Summer's.

'I'm sorry nothing worked out as planned here,' she said.

'What do you mean? I've been flat out in the café for three weeks instead of one. I'm thinking about taking the whole of January off to recover.'

'You know what I'm talking about.' Claire elbowed her gently in the ribs. 'Me allowing Tania to dictate that we come down here, letting her trick me into thinking she'd be away when we arrived, and then – well, the unexpected end to that already uncomfortable story. Not to mention the weather turning villainous on us. Our festive jaunt to Little Venice hasn't been smooth sailing.'

'And it's been all the better for it,' Summer said.

Claire narrowed her eyes. 'Don't humour me, Summer. I can take it.'

'I'm serious.' They stopped at a drinks stand and ordered two gingerbread lattes. 'I wasn't exactly delighted to see Tania, but it gave Mason a chance to talk to her, and I know that's been a relief for him. Obviously, none of us were expecting her to actually be investigating Ryder for drugs, but from a selfish point of view . . .' she shook her head, 'it's brought Mason and me closer together. I didn't think that was possible, but it made me realize I was still feeling insecure about some things, and it gave me the push I needed to be honest with him. Even if, at the time I opened up, he had spent the previous six hours crouching in the freezing cold waiting for a glimpse of a bird of prey.'

'Boys and their toys, eh? Though Mason isn't as straightforward as most. And you're not sad you won't be in Willowbeck for Christmas?'

'It's not what I'd planned, but sometimes the unplanned things are the best things.' She felt in her handbag, and pulled out the small navy box that housed Mason's ring.

'Why have you got that with you?' Claire squealed.

'Because I couldn't think of anywhere on the boat I could put it where Mason wouldn't find it. Don't worry, I'm not going to dangle it near the gorilla cage.'

'He rifles through your underwear drawer?' Claire raised an eyebrow. 'This latte by the way? Not a patch on yours.'

'Thank you!' Summer beamed. 'And I agree, it needs a bit more syrup, and a bit less milk. But my cabin on board *Madeleine* is so small, we share a tiny cupboard for our clothes. Nowhere's safe except my handbag.'

They sat on a bench on one of the wide esplanades watching families and couples, some strolling, some rushing to the next enclosure, dads in Santa hats, children with helium balloons in the shape of dinosaurs and parrots. There was a general air of Christmas merriment, the excitement of being at the zoo multiplied by the festivities. A family with four small children turned and stared as a man walked past leading two reindeer, the bells on their harnesses jingling.

'Is Santa here?' one of the children shouted. 'Is he?'

The man, wearing navy overalls with the London Zoo logo on, turned to him with a smile. 'Two thirty next to Penguin Beach. We might have a special guest. Obviously, he's very busy at this time of year, but you never know.'

'What will you do about your proposal now?' Claire asked, once the children's screams of delight had died down, and the reindeer had moseyed out of sight. 'Wait until you're back in Willowbeck?'

Summer put her latte on the bench and opened the small, velvet box, running her finger over the etched tree on the ring. 'I think so,' she murmured. 'We'll be travelling on New Year's Eve, and while I don't want to wait any longer than I have to, I still want it to be special – I don't want to rush it.' She looked up at Claire, whose lips were pressed together, trying to suppress a grin. 'What? What is it?'

'I'm so happy for you, Sum. You and Mason – you belong together. And he'll love the ring, I know it.'

Summer felt the familiar jiggling in her stomach, but this time it wasn't nerves, it was pure excitement. Claire was right, and as soon as they were back in Willowbeck, she would make her proposal – the event that had been delayed again and again and again – a reality. 'Where do you want to go next?' she asked Claire.

'Komodo dragons,' Claire said. 'There's nothing like seeing a couple of huge lizards with deadly saliva to get you in the Christmas spirit.'

When they left the zoo it was close to being dark, and they had to hurry through Regent's Park before the gates were shut. The air was cold and the sky was full of pink-tinged cloud. The air felt like snow, and while snow meant it was too warm for the canal to ice over again, Summer didn't want anything to disrupt their journey back to Willowbeck.

'I wonder how Mason's been getting on,' she said.

'What do you mean?' Claire asked, giving Summer a strange look.

'He said he had a few things to get finished. I'm not sure he's got my Christmas present yet.'

'Boys, eh? They always leave it until the last minute.'

'Are you expecting anything from Ryder?'

'For the last time, Summer, there is nothing going on with me and him.'

'I think your relationship is the most ambiguous thing about the roving traders, especially now his business dealings have been outed as being less-than-dodgy.' She laughed. 'Poor Ryder, he was really stung about that.'

'I'm going to do it, you know. Paint his boat like Del Boy's van. It would be hilarious.'

'Next time you're in Willowbeck,' Summer said. 'We can get Mick at the boatyard to help.'

'You're on.' Claire held out her hand for a high five, and Summer obliged.

They turned the corner and Summer could see the railings at the end of the road. They were almost back at the canal; back with Mason, Latte and Archie, a cosy Christmas Eve with a tapas-style meal and a bottle of wine. She grinned.

'What time do you want us round tomorrow?' Claire asked, slipping her phone out of her pocket, typing something quickly at her side.

'About one. Ralph's coming over earlier to help prep the food.'

'Sounds good,' Claire replied. 'And what are we all bringing again?'

Summer rolled her eyes. 'We've been through this about a gazillion times.'

'I know I know, just humour me.' Claire stopped walking, forcing Summer to do the same. They'd agreed to have Christmas lunch together, and Summer had offered to host it in the café, as it had the most space and was more formal than the cushions and beanbags on board *The Wanderer's Rest*. Summer, Mason and Ralph were doing most of the cooking, and everyone was bringing a dish to contribute to the meal.

Claire had told her family that with the waterways so disrupted, she wouldn't be able to visit them until closer to the New Year. She couldn't leave *Water Music* in Little Venice, where the moorings would be in high demand, so she would wait until the roving traders were settled somewhere else before making the journey. She hadn't seemed too disappointed, and Summer was glad they would be able to spend some of Christmas Day together.

It would be the ideal way to end their stay in Little Venice, a farewell before they all went their separate ways. Summer listed all the agreed dishes off on her fingers, but Claire wasn't paying attention, her gaze darting everywhere but mostly at her phone. It buzzed quietly, and Claire grabbed her hand.

'That's grand, Summer. Great. Let's get going, shall we? I'm so looking forward to tomorrow – the dessert part, especially, but don't tell Ralph that.'

'Are you OK?' Summer asked. 'You seem a bit distracted.'

'What? Oh, yeah, I'm fine, really fine.'

They reached the end of the road and, beyond the railings, the canal was laid out below them, the iconic blue bridge to their left.

Summer frowned. 'Aren't there more lights than usual?'

The railings, the narrowboats, the bridge – everywhere – seemed to be adorned with fairy lights, the glow almost blinding, the scene lit up like daylight. Summer took a step forwards. She could sense Claire behind her.

'No,' she murmured, 'hang on.'

Slowly, her eyes took it all in.

Not only was the whole place covered in fairy lights, but there were lanterns floating on the water. Shaped like small cubes, they were different colours; yellow and blue, red and green and purple, orange, white and pink. They were flickering softly, creating a sea of colour and light, like the most vibrant tulip field, only more magical against the darkness.

Summer gasped, her hands clutching the railing. 'Who's done this?' she asked, turning to Claire. 'Is this a Christmas Eve tradition in Little Venice?'

Claire was grinning. She shook her head and pointed to the bridge.

Music started up from somewhere. Summer couldn't make out what it was at first, and then the tune hit her. It was 'Don't You Worry' by Lucy Rose. Her heart started hammering. It was her favourite song. Why were they playing her favourite song?

'The bridge, Sum,' Claire whispered, and Summer looked.

She'd been distracted by the fairy lights, but now that she peered beyond them, she could see someone standing on the bridge. There was no traffic crossing it, no pedestrians drifting over it, stopping to look down at the water as they usually did. There was only one person. Someone distinct, someone whose silhouette she knew so well, with his mane of curls, his way of standing up straight but somehow always managing to look relaxed, easy, approachable.

253

A lump formed in her throat. Claire gently pushed her forward.

Summer walked slowly up the pavement towards the bridge, her hand trailing along the railings. She caught Mason's eye and he smiled, held her gaze as she walked towards him. The music got louder, she sensed there were people standing, watching, but she could only focus on Mason, on the twinkling lights, the flickering lanterns.

She reached the bridge and stopped, facing the centre.

Mason was standing in the middle wearing a navy shirt, smart jeans, black boots. He was lit from both sides, the fairy lights making him seem magical, almost like a mirage. Archie and Latte were sitting at his feet, their leads tied to the railing. They seemed quiet, subdued. Waiting.

Mason's smile widened, and he held out his hand to her.

Summer swallowed, felt the prickle of tears at the corners of her eyes.

She stepped onto the bridge, hearing the slight echo of her footsteps, feeling the reverberation through her boots. She walked slowly across the bridge towards him, and took his hand.

As she did, Mason dropped onto one knee.

Summer's breath stalled in her throat. Cheers and whoops drowned out the music.

'Summer Freeman,' Mason said, his voice clear, his dark, intense eyes – the eyes that had first made her notice him, made her feel that warm, nervous energy inside – holding hers. 'I love you, more than I thought it was possible to love someone. You make me laugh, you make me feel loved; you make me happy in a way that I thought I'd lost forever. And so I wondered if, on this cold Christmas Eve in Little Venice, you would do me the honour of agreeing to marry me, to live with me on board *The Sandpiper*, to come to Paris with me in the spring, and to be happy with me until the end of time?' His eyes were bright, brimming, and Summer could barely speak as the tears coursed down her face.

'Yes,' she said. It came out as a whisper. She cleared her throat and tried again. 'Yes,' she said, loudly. 'Yes, Mason Causey, I love you and I will marry you. Nothing would make me happier.'

Mason's smile set off fireworks inside her. He reached into his pocket and pulled out a small, velvet box. He opened it, and inside was an engagement ring, its blue, cushion-cut sapphire stone glinting in the glow of the fairy lights. 'It's not traditional, but—'

'I love it,' Summer said, as he slid the ring onto her finger. 'I love it, I love it!'

He stood and looked down at her, their noses touching, and he traced the line of her jaw, tilted her chin upwards and slowly, so slowly, brought his lips down to meet hers.

Sound erupted around them, but she blocked it out and leaned into the kiss, which felt as good as it always had, but somehow new, different, more intense. Mason kissed her harder and she responded, discovering how difficult it was to have a passionate kiss when both of you were grinning, but they did it anyway, laughing and kissing and holding onto each other, in the middle of the blue bridge. When they finally pulled apart, Mason's cheeks were wet with her tears, and Summer thought her heart would burst from happiness.

'Mason, this ring . . .' she held her hand up, mesmerized by the deep colour, the sparkle of the stone. 'It's the most beautiful thing.'

'Not to me,' he said softly. 'But it does complement you. And there's something else.'

'What else? How can there be? Are we really going to Paris?'

'I thought we could celebrate our engagement when it gets a bit warmer. But that's not the *something else*.'

He reached down for a long, cardboard tube that was leaning against the bridge wall. Archie pawed at his legs, and Mason stroked his dog between the ears before taking the lid off the tube and pulling out a rolled piece of paper.

'Hold this end,' he said, and walked away from her, unravelling the paper.

Though they were only lit by fairy lights, she could make out some of the detail. At the top it said *Plans for Madeleine – the Canal Boat Café*. On it were detailed technical drawings of her boat, the top image showing what it looked like now, with the café taking up half the boat, and her living space towards the stern deck. Below it, the image was repeated, but here it showed the café extended, with more seating, including benches running down the sides, the living space gone and a new kitchen where her cabin used to be, a hatch opening out onto the behind-the-counter area of the café, a small bathroom still in place at the stern end.

'Mason, what . . .?'

'It's just one idea,' he said, 'for how your café could look. I want to live with you, Summer. I'd love you to officially move onto *The Sandpiper* with me, and I want you to have the freedom to fulfil all the dreams you have for you r beautiful café. It's so successful already, and I want to help with that. I worked with Mick on some plans before we left

Willowbeck. He finished them and sent them to me here. But we don't have to do this, you don't have to give up your boat if you still want to live on it, I would never try to take away your independence, but—'

'This could be my café?' Summer stared at the plans, the proposed layout of her café, increasing the capacity by at least double.

'And you'd be on *The Sandpiper*,' Mason said again. 'But I know I have to go away for work sometimes, so Mick's suggested having a sofa bed in the kitchen. It isn't as comfortable, but there are a hundred ways we could alter the design, this is just an initial idea we came up with.'

'Oh my God, Mason!' The tears started all over again.

'Do you like them?'

She inhaled. 'I'm not sure what the most beautiful thing is any more. I love them. I'd love my café to look like this – if my café looked *half* as good as this, I'd be over the moon.'

'You don't mind moving properly onto *The Sandpiper*?'

'I've missed *The Sandpiper*,' she said through her tears. 'And it would only be a formality. Besides, husband and wife should live on the same boat.'

She stared at the plans, running her fingers over the detailed, exquisite lines of her potential new café, then Latte yipped loudly, so they rolled them up and placed them back in the tube. Summer kissed Mason again.

'Are you done yet?' called a familiar voice from the side of the bridge. 'We want to start celebrating, and our feet are going numb!'

'Two secs, Claire! You did a great job, by the way.' Mason gave her the thumbs up.

'So the zoo,' Summer said slowly. 'That was a distraction?'

'Claire's helped with the whole thing – and you partly have her to thank for the ring. We snuck out one day when you were in the café, and she took me to a few jewellers she'd come across when she was shopping with you. And, today, I needed you to be somewhere else. I had to get everything in place, with the help of Ryder, Jas and the others. The lanterns take a long time to light and float.'

Summer laughed. 'They're beautiful.'

'Ryder's surprisingly creative.' Mason raised a sceptical eyebrow. 'He told me he's been decorating the old river wardens' huts along the waterways whenever he comes across them. He said that with not much effort he's been able to completely transform them.'

Summer's mouth fell open. 'That was *him*?'

'And Harry, Greg and Tommy are here somewhere,' Mason said, peering towards the crowd that had gathered along the railings. 'They said they couldn't miss it. They've got a hotel in the area, but I thought they could join us for lunch tomorrow.'

'Even *Harry* was in on it?' Summer spun round and peered into the darkness. She spotted her friend's long, brown hair and a smaller figure beside her, bouncing up and down. 'Harry!' she called.

'I'm so happy for you, Summer!' Harry shouted back.

As Summer looked closely she could also make out a large man with white hair and a beard, wearing a dark red overcoat. She was sure that if she took a couple of steps towards him, she'd be able to see his half-moon glasses and grinning face. She wondered if he was disappointed he couldn't get any more mince pies, and how he had known to be here, at the canal's edge, tonight.

'We'll go and see them soon,' Mason said. 'But I don't

want this moment to end just yet.' He crouched down, and handed Summer two glasses. Standing again, he popped the cork on a bottle of champagne, and poured it.

'How long have you been planning this?' Summer asked.

'A while.' Mason's shrug was sheepish. 'Since I took you to the lake in Haddenham Country Park. I've known for a long time that you're the one, Summer, but after that day, I started to seriously think about how and when to ask you. I was going to do it in Willowbeck, so when you told me about Little Venice, I . . . I was frustrated. I'm sorry.'

Summer laughed. 'So that's why you were grumpy?'

'I had all these ideas about how it would work. I just had to rethink them.'

'You did a better job than me.'

'What do you mean?'

'At rethinking your plans,' Summer said. 'Champagne is good for everything, isn't it? Renaming boats *and* people. I may have been practising the name Summer Causey in my head, might even have tried out my signature a couple of times.'

'Oh you have, have you?'

They clinked glasses, and Summer felt the bubbles on her tongue.

'And I have something for you too, which I was also planning on giving you on Christmas Eve in Willowbeck, and then on New Year's Eve, and then – everything got delayed because of the weather.'

'What are you talking about?' Mason gave her a perplexed smile.

Summer reached inside her handbag, pulled out the box and then dropped onto one knee, putting her champagne glass on the floor. She opened the ring box, watching as Mason's confusion turned to realization.

'Mason Causey, I know you've already proposed, and I've accepted, so this is all very redundant, but I wondered if you'd do me the honour of wearing this ring, because I was going to ask *you* to marry *me*, but you've beaten me to it. Though to be fair, the lanterns and lights and music and friends beat all my ideas hands down.'

Mason stared at her, then at the ring, then at her again. He shook his head slowly. 'You were going to propose to *me*?'

'I wanted to be with you from the first moment I saw you, and that's never going to change. It may have taken us a while to get here, and it's been a bit like a rough sea in places, but I think – I hoped – we would always end up here. You're my ideal nature buff, Mason Causey.' She took his hand and slipped the ring onto his finger.

He held it out, staring at it. 'It's perfect.' He ran his finger over the tree etched into the metal. 'Sure you're not disappointed I didn't turn out to be a buff naturist, after all?'

Summer laughed. 'There's still time,' she said, wrapping her arms around him. 'You've already got the buff part sorted.'

'Flattery will get you everywhere.' He kissed her again, and Summer lost herself in his embrace, knowing her friends would wait for them.

As the music played, changing from Lucy Rose to 'We Wish You a Merry Christmas', and the fairy lights twinkled, and the lanterns floated on the water, twisting and spinning, filling Little Venice with colour, the first flakes of snow fell onto their coats and cheeks, settling in Mason's hair, making the dogs bark excitedly.

They broke apart and looked up at the sky, at the flakes falling down towards them.

For a moment, both of them were dumbstruck, and then Mason shrugged and grinned at her, a grin that, Summer knew, would always melt her in the same way that the snowflakes were melting on her skin.

'I'm sure we'll get back to Willowbeck eventually,' he said, and kissed her again.

Chapter 18

It was Christmas Day, and the canal boat café was full, but this time it was packed with friends rather than customers. The coffee machine was on in preparation for the last course, but for now, it was champagne that was flowing round the table where Summer and Mason, the roving traders and Harry, Greg and Tommy sat. Christmas music played softly in the background, and *Madeleine's* sparkly bunting glittered in weak sunlight that bounced off a thin layer of quickly fading snow.

It had continued to fall the night before, though it hadn't settled properly until the small hours, when the night was at its coldest. Now it was beginning to disappear, having done its job of giving Little Venice, Summer, her friends and her new fiancé, the almost mythical delight of waking up to a white Christmas.

Summer looked at Mason, who was topping up everyone's glasses, his purple Christmas cracker hat sitting wonkily over his curls. Her fiancé. That's what he was now. Against all the odds, despite all the problems and delays they'd faced, and despite it happening in a way that wasn't at all how she had planned it – mainly because he had asked her, instead of the other way round – they were engaged.

Summer would remember it forever.

Standing on the blue bridge in Mason's arms, Latte and Archie at their feet, and the celebrations afterwards in the Riverside Inn, which included not only their roving trader friends but Harry and Greg – until they had had to take an already over-excited Tommy back to their hotel to bed – and Alan, which was dress-down Santa's real name. Even Archie and Latte had been allowed in, news about the proposal spreading quickly due to it being anything but low key – Mason had even arranged for the road over the bridge to be closed for an hour so that traffic wouldn't get in the way.

Afterwards, they had made it back to *Madeleine*, high on happiness, and settled the dogs down for the night. It was the first time they had been alone since he'd asked her, and they'd had a few hours for it to sink in, to realize that they would be spending the rest of their lives together. Summer shivered as she recalled the emotion, the intensity once they had closed the cabin door, and looked down at the table, hoping she wasn't blushing.

'Summer,' Tommy asked, startling her out of her reverie, 'why do I have to eat the Brussels sprouts?'

Summer was taken aback by the question, and glanced at Harry, who rewarded her with a shrug. 'Because,' she said, 'you have to balance out dessert with vegetables. If you don't eat all your veg then you won't be able to have as much Christmas pudding.'

Tommy folded his arms and raised his chin. 'I don't like Christmas pudding anyway,' he said.

Summer tried not to laugh at how precocious her friend's

son had become. 'What about my macarons, you like those don't you?'

He nodded, his confidence slipping.

'Well then, if you want to try every flavour you have to eat your greens.'

Tommy sighed and slowly, as if it was a monumental effort, speared a sprout with his fork.

Summer and Harry exchanged a grin, and then, as the conversation moved on to where everyone was heading after Christmas Day, and what the state of the canal would be on the journey out of London, Summer's eyes drifted back to Mason.

He smiled at her, and Summer felt a lump in her throat. She would have to get a grip – she couldn't well up every time her fiancé looked at her. And then she thought of everything that she had to look forward to – Paris in spring, the changes to *Madeleine,* moving properly on board *The Sandpiper* with Mason and, to top it all, marrying the man she loved. She returned his smile, wishing she could reach out and take his hand.

They were at either end of the large table that Jas and Ryder had constructed out of all the smaller ones in the café, because Claire had said that she couldn't trust them to be next to each other and pay anyone else any attention. She had only realized, halfway through the starters of caramelized onion tart and Ralph's tomato chutney, that being opposite each other was perhaps even worse, and was giving them regular reminders that they weren't the only two people in the room.

'Oi, you two,' she said, chucking a red napkin in Summer's direction, 'stop making googly eyes at each other. It's putting everyone else off their lunch.'

'It's not putting me off,' Harry said, sighing. 'I think it's the most wonderful thing ever.'

'Of course it's wonderful,' Claire said, 'I never said it wasn't. I'm just wondering if we should have left them to have Christmas Day all by themselves, in their post-proposal bubble. Y'know, no clothes required, that sort of thing.'

Mason grinned. 'I'm not sure I'd want to risk cooking a full Christmas lunch naked; there's too much potential for complete – and very painful – disaster.'

'Exactly,' Ralph said. 'Pigs in blankets are a no-no, and I'm talking from experience.'

'Ew.' Summer grimaced, and the table descended into laughter.

Tommy looked perplexed, and Harry patted him on the head. 'I'll explain later,' she said, and he shrugged and mopped up the last of his gravy with his final Brussels sprout, giving Summer a triumphant look.

'Y'know,' Ryder said nonchalantly, running a hand through his hair as Ralph and Summer started to clear away the plates, 'if you're feeling a bit bereft in the love department, Claire, I could always help out.'

Claire stared at him, and Summer paused in the doorway, her heart in her throat. She couldn't read her friend's expression, but there were pinpoints of colour on her cheeks.

'Oh what,' Claire said bolshily, though there was a definite tremor in her voice, 'have you got a friend you can set me up with? I'm not interested, Ryder.'

'That's not what I meant at all.' He moved closer to her, and lifted his left arm above their heads. He was holding a piece of mistletoe, and Summer's breath stalled, waiting for Claire's reaction. She had always suspected that they cared a lot for each other, but were both too stubborn, too fiercely independent to admit it. Was Ryder finally relenting? Surely he wouldn't wind Claire up in this way – that would be too cruel even for him.

'Ryder,' Claire said, her eyes wide. 'What are you—?'

'I would have thought that was obvious,' he said, leaning in and kissing her on the lips, unconcerned that everyone's eyes were glued to them. After a moment's hesitation, Claire kissed him back. It wasn't long – she was much more self-conscious than Ryder – but the passion was obvious. Summer resisted the urge to squeal, and then Tommy started clapping, and soon everyone was joining in. Claire's whole face turned red and Ryder gave a rather awkward bow at the table.

'About. Bloody. Time,' Jas said. 'You'll have to actually get a bed now, will you, Ryder?'

'Or just upgrade my suite at the Hilton to a king-sized?' He raised an eyebrow, and everyone laughed.

Summer caught Claire's eye and she grinned, her eyes bright, and shook her head as if she couldn't believe what had just happened. Summer would have to find time for a private debrief with her before they started the journey back to Willowbeck tomorrow. She skipped into the kitchen, checked on the Christmas puddings in the oven, and gave Latte and Archie, who had followed her, a pig in a blanket each out of sheer delight.

She was marrying Mason, Claire and Ryder were finally admitting their feelings for each other, and after a glorious, eventful few weeks in London, they would be heading back to Willowbeck tomorrow. They would be reunited with Valerie and Norman, Dennis and Jenny; *Madeleine* would be back in her rightful place next to *The Sandpiper* — Summer serving her regulars, getting bacon from Adam in the butcher's — there would be moments of utter stillness where the sun glinted off the water, and the only sound was a blackbird singing.

She stopped for a moment in the café doorway, watching her friends as they chatted and laughed; Doug rubbing his stomach as if trying to make room for dessert after their gargantuan main course, Jas stroking Chester, his Irish Wolfhound, under the chin while surreptitiously feeding him his last sprout. Harry and Greg putting their Christmas hats on top of Tommy's, so that he had a tower of them on his head, Claire and Ryder linking hands under the table, out of sight of everyone except Summer.

Mason looked up, catching her eye, and she felt the butterflies dance inside her. She was marrying this man; he was going to be at her side for the rest of their lives, whatever fate dealt them. She could open her café every morning safe in the knowledge that he would appear for his bacon sandwich, that when she finished she would find him on the deck of *The Sandpiper*, scribbling an article in his indecipherable handwriting or taking a photo of the heron that sometimes fished from the riverbank, Archie at his feet, waiting for the next opportunity to cause mischief.

Winter in Willowbeck, Paris in spring, and perhaps a summer wedding, rose petals drifting down the river, an archway of peonies and sweet peas on the brick bridge. Was it possible to get married on a narrowboat? Summer would have to start researching. She couldn't wait.

Mason stood slowly, his gaze still holding hers, and banged his spoon against the side of his glass. The café quietened, everyone turning towards him, and he suddenly looked nervous, clearing his throat and adjusting his paper hat.

'Firstly,' he started, 'well – Happy Christmas. I think I can safely say that this is turning into one of the best I've ever had, and I wanted to say how lucky I am to have been able to celebrate – last night, as well as today – with all of you. The last few weeks have been . . .' he searched for the word, and everyone tried to help him out.

'Awful?' Doug asked.

'Freezing,' Ralph tried.

'Superb,' Ryder said, lazily.

Mason laughed. 'Ryder's closest to the truth, despite a few complications along the way. I know some of you thought that I was reluctant to come on this trip to begin with, but that was only because I'd been planning to propose to Summer in Willowbeck, and it forced me to start again from scratch. But it couldn't have turned out any better, and that is, in large part, down to all of you. So thank you, for accepting me into your group, and for helping me to make yesterday as perfect as I had imagined it, but far better than I believed it would actually be. I know that's due as much to your love for Summer, as it is your kindness to me.'

He swallowed, gave them a lopsided smile, and raised his glass. 'To good friends, safe journeys, no more frozen canals and, I know you've indulged me already, but just one more, I promise – to my fiancée Summer Freeman, who has brought us all together, and who has made me happier than I thought possible.'

Everyone raised their glasses as Summer walked back to the table, lifting her own.

'To good friends, safe journeys, no more frozen canals and Summer Freeman!' They stood, clinked their glasses together and drank, Summer grinning self-consciously.

'A Merry Christmas to us all,' Ryder said. Everyone echoed his words, which Summer had a suspicion were straight out of *A Christmas Carol,* and another toast was made.

'What happens now?' Tommy asked.

'Pudding will be ready in about half an hour,' Summer said.

'And after that,' Ryder leaned across the table towards Tommy, 'it's storytelling time. We turn all the lights off and tell each other spooky tales in the dark.'

'On Christmas?' Tommy asked. 'Isn't that for Halloween?'

'What you need to realize, young man,' Ryder said, 'is that we're not predictable. As we're all together, it would be remiss not to spend at least a small amount of time regaling each other with stories. But Tommy, you don't need to think of something scary, in fact, Christmas is full of magic and mystery when you think about it. None more so than the fact that this beautiful woman,' he said, glancing at Claire, 'returned my kiss. It seems on Christmas Day, even the slimiest of frogs can be princes. What's your favourite part of the festivities?' he asked Tommy, while the rest of the table was stunned into silence by his frankness. Claire was open-mouthed, her eyes shining.

'My favourite bit is—'

Tommy was cut off by the door opening and a loud voice shouting 'Ho ho ho!'

Everyone stared as Santa Claus walked into the café in his red and white suit and hat complete with fur trim, and with a sack slung over his shoulder.

'Is there a Tommy Poole in the room?' he boomed, and Tommy gasped, his hand shooting to the ceiling as if it was rocket-propelled.

As Alan walked over to him, he gave Summer a quick wink, and she returned it.

'Don't worry,' he said, 'I've not forgotten the rest of you. I can see that despite the wrinkles, the attempts at running businesses and trying to be proper adults, you're all still children at heart. You'll all get your gifts. But I must say,' he said, bending over at the waist, feigning extreme weariness, 'one of your delicious mince pies wouldn't go amiss on this, my busiest day of the year.'

'Coming right up, Santa,' Summer said, grateful for a reason to disappear into the kitchen so she could hide her amusement at the reaction to Alan's appearance.

He had cornered her in the pub to congratulate her on her engagement, and she had ended up telling him her ludicrous suspicions about who he was. He had laughed in a very Santa Claus-like way, and had said that he'd love to pop in on Christmas Day and see them all before they left London. Summer hadn't been counting on him going to this much effort, but she wasn't entirely shocked that this was how he'd chosen to say goodbye to them. She wasn't sure anything about Little Venice could surprise her any more.

By the time everyone had received their presents, said goodbye to Santa and left *Madeleine* to return to their boats and hotels, it was close to six o'clock. Summer and Mason stood on the bow deck, his arm around her, their breath misting in the cold, dark evening. The snow had gone, and the sky was a crisp, midnight canvas, the first stars beginning to wink and sparkle, reminding Summer of countless nights she and Mason had watched them from the roof of *The Sandpiper.*

Little Venice was quiet, most people snug in their houses and flats, or on their boats, resting after overdosing on roast potatoes at lunch, warming up after a bracing walk, or just sitting round the table to start Christmas dinner. Summer loved to think of them, of fellow liveaboards and the hundreds of people who had graced her café over the last few weeks, all safely inside, the happiness and cheer, children playing with new presents, a box of fancy chocolates being passed around.

'Shall we take Archie and Latte for a walk, fiancé of mine?' she asked, turning to whisper in his ear.

'I suppose we should,' he replied. 'Except after eating all that Christmas dinner they're probably as keen to snooze as I am.'

'All the more reason to take them. And is it really snoozing that you're interested in?'

Mason pretended to think about it. 'Well, maybe not *snoozing* exactly, though that second helping of Christmas pudding is making me feel a bit lethargic.'

'A walk would do us all good, then. We can take the dogs up the towpath, see the sights of Little Venice one last time, and then, when we get back – who knows? The kitchen's all tidied thanks to Claire, Jas and Ryder, so the evening is our oyster.'

'Claire and Ryder,' Mason said, shaking his head, wrapping his arms tightly around Summer so that she could feel the firmness of his torso through his thin jumper. 'Who'd have thought it?'

Summer laughed. 'Everyone thought it, forever, but nobody believed it would actually happen.'

'Christmas magic,' Mason said.

'Or Ryder being infected by your wonderful, romantic proposal, and realizing that life's too short not to tell people how you feel about them.'

'So Mason magic, then?' he asked, looking innocently down at her.

Summer sighed laboriously. 'Are you going to claim that's a thing now? That you're the new Cupid?'

He grinned, making her insides shimmy, her body yearn to be even closer to him. 'Nope,' he said. 'My work is done. I only ever had one person in my sights, and she said yes. I still can't quite believe it, that I could be so lucky, but I have everything I want right here.' He cupped her face, his thumb stroking her cheek, and brought his lips down to hers.

Their kiss was long and lingering, and by the time they broke apart, Summer wondered whether she would have the willpower to keep her hands off him long enough to take the dogs for even a short walk.

They went inside the café, which was pristine once again, ready for the next day of trading, wherever they had time to open for a few hours on their long journey back to Willowbeck. The only sign of the party was a row of the café's mugs lined up on the counter, the paper hats from all their crackers sitting round them so that it looked like a line of colourful crowns. Tommy's doing, Summer assumed, though with Ryder, Claire and Jas around, she couldn't be sure.

She followed Mason through the kitchen and into the living space, and peered over his shoulder at Archie and Latte, lying spread-eagled on the sofa, bellies exposed, legs akimbo, Archie snoring softly.

'Should we wake them?' he asked. She could hear the answer, and his reluctance to admit it, in his voice.

'If we don't take them now, we'll only have to do it later, and I might not want to move later.'

'Especially after we've finished the bottle of champagne I hid at the back of the fridge. And the box of chocolates Santa gave us.'

'Mason! You hid one of the bottles of fizz?'

He shrugged. 'We didn't run out this afternoon, did we?

It all went swimmingly, and besides, I've been thinking about tonight. You and me, celebrating our engagement, just the two of us. We need champagne for that and, the way I've been imagining it,' he leaned in, his voice low, 'not that many clothes.'

Summer shivered. 'That sounds . . . OK,' she said lightly. 'Quite an impressive follow-on from yesterday's efforts.' She looked at her ring for about the millionth time, the beautiful sapphire glinting in the light.

Mason raised an eyebrow. 'Glad you think so. But first, so we can enjoy our champagne without being interrupted by these two fur-balls, we should take them out. They'll thank us for waking them, I'm sure.'

Summer looked down at their pets, the mischievous terrier and diva Bichon Frise that – for the moment at least – completed their wonderful little family. 'The things we do for those dogs, eh?'

'Yup,' Mason said, handing her Latte's lead, crouching in front of Archie, stroking the fur between his ears to wake him. 'If only they appreciated it more.'

Once they had pulled on their coats and gloves and attached the leads to their dogs' collars, they stepped out onto *Madeleine*'s bow deck. The sky was full of stars now, twinkling down on them like festive glitter. A narrowboat moored on the opposite side of the canal had a full sized Christmas tree on its deck, its coloured lights pulsing gently in the dark, and somewhere nearby, someone was playing 'Silent Night,' its familiar tune drifting through the still, cold air.

Little Venice was settling into a quiet, contented Christmas evening, and Summer felt a swell of joy, of excitement, of gratitude for all that had happened, and for what her future

273

would hold with her soon-to-be husband, their two dogs, *Madeleine* and *The Sandpiper*. At that moment, she thought she must be the happiest person in the world.

'Summer,' Mason said, his voice low as if not wanting to disturb the peacefulness of the scene.

'Yes?' she asked, looking into his dark eyes.

'I love you.'

He handed her Archie's lead, and took something out of his pocket. Summer frowned, and then realization hit her when he pulled it firmly down onto her head, the snug warmth immediately comforting against the cold.

The polar bear hat.

He stood back to admire his handiwork, and then kissed her. 'There,' he said. 'Perfect.'

Summer rolled her eyes, but as Mason hopped down onto the towpath, took Archie's lead and then held out his hand and wrapped his fingers around hers, the pale of his skin visible through the ever-growing hole in his glove, she realized that, actually, he was right. And if perfect included a white, fluffy hat with polar bear ears, then who was she to argue?

THE END

If you enjoyed your
Canal Boat Cafe Christmas journey,
hop on board for magical trip on
The Cornish Cream Tea Bus.
Turn the page for a delicious extract ...

Chapter 1

My Dearest Charlie,

Gertie is yours, to do with what you will. I know that you cherish her, but you do not need to keep her. She is a gift, not a millstone around your neck. If the best thing for you is to sell her and go travelling, then that is what you should do.

I have so much to say to you, but my time is running out. I hope that these few words will be enough to show you how much I love you; it's more than I ever thought possible.

Look after yourself, think of all the happy times we spent together, and know that you can do anything if you believe in yourself enough.

Remember, my darling niece, live life to the full – you only get one chance. Make the most of your opportunities and do what is right for you.

All my love, always,
Your Uncle Hal x

Charlie Quilter folded the letter and pushed it into the back pocket of her jeans. She blinked, her eyes adjusting to the gloom, and tried to stop her heart from sinking as her dad stopped beside her in the garage doorway. His sigh was heavy, and not unexpected: he had been sighing a lot lately. She could barely remember a time when his narrow shoulders hadn't been slumped, and she had forgotten what his laughter sounded like. But on this occasion, she felt the same as he did; the sight before them was not inspiring.

The 1960s Routemaster bus, painted cream with green accents, looked more scrapheap than vintage, and Charlie could see that its months left in the garage without Uncle Hal's care and attention had had a serious impact.

'God, Charlie,' Vince Quilter said, stepping inside the garage and finding the light switch, 'what are you – we – I mean . . .' He shrugged, his arms wide, expression forlorn.

Charlie took a deep breath and, despite the February chill at her back, unzipped her coat and unwound her thick maroon scarf. The wind assailed her neck, newly exposed to the elements after the pre-Christmas, post-break-up, chop-it-all-off graduated bob that – she now realized – had been an ill-advised choice for this time of year.

'We're going to fix her,' she said purposefully, putting her bag against the wall and laying her palm flat against the bus's cold paintwork. 'We're going to restore Gertie, aren't we, Dad?' He was staring at the workbench where all Hal's tools were laid out, rubbing his unshaven jaw. Hal's death had hit him harder than anyone else, and while Charlie felt her uncle's loss keenly, she knew it was nothing compared to what Vince was going through. 'Dad?' she prompted.

'Sorry, love. That we are.' He started rolling up the sleeves of his jacket, thought better of it and took it off instead. He switched on the heater and rubbed his hands together.

Charlie felt a surge of hope. She hurried over to her bag and pulled out a flask of coffee and a Tupperware box. 'Here, have a brownie to keep you going. I thought we could do with some sustenance.' She took off the lid, and a glimmer of a smile lit up Vince's face.

'Always thinking ahead, huh?'

'This was never going to be the easiest task in the world, practically or emotionally. Brownies baked with love – and hazelnuts and chocolate chip, because that's your favourite kind.'

'Your food is the best, because it's baked with love and extra calories,' her dad said, taking one of the neatly arranged squares. 'That's what he always said.'

'Yup.' A lump formed unhelpfully at the back of Charlie's throat, as it had been doing at inopportune moments ever since her uncle Hal had been diagnosed with an aggressive cancer at the end of last summer. So many things reminded her of him, and while dealing with practicalities – assessing the state of his beloved Routemaster bus, for example – were easier to focus on without the emotion overwhelming her, his sayings, his nuggets of wisdom, always knocked her off kilter. They were so ingrained in her family now, but it was as if she could hear Hal's voice, his unwavering cheerfulness, whoever was saying the words.

'Love and extra calories,' she repeated, wincing when she noticed a deep gouge in Gertie's side. 'How did he get away with being so sentimental?'

'Because he was straightforward,' her dad said through a

mouthful of chocolate and nuts. 'He said everything without embarrassment or affectation. He was a sixty-eight-year-old man who called his bus Gertie. He meant it all, and was never ashamed of who he was.'

Uncle Hal had given scenic tours on Gertie, the vintage double-decker Routemaster, that were legendary throughout the Cotswolds. He was an expert bus driver and a world-class talker. Everyone who took one of his tours left feeling as if they'd made a friend for life, and the testimonials on TripAdvisor were gushing. His untimely death had left a huge hole in the Cotswold tourist trade, as well as his family's life.

And now Gertie belonged to Charlie; left to her in Hal's will, for her to do with whatever she wanted. At that moment, all she could see in the bus's future was being dismantled and sold for spares, but she was not going to let that happen. She couldn't imagine herself taking over her uncle's tours, even though she had spent many hours on them and had been taught to drive the bus as soon as she was old enough. Her expertise was in baking, not talking.

Her dad finished his brownie and started examining Gertie's engine. As a car dealer he knew his way around vehicles, but had admitted to Charlie that he wasn't that knowledgeable about buses. Charlie had argued that it was just a bigger version, and nothing could be that different.

She cleaned the chocolate off her fingers with a paper napkin and climbed on board the bus. It had taken on a musty, unloved smell, and was bone-achingly cold. Charlie walked up the aisle of the lower deck, her fingers trailing along the backs of the forest-green seats, and opened the cab.

Her dad appeared behind her, wiping his hands on a rag.

'The engine seems in good enough shape, but I only know the basics. And in here?' He gave another melancholy sigh.

'It's going to be fine,' she said. 'She needs a bit of sprucing up, that's all. A few things need fixing, there's some cosmetic work, knocking a couple of panels back into shape, and then Gertie will be as good as new.'

'I could give Clive a call,' Vince said, worrying at his scruffy hair, 'get him to come and give her a once-over, see what condition her vital organs are in.'

'And in the meantime, I'll tackle in here. We've got the Hoover, cleaning sprays, and I can make a list of what needs repairing. The toilet probably needs a good flushing out.' Charlie made a face and her dad laughed.

'You sure you want to start that now?' he asked. 'Shouldn't we find out if she's salvageable first? You don't want to waste your time cleaning her if the engine's buggered.'

'Dad, the engine is *not* buggered. She's fine. Hal was driving her right up until . . . he wasn't any more. He never mentioned anything being wrong with her.'

'Yes, but you have to agree she looks—'

'Neglected,' Charlie finished. 'Which is why we're here. I guarantee that once we've given her a bit of love and attention, things will look a hundred times better. Gertie is going back on the road, that's all there is to it.' She grinned, and it wasn't even forced. She had almost convinced herself.

Her dad looked at her fondly. 'You're a wonder, Charlie. Anyone else faced with these circumstances – with this,' he gestured around him, 'and Hal, and everything you've been through with Stuart – would start a lengthy hibernation, and nobody would blame them. Instead you've baked brownies and dragged me here, and you're not going to leave until Gertie's gleaming. You don't even know what you're going to do with her when she's restored!'

Charlie's smile almost slipped at this last point, because that was worrying her far more than the state of Gertie's engine or how many panels needed replacing. What on earth was she going to do with a vintage, double-decker bus, when she worked in a café in Ross-on-Wye and her main skills were baking and eating? 'I'll think of something,' she said brightly. 'One step at a time, Dad. Fix Gertie, and *then* decide what to do with her.'

She put the key in the ignition and a satisfying thrum reverberated, like a heartbeat, through the bus. The engine was working, at least. She cranked the heating up to max – she didn't want her fingers to fall off before she'd polished the metalwork – then turned on the radio.

'Gold' by Spandau Ballet filled the space, and Charlie took her dad's hands and pulled them up in the air with hers. She forced them into an awkward dance down the aisle, bumping into seats as they sashayed from the front of the bus to the back, and sang along at the top of her voice. Soon they were both laughing, and her dad let go of her hands so he could clutch his stomach. She dinged the bell and tried to get her breathing under control. When Vince looked up, Charlie could see the familiar warmth in his eyes that she had been worried was gone for good.

It was impossible not to feel cheered in Gertie's company. Hal had been convinced there was something a little bit magical about her, and while Charlie had always argued that it was Hal who inspired the laughter on his tours, at this moment she wondered if he was right.

They could do this. No question. Despite all that had

happened to her over the past few months, she knew she could restore Gertie to her former glory. What came next wasn't so certain but, as she'd said to her dad, they could only take one step at a time. Right now, they needed to focus on bringing the bus back to life.

They worked all morning, and even though Charlie knew the bits they were fixing were only cosmetic, and a small part of her worried that when Clive came round he would tell them that the engine was too old, or there was too much rust in the chassis, or any one of a number of things that meant Gertie would not outlive Hal, she felt so much better for doing it. The radio kept them buoyed, and at one point her dad even whistled along to a Sixties tune, something that, only a day before, Charlie and her mum would both have thought impossible.

The simple act of working on Uncle Hal's bus was taking the edge off their grief. It reminded Charlie how much she had loved spending time with him, a lot of it on board this very bus, and how big an influence he'd been on her. That didn't have to stop just because he was no longer physically with her. Hal would be part of her life for ever.

It was after one o'clock when Vince announced he was going to get sandwiches. Charlie ordered an egg mayo and bacon baguette and, once her dad had strolled out of the garage with his jacket done up to his neck, she climbed to the top deck of the bus. She sat above the cab – her favourite position as a child because she could pretend she was driving – even though, inside the garage, the view was less than inspiring. As she did so, she felt the letter in her back pocket. Hal had left it for her in his will, and it had been folded and reopened so many times the paper had begun to wear thin along the creases.

It no longer made her cry, but the words still affected her deeply. He had never married, had never had a family of his own, so she had been like a daughter to him. Losing him had been a huge blow – his cancer diagnosis a mind-numbing shock followed quickly by practicalities as his condition worsened and he needed more care – but at least she had been able to spend time with him, to let him know how much she loved him and how much he had shaped her life. And she would always have his letter. It was bitter-sweet, but so much better than the irreversible cut-off of losing someone suddenly.

She was still lost in thought when she heard a woman calling her name, followed by a high-pitched yelp. Charlie ran down Gertie's narrow staircase and out of the open doorway.

'How are you doing?' Juliette asked. Before Charlie had time to reply, Marmite raced up to her, his extendable lead whirring noisily, and put his tiny front paws on Charlie's shins. Charlie scooped the Yorkipoo puppy into her arms and closed her eyes while he licked her chin. However miserable some aspects of life had been recently, Marmite never failed to bring a smile to her face. He was six months old, and more of a terror with every passing day.

'OK, I think,' Charlie said. 'But don't look at the outside, come and see what we've done inside. Dad's getting someone to take a proper look at her, and in the meantime we've been giving her a polish. He's just gone to get lunch.'

'I know,' Juliette said, unclipping Marmite's lead and following Charlie onto the bus. 'I saw him on my way here. He's getting me a sandwich, too.'

'So you can stay for a bit, before you go back to Cornwall this afternoon?'

Juliette nodded. 'It's been so good seeing everyone. But I'm still not sure, Char, how you're really doing. What's going on up here?' She tapped Charlie's forehead. 'You're putting on this amazing front, but I need to know before I go home that you're OK.'

'I'm fine,' Charlie said. 'This morning has helped a lot. Dad was concerned that Gertie wouldn't be salvageable, but just look at her! She might need a bit of work under the bonnet, some patching up, but it's given me hope.'

Juliette surveyed their morning's work, the metal uprights gleaming, the walls clean, the seats vacuumed to within an inch of their lives. 'She looks great, Char, almost as good as new. But I'm not as convinced about you. Since I've been back you've been so busy, working at The Café on the Hill, helping with the catering for the funeral. You haven't stopped, even for a day. You should be taking some time out.'

Charlie groaned. 'Why does everyone think that's best for me? Keeping busy is what helps in this kind of situation.' She led Juliette to a seat halfway down the bus. Some of the chairs were sagging dangerously, but this one, she had discovered earlier, was still fairly firm.

'Are you *sure* you're OK?' Juliette said after a minute. Her voice was low, her slight French accent always adding a seriousness to her words, though in this case it was probably intentional.

Charlie remembered the first time she had heard Juliette speak, on a packed train from London to Cheltenham; she'd been chatting with someone on the other end of her mobile, and had occasionally slipped into French. Charlie had been sitting next to her, and after Juliette had finished her call and offered some expletives in both languages, Charlie had asked her those same words: *Are you OK?* Juliette had been reserved, embarrassed that she'd been entertaining the whole carriage, and so Charlie had told her how *she'd* had a no-holds-barred telephone row with her then-boyfriend in a hotel doorway, not realizing that a wedding party were waiting to get past her into the ballroom, and how some of the guests had looked quite shocked when she'd finally noticed that they were watching her.

She'd made Juliette laugh, and by the time the train had pulled up in Cheltenham, they had swapped numbers and agreed to meet up. That had been almost seven years ago, and their friendship was still strong despite Juliette's move to Cornwall two years before, with her boyfriend Lawrence. Charlie was still touched that Juliette had come back for Hal's funeral, staying for a couple of weeks to catch up with friends in the area. She had been on Gertie countless times when she'd lived in Cheltenham, and Charlie hadn't asked her if *she* was OK.

'I'm not doing too badly,' she said now. 'I've been getting on with stuff, which is better than wallowing in the empty flat, or at Mum and Dad's. Dad's so cut up about losing Hal. Today is the first time I've seen him smile in what feels like for ever.'

'I know you're worried about Vince, but you have to think about yourself, too.' Juliette put a hand on her shoulder. 'Because it isn't just Hal, is it? It's only been a couple of months since you and Stuart . . . finished. And you're in the flat, hosting viewings, unsure where you're going to go once it's sold. I know you don't want to go back to living with your parents, and you can't live on Gertie, as tempting as it is.' She laughed softly.

'That's looking like one of the better options, actually,'

Charlie said, chuckling. 'What *am* I going to do with her, Jules? I can't be a tour guide. I'm a baker, a caterer. I don't have the gift of the gab like Hal did. But, despite what he said in his letter, I can't sell her.' She rubbed her hands over her eyes, realizing too late that they were covered in cleaning spray.

'This is why you need time,' Juliette pressed. 'You need to stop thinking for a bit, give yourself some space before you make any big decisions. The place in Newquay wasn't brilliant, but our new house in Porthgolow, it's perfect, Char. It's so close to the sea. It's beautiful and quiet, and the people in the village are friendly. Come and stay for a couple of weeks. Bea would give you the time off, wouldn't she? The hours you've put into that café, you're probably owed months back in overtime.'

'Working is good for me,' Charlie insisted but, even as she said it, the thought of returning to the café in Ross-on-Wye, even with its spring-themed window display and the ideas she had for seasonal cakes and sandwiches, didn't fill her with as much joy as it should. There were too many other thoughts crowding her mind.

'Take a break,' Juliette continued. 'Come and stay with Lawrence and me. I'm sure Marmite would get on fine with Ray and Benton. They're easy-going cats, and Marmite's still so small. And the most adorable dog in the world, by the way. I'm so glad you've got him to look after you.'

Marmite was sitting on the seat in front of them, scrabbling at the back of the cushion as if there might be a treat hidden somewhere in the fabric. Charlie picked him up and settled him on her lap, rubbing his black-and-tan coat. She pictured the two of them walking along a sandy beach with crystal blue water beyond, to a soundtrack of seagulls and crashing waves. It was certainly a better image than this bland, functional garage or the flat she had shared with Stuart, now empty and soulless. She didn't want to run away from the hard things in life, but she knew her friend was right.

'Let me talk to Bea,' she said decisively. 'I'll see if I can get a couple of weeks off.'

Juliette's face lit up. She ruffled Charlie's hair, which had been enhanced from its natural reddish hue into a vibrant copper at the same time as the drastic haircut. 'The next time you're in the café, you promise me you'll ask her?'

'I will, I—'

'Room for a little one?' Her dad appeared in the doorway, along with the salty tang of bacon.

'Thanks so much, Vince,' Juliette said, accepting her baguette and a coffee.

'You convinced Charlie to come and stay with you yet?' he asked, taking the seat in front and turning to face them.

'Almost,' Juliette said. 'She's agreed to ask Bea for some time off.'

'Bloody hell! You've actually got her considering a holiday? Or have you tempted her down with some sort of Cornish cooking competition?'

'No competition,' Juliette said through a mouthful of cheese sandwich. 'No work. An actual holiday.'

'I am here, you know,' Charlie said, lifting her baguette out of Marmite's reach. The dog put his paws on her chest and sniffed the air, whimpering mournfully.

'It doesn't hurt to hear the unvarnished truth occasionally, love,' Vince replied.

'I've never . . .' she started, then sighed and unwrapped her lunch. She didn't want to argue with her dad, and she knew they both had her best interests at heart, even if they were being irritating about it.

'This is cosy, isn't it?' Juliette said. 'Having a picnic on board Gertie. Hal could have started something like this, including sandwiches and cups of tea on his tours.'

'Enough people brought their own food, didn't they?' Vince laughed. 'He was getting fat on all the sausage rolls and packets of Maltesers that went around.'

'But a few tables in here instead of front-facing seats, a tea urn, the beautiful views outside the windows. It'd be ideal, wouldn't it? If the weather was cold, or you didn't want wasps in your cupcakes.' Juliette grinned. 'You could see the countryside from the comfort of the bus.'

Charlie returned her friend's smile, her synapses pinging. She couldn't be a tour guide. She knew how to drive the bus, she had the right licence and kept up to date with her top-up training, but she hadn't done it every day for the last thirty years; she was inexperienced. But what she could do, almost with her eyes closed, was feed people. She could make cakes and pastries and scones that had customers squealing in pleasure and coming back for thirds.

And Gertie *was* cosy. With a bit more polish and a couple of personal touches, the bus could even look quite homely. It could be somewhere you'd enjoy spending time, and not just for a journey around the winding lanes of the Cotswolds.

'All right, love?' her dad asked, his eyebrows raised quizzically.

'Earth to Charlie!' Juliette snapped her fingers, and Marmite let out a tiny growl.

'I think I've got it,' Charlie murmured.

'Got what?' Vince asked.

A smile spread across her face. This might be the answer

she had been looking for. If it worked, she would have to reward Juliette for the flash of inspiration, so bright that it was like a meteor sailing across the sky.

'I think I know what I'm going to do,' she said, patting the seat next to her. 'I think I've found a way to keep Gertie on the road.'

Chapter 2

'Have you completely lost it this time, Charlie?'

At least Bea Fishington wasn't one for mincing her words.

'I don't think so,' Charlie replied, following her from the kitchen into the main café, carrying a plate of freshly baked raspberry flapjacks. 'I think this could be a real turning point, for me and Gertie – and for you and The Café on the Hill.'

Bea folded her arms over her large chest, the silk of her cream blouse straining across it. 'Serving cakes on your uncle's bus? I know you're sad about losing him – completely understandable; he was a gentleman – but you're looking for harmony where there is none to be found.'

'I disagree,' Charlie said, sliding the flapjacks into place behind the glass counter. 'It would be a way to get this place known, to expand its range beyond these four walls.' She gestured to the smart, well-appointed café. The walls in question were slate grey, complemented by a black-and-white chequerboard floor. Accents around the room in lemon yellow and sky blue gave it a modern twist. There were high benches in the window and a mixture of squashy sofas and upright chairs, inviting lone workers with laptops, couples, large families and groups of friends.

Early in the morning on a dull Monday at the beginning of March it was quiet, with a couple of post-school-run mums drinking lattes and two men with grey hair sitting by the window sharing a toasted teacake.

Bea glared at her, but Charlie stood up straighter and refused to look away. She had a height advantage over Bea – over most other women, if she was honest – and a determination that had got her into trouble on more than one occasion. But she knew this was a good idea. The area around Cheltenham and Ross-on-Wye, England's glorious, green Cotswolds, was always hosting fairs, festivals and myriad other events, where a beautiful vintage bus selling cakes would be popular. Every time Charlie had moaned to Hal that she had nothing to do at the weekend, that Juliette was with Lawrence or Stuart was staying in London for some posh bankers' do, Hal would reel off a list of all the classic car shows and autumn fêtes and dog owners' carnivals that were happening, leaving her with no room to complain.

'I'm not after world domination,' Bea said, turning to the coffee machine. 'I know you're ambitious, Charlie. I could see that from the moment I met you, and I have no doubt that you'll be running your own café or catering empire before too long. But selling cakes from a bus? It sounds too tricky. How would you store ingredients, make drinks en masse?'

'People live on buses,' Charlie countered. 'They cook and shower and sleep on buses, so selling a few coffees and scones couldn't possibly be a problem.'

'You say that like you've not researched it at all.' Bea frothed the milk, pausing their conversation while a loud whooshing sound filled the space between them.

'That's what Google's for.' She grinned and shrugged, her smile falling when Bea didn't return it. 'I'm going to speak to Clive, one of my dad's friends, tomorrow. He's coming to give Gertie a once-over anyway, and he's refurbished a few buses, so he'll know exactly how I can get a coffee machine and a fridge installed on it.'

Bea handed Charlie a cappuccino, and she sprinkled it with chocolate dusting. 'Is it even laid out like a café?' she asked.

Charlie leaned against the counter and blew on her drink until a dent appeared in the thick froth. 'It's got front-facing seats. But I thought, to begin with, I could just serve from it. People can sit on the bus if they like, but I'll treat it like a takeaway food truck, just to see if it's possible. Then I can think about modifying it properly. The Café on the Hill could have an offshoot, like a cutting from a plant. The Café on the Bus. It has a nice ring to it, doesn't it? And you *know* the food will be good quality; I've never let you down in that respect, have I? Why not spread your wings? Give yourself some wheels, expand your horizons.'

'You have put so many mixed metaphors into that sentence, I don't know where to begin.'

'Begin by saying *yes*, Bea. Just to the Fair on the Field. People in Ross-on-Wye know your café. It's big enough to be a proper test, and small enough that if it all goes hideously wrong – which it won't,' Charlie added quickly – 'then your reputation won't be dented. One event, one chance.' She clasped her hands together in front of her.

'And you're definitely speaking to this Clive person

tomorrow? There can be no cut corners with food hygiene or health and safety. Everything has to be done properly.'

'It will be,' Charlie said.

Bea's shoulders dropped, her lips curving into what could almost be considered a smile. 'I'll need to see plans. Exactly how it's going to work. Then I'll make a decision.'

'Of course,' Charlie said, nodding.

'And just the Fair on the Field. One gig, and we'll take it from there, OK?'

'OK. Absolutely. Thank you, Bea. You won't regret it.'

'I'd better not,' she muttered.

Charlie went to adjust the window display where one of her daffodils, lovingly crafted out of tissue paper and card, had drooped and was giving off a despondent air. Her pulse was racing. Serving cakes on Hal's bus, to the general population, at a public event. Somehow, in light of Bea's cold, logical reality, it seemed like the most ludicrous idea on the planet.

But people *did* live on buses. They travelled around in their portable houses, where they had all the mod cons. Some were even luxurious, like tiny five-star hotels. Surely fitting a few basic appliances wasn't too far beyond the realms of possibility? Well, she would find out tomorrow. She hoped that Clive would make it easy for her.

After not having been in Hal's garage for months, Charlie was back there for the second time in less than a week. Today, she had the sun at her back. It was a weak March sun that couldn't cut through the cold, but it was welcome nonetheless, as were the sounds of metal against metal and her dad chatting to Clive while he did something unfathomable to Gertie's engine.

Everything about today was an improvement on last time, except that Juliette wasn't here. She was all the way down in Cornwall, with Lawrence, her cats and a sea view. Charlie would go and see her – of course she would. But she couldn't go now, not when she had the fire of possibility lighting her up.

Clive had assured her and Vince that Gertie wasn't destined for the scrapheap, and that he would be able to have her back to her best in a day or so. He'd also been more positive than Charlie could have hoped about the other alterations she wanted to make.

'So you really think it's possible?' she asked, when there was a lull in the conversation. 'Putting in a serving hatch and a coffee machine. A fridge, even?'

'Oh, it's doable,' Clive said, standing up. He was a short man with silver hair, ruddy cheeks and cheerful blue eyes. 'I can't get it perfect with your budget and timescales, but for the Fair on the Field it'll see you right.'

'Thank you,' Charlie said. 'And it's safe, is it? What you're going to do?'

Clive chuckled and tapped his spanner against his chin. 'It won't put her at risk of explosion if that's what you're worried about. Ideally, she'd need a generator and an extra water tank, some of the seats ripped out, but you can come to those if it's worth pursuing.'

'That's great!' Charlie did a little jump. Marmite barked and attacked her boot.

'Your mum's going places,' Vince said, picking up the Yorkipoo and rubbing his fur. 'Shame it's not Cornwall, though.' He gave Charlie a sideways glance.

'I'll go and see her,' Charlie protested. 'But the Fair on the Field is the perfect opportunity to test this idea out. I can visit Juliette anytime, and Cornwall will be nicer in the summer. Also, if I do it once the flat's sorted, I'll have more holiday money.'

'It's not gone through yet?' her dad asked, putting Marmite on the floor.

'Nope. We've got buyers, but God knows what Stuart's doing. I need to call the solicitor and see where we're up to.'

'It's a lot to be dealing with, love. Are you sure trying Gertie out for this café bus business is the best step right now? I was surprised that you even wanted to come and look at her so soon, and this new venture is going to be a lot of work. Don't you want a bit of breathing space? Coast along while you sort out the flat and let life . . . settle?'

'I can't let go of this idea now,' she said. 'It's in my head, and I'm going to be *un*settled and fidgety until I've tried it. One event, then I'll have some idea if it's worth more investment – of my time and, maybe, a bit more money. Besides, Bea might have changed her mind by tomorrow. I need to strike while the iron's hot.'

Vince looked at her for a long moment, then nodded. She could see the concern in his eyes, but she knew that he wouldn't push it.

Everyone dealt with loss in different ways. It wasn't great timing that her relationship with Stuart had imploded soon after her uncle had become ill, but at least it couldn't get much worse. And her biggest fear – or the one it was easiest to focus on, at least – Gertie and what would happen to her, was on the way to being solved. Her dad couldn't be against her revitalizing Hal's pride and joy. He was worried about her, but there was no need for him to be.

'Oh,' she said, 'I almost forgot. I brought snacks.' She dug in her bag and pulled out the box of orange and chocolate-chip muffins she'd made early that morning. Clive downed tools immediately. Marmite pawed at her legs, and she gave him a couple of puppy treats.

While they were eating, Charlie took her time to walk slowly around Gertie. Clive still needed to fix the panelling, but with the sunshine hitting her glossy cream paint and reaching through the windscreen to alight on the newly polished metalwork, the bus was looking a lot better. Almost like her old self.

And soon, she would be transformed again. The changes would be small, but significant. They would allow Charlie to give the Routemaster a brand-new lease of life. And everyone deserved a second chance.

As Clive and her dad gave her the thumbs-up for her muffins, she felt the first flutterings of excitement. This could be the start of something great, for her and for Gertie. When you're down, the best course of action is to get up, and aim higher than you've ever aimed before. Charlie Quilter had never been one for wallowing: she was going to prove to everyone just how bad at it she was.

Chapter 3

The Fair on the Field took place at the bottom of the hill on which Ross-on-Wye town centre proudly sat. It was a beautiful spot, with the River Wye wending along the bottom of the field, and the buildings of the town looking down on it from up high. When Charlie had phoned up to book a space, the organizers had assured her that, despite being close to the river, the ground was firm enough for Gertie; they'd had enough food trucks over the years and never had a problem. Even so, her pitch was at the edge closest to the road, where the ground was more solid. But it had rained heavily during the night, and while the sun was shining down on them now, as if the torrential downpour had never happened, Charlie could feel the wheels spinning as she navigated Gertie over the bumpy grass to her slot.

At least she knew how to drive the bus. Her time spent on the vintage Routemaster had started when she was little, Hal teaching her how to steer in car parks from his lap and, once she was old enough to legally drive, being patient with her about turning circles and visibility, how much space she needed to manoeuvre it into a tight spot. He'd encouraged her to take the bus driving test soon after she'd passed her car test with flying colours, and she was proud of her ability to keep the ride as smooth as possible, to not panic when faced with the narrowest of lanes.

'OK, Sal?' she called back into the bus, where Sally, The Café on the Hill's newest staff member, seventeen years old, and with a pile of caramel curls on top of her head, was sitting quietly.

'I'm fine,' she replied, her high voice rising further as they went over a large rut in the grass.

Charlie grinned. They had made it. Clive's hard work had paid off and now, with only the loss of a couple of downstairs seats, she had a small preparation area, and an under-the-counter fridge where she could keep chocolate éclairs and fresh cream cakes. She had made individual portions of Eton Mess and Key Lime pies, and a range of flapjacks, brownies and millionaire's shortbread. Clive had also installed a fresh-water tank. It was small, but it meant she could have a proper coffee machine with a milk frother.

Everything was fairly cramped, but that didn't matter because she wasn't going to invite people onto the bus. What remained of the downstairs seating was taken up with her trays of goodies, and one of the long windows was now a serving hatch. She could unclip it and pull it up, securing it inside the bus while she served through the opening, as with any other food truck. It was perfect.

Gertie was a half-cab Routemaster, with the traditional hobbit-sized door on the driver's side, used to climb into the cab, and the main doorway and stairs at the back of the bus. When Hal had given her a makeover a couple of years ago, he had made the cab accessible from inside the bus – he told Charlie he was getting too old to hoick himself over the wheel arch – and installed a tiny but functional toilet under the stairs. Clive had made Gertie as good as new and, with the extra additions, she had everything she needed, Charlie hoped, to work as a café bus. But this day would prove it either way; she was determined to make a success of it.

She slowed the bus down, and a young man in a fluorescent jacket waved her into position. Sally arranged the trays of bakes strategically around the serving hatch while Charlie jumped down from the bus and, registering nervously how spongy the grass was, slid her menu into the frame Clive had bolted on next to the opening. She was offering a selection of sweet and savoury treats, including a sausage roll with flaky pastry and a herby sausage-meat filling. Ideally they'd be served warm, but they tasted delicious cold as well.

'Ready to go?' she asked Sally, who was smoothing down her apron and staring at the sausage rolls as if they might bite. 'It doesn't open officially for another half an hour, but it may be that other traders will want a snack before the general public arrive.'

Sally had only been working at The Café on the Hill for two weeks, and behaved as if everything was a potential threat. Charlie knew she'd come out of her shell sooner or later, and thought that a day spent at a fair, where almost anything could happen, would be good for her.

'I've arranged all the cakes and pastries,' Sally said, giving Charlie a nervous smile.

'They look great. Shall we go and hang the banner up?'

She'd had it made at one of the local printer's; a beautiful sign in tarpaulin-weight material that would run the length of the vehicle, declaring it to be The Café on the Bus in burgundy writing on a cream background. Beneath it, in a forest-green font, it read: *An offshoot of The Café on the Hill.* It had brass-capped eyelets threaded through with thick chord, so she could attach it easily over the upper deck windows. Even Bea had widened her eyes appreciatively when she had showed her, rolling it out along the tabletops in the café.

She had also added a couple of photos of Gertie to The Café on the Hill's Instagram page, and had received 117 likes on the picture she'd posted yesterday. It needed work, but it was a solid start.

Now Charlie led the way up the narrow staircase, the metal rail cool under her hand, and passed one end of the banner to Sally.

'We're going to have to hang it out of that end window, and then I'm going to have to grab it and unroll it outside, going to each window in turn to get it running the whole length of the bus. So just hold on, OK?'

'OK,' Sally parroted back.

It was hard going. She had to lean her arms out of adjacent windows so she could hold it up and then unfurl it further, but after ten minutes of sweating and muttered swearing, she was tying her end of the banner firmly onto the window. It was the right way round. It wasn't upside down. Quietly triumphant, they rushed outside to look at their handiwork, and Charlie grinned. 'The Café on the Bus,' she declared. 'We are open for business!'

Within two minutes of the banner going up, she had a queue of five people looking eagerly up at her through the serving hatch.

'What's this, love,' said an old man with a flat cap pulled low over his eyes. 'Hal's old bus getting a new lease of life?'

'Absolutely,' she replied. 'He left it to me, and I'm giving it a fresh start as a food truck. What do you think?'

'I think my Daphne will miss the tours,' he said, accepting a sausage roll and a black coffee in a sturdy takeaway cup. Charlie hadn't had time to get them branded, but had picked out cream and green cups to tie in with the bus's colour scheme.

'Lots of people will,' Charlie admitted. 'Hal ran brilliant tours, but I can't do that.'

'Someone else could mebbe take them on, then,' he added thoughtfully, and bit into the sausage roll. He eyed it appraisingly, and then her, and then shrugged. 'Not sure it's meant to be a café bus, like.'

Charlie kept her smile fixed. 'I'm just giving it a go. This is our first outing together.' She patted the side of the bus, feeling like something out of a cheesy Sixties film.

'I say good luck to you,' called a tall man in a navy fleece from further back in the queue. 'Coffee out of a bus is a marvellous idea. Gives it a bit of individuality. You going to serve three-course dinners from your little window, too?'

'Oh, shush your mouth, Bill Withers,' said a bright-faced, plump lady Charlie recognized from the chemist's in town. 'This young lass is using her initiative. Would you rather the bus stayed locked away in a garage until it rusted to nothing? We all know Hal wouldn't have wanted that.'

'I just think it's hilarious,' Bill countered, while Charlie tried to serve and not let embarrassment overwhelm her. 'Serving food from Hal's old bus. Whatever next? Driving to work in the Indian takeaway?' He laughed a loud, unbridled laugh that had several people turning in their direction.

'Oh, don't mind him,' the woman said as she reached the front of the queue. 'He's so far stuck in the past he should be wearing black and white.' She rolled her eyes, and this time Charlie's smile was genuine.

'It was only an idea,' she replied. 'Hal left me the bus, and I wanted to put it to good use, to have it out in the open, like you said. I'm a baker, so I thought I could combine the two.'

'And it's a *grand* idea,' her supporter said, accepting a slightly haphazard-looking Eton Mess that was living up a bit too well to its name – Charlie would have to do something to keep her puddings upright when they were driving across rough ground. 'You iron out a few . . . wrinkles, and it'll be a triumph. Don't listen to the naysayers. You do *you,* and let everyone else worry about themselves.'

'I will,' Charlie said. 'Thank you for the vote of confidence.'

The morning passed quickly, and Charlie had a constant stream of people buying coffees, flapjacks and Bakewell tarts, and the sausage-roll stock was depleting quickly. Music had started up from somewhere, and there were families and groups of friends, people with dogs on leads milling about the field. A falconry demonstration was taking place in the cordoned-off square they were calling the arena, and Charlie knew that, despite all the hustle and noise, Gertie stood out. She was taller than most of the other food trucks, striking with her cream and green paintwork and, if nothing else, word of mouth was doing its job regarding her cakes.

'What do you think, Sal?' she asked. 'Are you enjoying yourself?'

'It's great,' Sally squeaked. Charlie would have to work on her confidence once they were back in the café.

She turned to the hatch, her head full of strategies for female empowerment, and her smile fell. There, first in the queue, was Stuart Morstein. He looked effortlessly handsome in his jeans, white shirt and navy jacket, his light brown hair pushed away from his forehead. He grinned at Charlie, and her insides shrivelled.

'A cheese scone and a latte, thanks, Charlie. Can I have the scone buttered?'

'No problem,' she said, through lips that wouldn't work properly. What was he doing here? Was it something to do with their flat? If so, why hadn't he called her? The last time she had spoken to the solicitor she had said the sale was going through, they were just waiting on some final paperwork. It was a typically vague answer, and she should have gone to Stuart to begin with, but she was avoiding him at all possible costs. He was obviously not affording her the same courtesy.

'How's it going?' he asked, while Charlie frothed the milk and Sally buttered a scone and put it in a paper bag with a green napkin and some Parmesan crisps.

'Good, thanks,' she said, wondering where Annalise, her replacement, was. Charlie wouldn't be surprised to discover she was too proud to come to the countryside, and lived her life entirely in London or on holiday in the Maldives. At least, she thought as she gazed at the man who until four months ago had been her boyfriend, being in the bus meant she could look down on *him* for a change.

Sally handed her the bag. Charlie leant out of the hatch to pass Stuart his coffee and scone, and the bus lurched forwards. Charlie was thrown sideways, scalding latte covering her hand, her shoulder bashing against the window frame. Behind her, Sally screamed, and Stuart took a step backwards, his features contorting in alarm.

'Shit.' Charlie tried to right herself and the bus lurched again, this time sending up a thick spurt of mud from the front wheel onto Stuart's jeans.

'We're *sinking!*' Sally screamed. 'Is it a sinkhole? Oh my God, oh my God, oh my God!' She ran through the bus and flew down the steps.

Charlie tried again to pull herself up and Gertie lurched for a third time, the front left-hand wheel sinking further into the mud. Stuart's latte cup was almost empty now, most of it dripping over Charlie's hand, and she had dropped the scone after lurch number two. Stuart was standing back, looking at her as if she'd turned into a monster, and he wasn't the only one.

A crowd had formed, and as Charlie scanned the faces of the people who were standing and staring, rather than helping, she saw that their expressions ranged between horror and glee.

After the third lurch the bus seemed to settle, and Charlie dragged herself to standing, which was difficult now that the ground below her was tilted.

'Jesus Christ, Charlie,' Stuart said, somewhat pompously, she thought. 'This bus is a death trap! Anyone could have been standing at the front.'

'The ground's too soft, that's all. And nobody would have got hurt even if they *had* been standing at the front. It hasn't rolled. It's just . . . sunk a bit.' She peered out of the hatch and looked at her submerged wheel. Would she be able to drive it out? Would anyone help with planks?

Her ex took a step closer, his hands on his hips. This was

classic Stuart: he would rescue her, fix her calamities and errors of judgement like the wonderful, patient human being that he was, and expect her to be eternally grateful. Charlie narrowed her eyes, preparing to do the opposite of whatever he suggested, when there was a flapping sound and the banner, which they had secured so tightly at the beginning of the morning, came free of its restraints and fell towards the ground. Except that Stuart was in the way, so it landed, quite expertly, on top of him, as if he was a fire that needed extinguishing.

'For fuck's sake, Charlie!' came Stuart's muffled voice from somewhere beneath the banner. Even though Charlie's audience seemed less than approving of her, and poor Gertie was clearly wedged quite solidly in the mud, and this probably meant that her time running The Café on the Bus was already at an end – the shortest-lived career in history – Charlie started laughing. Once she'd started, she couldn't stop, tears of mirth pouring down her cheeks as she surveyed the carnage from the hatch window, trying to keep her footing on the lopsided floor. As Stuart emerged, flustered and fuming, Charlie hid inside her bus, where scones and flap-jacks were scattered like autumn leaves, and the coffee machine was beginning to leak.

'Shit,' she said. 'Shitting hell.' The sight was sobering, and her laughter left her as suddenly as it had started.

She heard footsteps and looked up, prepared to brace herself against her ex-boyfriend's anger, and found another man standing in the doorway, his movements hesitant as he tried not to succumb to gravity and fall into her.

'Hello,' she said, wiping her eyes. 'How can I help?' In the circumstances, it was a ridiculous thing to say. She wasn't in a position to help anyone.

'Are you all right?' He had dark blond hair crafted into some sort of quiff, and was wearing a denim jacket over dark cords and a black T-shirt with a green logo on it. His skin looked impossibly smooth above the designer stubble, and his hazel eyes were warm.

'I'm OK,' she said, raising her arms hopelessly.

'I've had this happen before.' He edged forward and held out his hand. 'Oliver Chase. I run The Marauding Mojito.' He gestured over his left shoulder. 'I've got experience of sinking, leaking, wasp swarms – you think it up, I've had it happen. But this is your first time?'

'First and last, I should think,' Charlie said, shaking his hand.

He gave her a gentle smile. 'No need to be so dramatic. First thing we need to do is get her upright. And I'd like to say I can help, but I'm a man, not a god. So . . . recovery?'

'I have a number in my phone.' Charlie walked hesitantly to the cab, holding onto anything she could, and took her phone out of the valuables box. She didn't know Oliver or The Marauding Mojito, but she was grateful for his calmness. Of course she would have made this decision on her own, but it was as if he'd sucked all her panic away.

He was peering out of the hatch towards the site of the submergence. Some of the crowd was still there, and Stuart was tersely dusting himself down, his ego more bruised than anything else. Charlie took a deep breath. It was a hiccup, nothing more. She could still do this.

And then there were more footsteps. She and Oliver both turned to see who else had come to help, and were met with a face that was very familiar to Charlie, and yet stormier than she had ever seen it.

Bea Fishington gripped onto the walls of the bus as if it was a sinking boat, still rocking violently.

'Oh Charlie,' she said, her expression a mixture of pity and distress, 'what on earth has happened here?'

Discover more delightful fiction
from Cressida McLaughlin.
All available now.

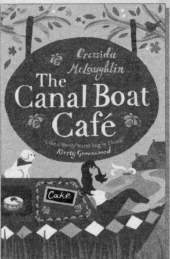

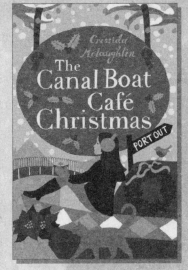